THE DEAD HUSBAND

Enjoy the read

RJ Brown

Books from Big River Press

Fiction

The Dead Husband
A Sally Sees Cozy Mystery
by R. J. Brown

Epitaph
A Submariner Thriller
by D. Clayton Meadows

Honor Defended
Citizen Warrior Book II
by D. H. Brown

Honor Due
Citizen Warrior Book I
by D. H. Brown

Creative Nonfiction

Standing The Watch
The Greatest Gift
A memoir by R. J. Brown

THE DEAD HUSBAND

by

R. J. Brown

A SALLY SEES COZY MYSTERY

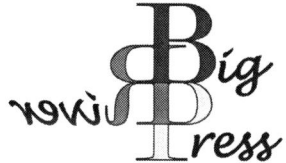

Published by Big River Press
P. O. Box 371
Clallam Bay, Washington 98326
http://www.bigriverpress.com

The Dead Husband: A Sally Sees Cozy Mystery, Book I
Copyright 2009 by R. J. Brown
http://www.rjbrownbooks.com

All rights reserved. No part of this book may be reproduced in any form or by any electronic or mechanical means, including information storage and retrieval systems, or transmitted by any means, electronic, mechanical, photocopying, recording, or otherwise, without written permission from the publisher, except by a reviewer who may quote brief passages in a review.

This is a work of fiction. All places, characters and events are either fictitious or used fictitiously. Any resemblance of the characters to real persons, living or dead, is purely coincidental.

ISBN-13: 978-0-9798744-7-5
ISBN-10: 0-9798744-7-5

Library of Congress Control Number: 2009926123

First American Paperback Edition

Printed in the USA on acid free paper

Cover Design by Big River Press

DEDICATED TO

The memory of "Tully," my family's live-in Nanny and Char through war and peace, who cared for me in ways no one else at home did.

All the unsung women who clean the world.

My adopted country which let me dream a new life, gave me the liberty to pursue what made me happy so I might gain contentment wherein I found myself.

My therapists and Human Potential Movement trainers who created safe spaces for me to look at my hardwiring and showed me tools to transform the quality of my life.

"Let the charwoman alone to be the first...
Let the laundress alone to be the second;
and let the undertaker's man be the third."
A Christmas Carol
Stave 4: The Last of the Spirits
Charles Dickens 1867

~charwoman:
someone you employ to clean your home
also charlady or just your char

THANKS TO

AFTER THE BIRTH of my first child at the end of a hot Chicago summer, I was bemoaning to my friend Bernie, how intensely I was missing the land of my childhood. Later that day he lugged his camp trunk up to my fourth floor apartment off Lincoln Avenue. In it was every one of Agatha Christie's paperbacks, and ever since, I've been keen on atmospheric cozy mysteries. Now, I want them to take me someplace I haven't been to meet new people and teach me something I didn't know.

My Reading Group for their enthusiasm and wise words: Dr. Alma H. Bond, Glenda A. Bixler, Lorna Collins, Kitty Mady, Karin Bergsten-Buret, Marjorie L. Carmony, and Lynn Lott who sent me this classic comment: "Your MS does not need as much work as you may think, though I did delete about a million commas... there were times I wanted to shake [it] and make them all fall into a pile and then shove them under my bed."

When you're a writer you inhabit your mind rather more than most folks. This means others must guard the cave, fiddle with computers and the Internet and leave you alone to write. For this I have my beloved and very much alive husband, D. H. Brown, himself a teller of fine tales.

GLOSSARY

Brit = an Americanism for anyone from anywhere in the UK.
Yank = a Britishism for anyone from anywhere in the USofA.

About the spelling of verb tenses as in learnt, smelt, leapt and the like: they're a hangover from my 1950s British education.

Loverly, my Mum, my Man and Mr or Mrs without a period (a fullstop in English English) are Sally's personal idioms.

a brace = a pair
a flat = an apartment
a grip = a soft travel or duffel bag
a plait = a braid of hair
a quid = a pound sterling circa 1960s
a tenner = a ten (bob) shilling note ditto
a tin = a can
a trice = in a moment, quickly
bed-sitters = a many-storied house converted into furnished living rooms with communal bathrooms
bonkers = crazy
brass tacks = nitty-gritty
bum = derriere, behind
bung hole = drain
chap/s = guy/s, man/men
chivvied = coaxed, bossed
chuffed = pleased, relieved
clinkers = coagulated burnt coal

everso = a lot
fortnight = fourteen nights = two weeks
GCE = General Certificate of Education circa 1950s
goal = jail, prison
guff = sass, a hard time
jiggy/ies = jigsaw puzzle/s
knocked-up = pregnant
loo, throne = toilet, rest/bath/powder room
midden = kitchen rubbish heap
Missus = the woman of the house
Mister = the man of the house
nackered = exhausted
nought = nothing (spoken as snout)
pong = strong or foul odor
portico = front porch with roof, columns and railings
pranged = pre-WWII term for crashing a car
scullery = once a room off the kitchen for prepping veggies and washing cooking pots and pans. Now refers only to the chores
starkers = naked
storey = the floors of a house
ticked-off = annoyed
wireless = radio

Please be aware
there are a few "passing expletives"
in this tale.

Chapter 1

DISCOVERY

CLEANING UP DEAD HUSBANDS is not part of my job description. At the time I wasn't worried about how he'd got there, all I could think of was he was my first... dead husband, that is.

Don't get me wrong, he wasn't *my* husband (I've never been married) although we'd liked each other well enough. You see, in this chapter of my life I'm earning my keep as a charwoman and this husband, or rather his huge house behind me is my first job of the week. Actually, I run a cleaning company, Sal's Gals, with eight other women.

The last time I'd seen Mel Birnbaum we'd been sitting in the sun in his Adirondack chairs out at the end of the kitchen breezeway, enjoying a post-clean chat. By the way, he thinks those chairs are the cat's meow. Well, given he's a dog man they'd have to be the dog's woof, wouldn't they?

Unlike in years past, all this summer no one besides Mel had been around when I came for my Monday clean. No Renee, his wife of nineteen years nor Claire, their now-graduated daughter.

Anyway, last week Mel and I had been satisfying our addictions for high octane espressos and strong Sobranie cigarettes, chatting about this and that. Up here in the Pacific Northwest it's always about the weather, with a new twist: all the tsunami evacuation signs popping up along the Strait of Juan de Fuca shore roads, and what one would do to our coastal communities.

Come to think of it, Mel had been in a bit of a grump, which was unusual. Not even my jolly company had gotten him out of it.

Now I was staring at the body of my friend which his dog had dug up out of the mud and dead leaves under the Madrona trees. Beyond was the chain link fence, the bluff ledge thick with withered sea grass, and the drop off to the beach some ninety feet below.

As my bum wicked up the damp from Friday night's rain, I pulled out my pack of smokes and lit up. Black Lab Borscht stopped pawing at his dead master's arm in its dirty white shirt.

"Ah, jeez, Mel," I breathed. I let my eyes drift beyond the contorted orange Madronas to the dazzling panorama of Discovery Bay. Across its vast shimmering blue, glowed a perfect four mountain day: a deep forest green coast behind which rose hazy green foothills to the gray-blue uplands, and then the mauve mountains with snowy patches on their northern faces, poking into an everso blue sky.

Tears suddenly spurted and I blotted them with my uniform sleeve. Borscht whined. I reached out and he stumbled over shivering, poking his muddy nose under my chin. I fondled his velvety ears.

"Poor old fella," I soothed. "You did good. Sit." He wiggled onto his haunches and panted, mournfully watching his still master. I stroked his thick fur as we sat together in the shade.

Naturally my mind decided to think about the other people who've died on me, so far. The first was my wore-out Mum, ages ago back in London when I'd been a young maiden getting my training at Moneypenny's Secretarial College. The second was just six years ago right here in Port Townsend, when my dear friend and lover Clay had shucked off his mortal coil sitting on his sofa in his sunroom, wrapped in one of my quilts.

Now here was Mel, with his curly black and silver hair and beard, nostrils and mouth all muddy. Looked like he'd drowned in the stuff. The spots of his skin that weren't smeared had a strange yellow cast. What made my stomach quiver were his wide open eyes staring up at his home. The whites were dull and damaged, as if something had punctured them. How on earth had he got here, half in and half out of his muddy grave?

When I'd arrived some forty minutes ago, even though Borscht hadn't been loping around the drive and Mel hadn't been sitting at the table under his aquamarine canopy with our first jolts of java at the ready, I hadn't given it much thought.

We had an agreement, this husband and me: I cleaned his pristine suite the first week of each month while he took off with his dog, to come back when I was done with his rooms and was attacking the rest of his home. When I was finished we'd have another cuppa before I left for my afternoon job.

Today, being the third week of the month, I'd simply opened the kitchen door with its keycard, punched in the code to disarm the alarm and hauled in my vacuum and tool basket. When I saw the brushed steel Gaggia espresso machine had been unused, that gave me pause. It's Mel's pride and joy and he couldn't start his day without a couple of frothy stiff ones.

Old habits die hard, and even though Renee hadn't been there on a Monday since spring when she'd put in an appearance for her daughter's high school graduation, I looked for her note with instructions and found instead no sign of any cooking, or anyone.

I'd set my boombox on the butcher block and punched on my music while I made sure the pockets of my uniform contained my necessities. Then I pulled on my purple cleaning gloves.

I was stuffing my tools into the dumb waiter in the entryway ready to start on the upstairs when the phone rang, like a xylophone.

"Hello? Dad?"

I pressed the speaker button on the system. The LED light indicated seven messages. Above that, the black and white monitor showed its split views of the gates off the main road and the Birnbaums' drive.

"Hi Claire, it's Sally. No one's about."

"Oh, Sal, I'm so freaked. Haven't been able to get hold of Mom or Dad since Thursday. Just voice mails. No one's calling me back. Where are they?"

"I just got here, dear. I think your mother's not here, and your father's car—"

"I've got it. Been out at Lake Quinault, closing the camp for winter. I was so beat when I got to the Gramps last night I stayed over. Wait! Got another call, maybe it's—"

I was left listening to air waves.

"Not them. Where are they?" I heard another voice in the background. "Call you later, Sal."And she disconnected.

Okay, that meant she was in Sequim at Mel's parents, a fifty minute drive west on Highway 101, if you didn't get stuck behind a school of sporting fishermen's pickup trucks towing their boats.

UNSUSPECTING OF HOW MY MONDAY was going to turn out I'd woken this morning in a jolly good mood because my Man had stayed overnight after a perfect weekend roaming around the Wooden Boat Festival. George Tullock's been Chief of Detectives for Jefferson County (locals shorten it to Jeffco) since before I moved up to Port Townsend.

After breaking our fast at the Salal Café on Water Street we'd parted company. He, off in his brand-spanking new Escalade to the Justice Center in Port Hadlock, and me to my Detroit wreck from the late '80s, so Wally tells me. And yeah, that's what he calls all his leasers. My Man calls it a beater.

On the way to the Birnbaums I'd cruised out of town along the back roads now refreshed by the first rain in two solid months. I'd swung around Chevy Chase Golf Course and on up to the ridge with its glorious panorama across Discovery Bay far below and the massive hulk of the Olympic Mountains on the horizon. The forest was logged back around the First World War and has since been sparsely settled, mostly down by river deltas and beaches.

Then I came to Bluff Haven's mile long red brick fence with its mossy epaulets guarding the estates tucked out of sight in the second growth.

I'd turned off the road and with a touch of the accelerator pulled up onto the tarmac apron beside the gazebo housing mailboxes, recycle bins and Dumpsters, in front of the wrought iron gate with its arch, central motion sensor light and security camera. Beyond, the estate road branches off around a circle of purple Heather, clumps of Pampas Grass sporting their plumes and a Monkey Tree.

With nary a care I'd popped my keycard in and out of the slot at the end of the gooseneck stand which has its own little camera, and made a face at Jerry in his security company office in Port Hadlock. Then I waited for the gate to rattle aside on its wheels. I let my beater coast forward until, as the metallic voice ordered, I halted while the gate closed, the blue and white bar raised up and the tire spikes retracted. Some security system, eh?

My destination was the last estate on the right at the end of Bluff View where I'd go through the same silly routine, minus the bar and spikes. On the way I pass three elaborate gates out of which, in all the years I've driven along this lane, I've never seen a resident come or go.

I'm always agog for the view of the bay and mountains as I ease along through the Rhododendrons, Mountain Ash and Vine Maples of the Birnbaums' quarter mile drive. At this time of year the tarmac's covered with orange berries which South American Pigeons love to chomp on before heading home for their second summer. Clever birds!

At the circle in front of the Birnbaums' vast cedar shingle home, I'd driven by their three stall garage and parked at the end of the flagstone breezeway to the kitchen.

Setting my tools down by the door I'd gone over for a dose of aromatherapy from Renee's wedding anniversary roses and Lavender bushes, which I'd already harvested. The roses have completely recuperated after their relocation from the parched Piedmont Hills overlooking Berkeley and the San

Francisco Bay. In their last bloom, they were dripping with dew-jeweled cobwebs and smelt divine.

That's when I first heard old Borscht barking from his gulag in the basement. Once upon a time this usually silent Lab, also a transplant from California, had had free range of the entire ten thousand square feet. A good-natured dog, he rarely forgot his rank in his pack until the year the woman of the house got a bee in her bonnet and quit nicotine, caffeine, cooking, and being around. The first time she was home, after four Mondays away that I knew of, she had a crew there tearing up the immaculate wall-to-wall carpeting. I'd had a tough time cleaning that day. The next week they were installing gleaming, squeaky wood floors. Over those Renee'd positioned artsy runners and expensive rugs.

Borscht's standing took a nose dive then. He'd slid and skid like Bambi on that ice pond, his nails leaving scour marks. When he got excited he'd try to dash around as of yore and rumpled the rugs, slamming into walls. Anatomy being what it is he'd also leak, usually all over those damn rugs. This so pissed off the nicotine-free Renee she'd exiled hound, and then husband.

Mel had promptly called in his own army of interior decorators who morphed the downstairs rec room into a black, white and chrome den. They expanded the half-bath into a full one and built a walk-through closet as a buffer between the laundry room. Unlike his wife, Mel had plush black carpeting laid down all over, except the bathroom.

Borscht got a wicker basket filled with a cedar chip pillow set beside the new wood stove and Mel got a wicker chair hung on a chain from a joist of the deck over his patio. He'd also replaced the nice normal staircase up to the kitchen with a vertigo-inducing spiral iron thing to prevent, so he said, his hound from ascending into enemy territory.

Each time I come to clean I say a sincere blessing for the large dumb waiter—no that's not a mute waitperson, it's a manually driven elevator that holds all my tools. It's in the hallway off the kitchen, services all three floor and, so far, neither husband nor wife have thought to rip out. Perhaps cuz the kitchen's the DMZ between their war zones and it's easier than carrying trays up and down stairs to their separate corners.

Chapter 2

DESERTED PARADISE

AS I SAT SMOKING and stroking Borscht's ears, dazed at the sight of my longtime friend in his muddy grave, a horrible thought slunk across my mind. With his master dead, Borscht's days here were numbered. Before his exile Renee'd often threatened to have "that mangy mutt" put down. He'd never had mange, or anything else that I knew of. Now he nudged his dry nose against my cheek and whined.

"Good dog," I murmured, pinching out my smoke and putting it, and a couple of butts I'd seen among the damp leaves in my baggie, stowing it in a pocket of my uniform.

The first person I needed to talk to was my Man. I pulled out my cellphone and hit speed dial.

"Jefferson County Chief of Detectives. How can I help you, Ms. Collier?" Ah, the transparency of caller ID. His formality warned me that we were being monitored, even recorded.

I cleared my throat, "I've found a dead body."

"Where?" His deep bass came back immediately.

"At the bottom of the garden." I was only trying to be exact.

"And that garden is where?"

"Oh, yeah, at the Birnbaums in Bluff Haven."

"On Discovery Bay Road?"

"Yeah, what should I do?"

Turns out there wasn't much, just sit tight, take Borscht up to the house and wait while George set the wheels of law enforcement in motion.

My next call got redirected to my client's voicemail.

"Renee, it's Sally. Monday. Ten-fifteen-ish. Just found Mel..." I swallowed a sob. "Under the Madronas. You better get home. I've called nine-one-one." I was about to disconnect when Borscht nudged me again. "Oh yeah, I'm taking Mel's dog home with me. You know where I live."

I watched him, now his usual silent self, sniffing at Mel's damaged eyes. That's when I remembered the cats. I'd been staring out of the dining room windows on the first floor wondering where everyone was, when a pride of tabbies had come slinking along in the grass at the edge of the septic drain field, heading down to the fence. I'd never seen cats anywhere here before. They'd scared off some crows who landed in the Madronas, in a riot of squawking. I looked up into the smooth, orange branches where bunches of red berries dangled. The crows were long gone.

"Hey, old boy, let's go." I felt I had to get out of there before I upchucked or bawled myself silly. I pulled on Borscht's chain collar, jingling his tags. "Come!" I mimicked the way Mel spoke to him, and we climbed the cedar chip path, back up the hill.

When I went to pull open the sliding glass door to Mel's den, I caught sight of my reflection with the sunny terrace behind me. I'm an English WWII runt, not a hair taller than five foot three with a sturdy pear-shaped bod dressed in the teal and mauve scrubs I sew up for work uniforms. I've always kept my wavy black hair short. Now, when did that silver streak in my widow's peak start showing? Never enamored of makeup, I don't spend much time in front of mirrors, mostly cuz there's nothing spectacular to look at.

I inherited my Pa's Welsh features of thick eyebrows, big brown eyes and square forehead and jaw, and my Mum's peaches and cream complexion. My nose is a nose without distinction, as are my lips even if George says I'm a real good kisser. I do like my hands. They're shaped like my Mum's though not nearly as worn as hers cuz she'd started hard housework when she was twelve, back before washing machines. I only started cleaning professionally six years ago, and I wear gloves.

I let Borscht loose inside Mel's apartment and went to find his box of treats beside his feed bag in the closet by the front door. While he daintily chomped down a handful, I filled his water bowl in the bathroom. He lapped it all up and I refilled it. After he had seconds, I pointed to his bed. He trotted over to it, flopped down and lay there watching me with his huge sad eyes.

I stepped outside again, slid the door almost shut and dodged the mud puddle on my way to Mel's hanging chair. When I settled into it something poked my hip. I dug beside the cushion and there was his tin of Sobranies. Inside were five smokes and his little gold lighter. I lit up.

"This one's for you, Mel. Wasn't the nicotine that got you in the end." It was a loverly smoke and I found myself yearning for one of Mel's lattes.

My cellphone chirped.

"This is Cindy at nine-one-one. That you, Sal?"

"Yeah. What's happening?" She's a dispatcher at the Justice Center in Port Hadlock and also a WOW, as in Wild Olympic Women. We're a quilting bee and every year we sew up a kingsize free-form quilt to raffle off to raise money to save the Salmon. Last week we'd reconvened after the long summer break.

"Deputy Haffey's out at the airport. Says he'll be there in fifteen minutes. Captain Tullock says to ask if you're in any danger."

I looked around. The place was deserted.

"Nope. I'll open the gates. Tell the deputy to make a right. It's at the end."

By the time we said goodbye the Sobranie was finished. I leant over to stub it out in Mel's bucket of sand, and poked at the butts already there. Four Sobranies and lots of Dorals, some with traces of lipstick on 'em. Had Mel had company? I took mine back and stashed it in my baggie with the others. Then I left the patio and headed up the outside flagstone steps to the kitchen.

I got my water bottle from my basket and drank while I watched the security monitor showing nothing new, wondering if this system recorded the comings and goings. I pressed the button connecting directly to Jerry's security company. By night, he's the bass guitarist in a group who plays a lively mix of country and rock. I first met him, years back, when he won a blue ribbon at the Sandcastling Festival I help organize each summer on a Fort Worden beach. He specializes in Escher-like visions.

"Sally Collier here." I told him when he answered. "Just found Mr. Birnbaum dead. I've called the police. They say I have to open both gates and leave the alarms off."

"What did you say?" Jerry's New York accent twanged loudly. I repeated myself.

"Jeez, Sal, that's... you sure he's really dead?"

"He's not breathing, not moving."

"Jeez!" I could hear a commercial for LeafGuard Gutters in the background. "Think the cops'll be calling me? I'll tag the discs. How far back do you think I should I go?"

"A week would be my guess."

Given the dampness down there under the Madronas it must have been Friday night during the rain cuz Saturday had been dry and overcast with yesterday much the same, although the clouds had blown off by sunset which had been an apricot-magenta vision. George and I had enjoyed it from one of our favorite sunset-watching spots near the new ferry dock.

There wasn't much more Jerry or I could do except watch the world come peering into the Birnbaums' private paradise.

I wanted to get off my feet, so I pressed the buttons for the gates and watched the monitor as they rolled open, then left the cool kitchen for the warm breezeway and sat in my chair in the Chat Pad, as Mel calls it. Then the tears came. Despite the heat I was shivering. I could almost taste one of Mel's espressos. I knew better than to help myself to one by starting up his Gaggia.

He'd had such a rich voice with a strong east coast accent. "Noo Joyzee," he'd say. And he'd loved mine. His sense of humor often got me giggling. He didn't talk about his work. I figured it had to do with investments cuz before he caught the computer bug I'd seen Blue Chip envelopes in his trash.

When the word murder popped into my mind I immediately thought of Renee. She had enough... er... drama, except she wasn't any taller than me and a featherweight, to boot. Besides, she'd never have gone out into all that mud.

Then the image of their darling daughter danced before my eyes. Well, she's her Dad's darling and her Mom's thorn. I've never known a grown woman so disturbed by her daughter's budding beauty. I've watched Claire grow from a chubby girl puppy into a model tall pretty, healthy maiden. She could have done it although I couldn't imagine why cuz she adored her father. You could see it whenever she looked at him with those big blue eyes she'd inherited from him. Her dirty blonde hair and dirty big mouth, however, were all Mom's.

Having emigrated in my twenties, the ways of American maidens have always been a mystery to me. Had I ever been that young? At her age I'd already been working for my keep. Or as carefree? I'd struggled to make my wages last the week. Callous as it may sound, Claire's safe little world was sure going to change.

AS I WAITED for the Jeffco deputy to arrive I thought about how the Birnbaums had once been good friends, although I hadn't actually seen husband and wife together since Claire's Sweet Sixteen party. They'd invited me over for cake and moral support, along with a handful of parents who liked to play Bridge. While the bevy of hormone-hyped girls took over the house we adults had huddled out on the deck off the dining room.

Everyone was drinking wine as Mel barbecued chicken wings, Claire's favorite food. I'd brought my

THE DEAD HUSBAND

Stanley thermos of tea. Haven't touched Al. K. Hol since I was a working girl in London. Don't like what it does to me, or anyone else for that matter. I thought Renee'd have a cow when Mel offered his tin of Sobranies around and most of us lit up.

I'd been getting back on my feet after relocating to the Bay Area from Chicago when I met the Birnbaums at a Human Potential Movement training. I'd signed up to find out why I made the lousy choices I did. We worked the exercises together and had taken a liking to each other. My kids had been in the creche seminars with Claire. Oh yeah, I have two. At the time June was seven, Cooper six and Claire had just had her fourth birthday.

I'd been cleaning the Oakland motel I lived in and making good money. Enough to get off Welfare, as it was called back then. Three months into my new career as a char I'd done the math, and the morning after a particularly mind-expanding seminar I'd dropped the kids off at school and gone to see my case worker. Gave her the yellow rose I'd plucked from a garden and signed myself off her case load.

Ever since I'd walked into her office with my papers from the Chicago Welfare office I'd felt sorry for the work-worn woman. She reminded me of why I hadn't gone back into office work after the kids' Dad left. With a genuine smile she'd taken the rose and then mentioned that my kids were still eligible for medical coverage. Thought I'd better not burn that bridge, too.

So life went on: I cleaned the motel and the Birnbaums' home. Sometimes my kids and I would stay the weekend with them, parboiling ourselves in their hot tub, romping with Claire. After I put the kids to bed, I'd join their Bridge tournaments. A card game, along with Canasta and Bezique, I learnt at

Moneypenny's.

Then one morning I'd come across Clay Zumbach in a unit at the motel. I'd taken a liking to him and he for me. Three months later I'd moved my family up here to Port Townsend, settled into one of his rentals and gone right back into an office by running his general practice.

I sent postcards to Mel and Renee, showing the lush land I'd found. The next summer they flew up and fell for the area, too. Mel had been enthralled by the sunsets. Renee'd loved the small town schools and the closeness to Seattle. They'd gone house hunting, found the Bluff Haven property and decided to build their dream home.

By the time they'd settled in I'd started Sal's Gals, my cleaning company, and had taken them on, for old time's sake.

If, Dear Reader, you're wondering how I, a Brit, as you Yanks still insist on calling me even though I'm a presidentially welcomed, hand-on-my-heart pledger-of-allegiance, standing up anthem-singing, voting American citizen got all the way to this paradise in the Pacific Northwest, it'll have to wait cuz right now a green and white cruiser followed by a black sedan has swung around Renee's roses and parked behind my beater.

Chapter 3

SHOW AND TELL

I'M A RUNT,(no vitamins or fresh milk or fruit for my first six years due to The War) so it's a given most everyone I meet is taller, and Deputy Haffey in his Smokey the Bear hat was no exception. I've never seen him without it so have no idea what color his shorn hair is, nor his eyes behind his wrap-around sunglasses. He certainly had a splendid summer tan with his left arm darker than his right.

Lois, one of my Gals, is dating him and filled me in on how he'd moved here from Ada, Idaho so he could take up sailing. Surrounded by a bay, an inlet, a sound, a strait and a gazillion islands Port Townsend's a good place for that, and hosts a yearly Wooden Boat Festival to which thousands of salty dogs steer their sailboats from all over the world.

As she tells it, he couldn't get over being seasick so he got back into law enforcement and in his free time, music: jazz to be exact. Lois met him in one of the taverns she cleans and says he plays a mean trombone. He was not carrying it. Instead his crisp beige summer uniform was festooned with the tools of his trade.

Someone with a familiar crest of black hair and pale complexion in a gray suit got out of the sedan. Deputy Haffey went over to him. Well, well, Bill Westin had moved up in the world. The ID he showed me was of a Jeffco detective. No longer the Port Townsend Police Officer who responded to my call after finding Clay dead in his sunroom.

Without a word I gestured for the chaps to follow me down the flagstone steps to the terrace. I was about to lead 'em further when Deputy Haffey got in front of me, forcing me to stop. He surveyed the slope and I squinted up at him, seeing myself reflected times two, in his mirror shades.

"We'll take it from here, ma'am." He growled.

"Wait here, Sally," Bill Westin touched my arm. "When I get back I'll take your statement."

They stepped over the terrace edge and started down the path to Mel's grave. I was a tad ticked-off that Haffey hadn't recognized me and by Bill's dismissal, so I sulked in the shade under the deck. Borscht was wagging his tail on the other side of the sliding door.

I settled into Mel's chair again and wondered how I was going to tell my Gals about this, and what their reactions would be. Joanne would pepper me with questions; Ethel would come up with a potage of French swear words; Annie would want all the gory details; Lois would have already pumped her beau for info; Zoe would likely come up with a sappy song to tease me with; Joy would be interested in the exact lay of the land; Sandra would have all her fears about dangerous clients confirmed and Judith, excellent char though she be, would want to know what plants had been damaged by the digging.

I got to my feet when I heard the jingle of the returning deputy.

"Please show me your driver's license, ma'am."

I dug my wallet out of my uniform pocket.

"You don't have a purse?"

"Not when I'm working. Why?"

He shrugged and wrote in his notebook.

"And your Social Security number, ma'am?"

I recited it. His "ma'am" was sawing on a nerve.

"Now, Miss Collier, how did you find the vic—"

"He's Mel Birnbaum. That's his apartment." I pointed to the glass wall, "Actually, the whole house is his. I've called his wife and left a message."

"Please give me that number. What time was that, ma'am?"

A single whoop of sound reverberating from the driveway shut off my babbling.

"That'll be the Cape George EMTs. Please go and wait by your car." Deputy Haffey lost interest in me.

"Bill said he wanted to... their dog's in there." I gestured to where Borscht was prancing.

"That's all right, ma'am, just wait up top for the detective. He'll be there soon. I'll call the animal shelter and ha—"

"No, please don't! He stinks, and I... he knows me... and well, the wife'll put him down. I'm going to wash him and take him home."

"That'll be fine. Just don't go in the house or leave the grounds." His radio screeched and he turned away. That was my cue to leap over, pull the sliding door open and hustle Borscht up top.

MEL'S GARAGE isn't one of those metal and aluminum carports you see tucked beside so many homes in this neck of the woods, like mine. No, his is a three-stall cedar shingled carriage house complete with a dovecote and cluster of satellite dishes on its roof. It has retracting doors, all of which I now remembered had been open and the stalls empty when I got here. Usually they're closed.

I latched Borscht to Mel's handy-dandy washing pen inside the first stall right by the drain, grabbed a bottle of shampoo from the shelf unit by the freezer and spread a line along his black back. With the nozzle of the hose in hand I watched the EMTs offload under the front door portico. When they realized no one was there they chatted into their radios, changed positions and rolled the gurney to the breezeway, hefting it down the steps.

I opened the nozzle and spent some time washing a miserable dog. Then I rubbed him with the drying towels and set him free. With much shaking from head to toe, he danced about the driveway grinning. I filled a plastic bucket from the faucet and put it down. He came over for a long lap and then dashed off to Renee's roses and the rhodies beyond.

As I tidied up I realized I was still wearing my cleaning gloves. I dried and stripped them off, tucking 'em into a pocket. My fingers were like white prunes, almost numb. Damn, I hate having my schedule screwed with!

Borscht came loping back, stopped to sniff and piss on all the tires on the vehicles and then he was ready to refill his radiator. I was ready for more nicotine. Borscht trotted over to where I sat in my chat chair, dropped his sopping jowl on my knee and wagged his tail. I was a goner.

"Lie down," I ordered gently. He sniffed around on the flagstones, found his favorite warm niche and flopped down facing me. Again, I wished for a swig of Mel's brew.

I thought for a nanosecond of letting Borscht loose. Old-timers I've met on my walks around this bay say people have been driving out here forever and throwing unwanted puppies and kittens out their windows. Discovery Bay Road's still mostly rural and undeveloped, although closer to town there's been a building boom and subdivisions have been popping up like mushrooms.

I've heard the packs of feral dogs as they roam the area, though never actually seen 'em. And the cats have thrived too. The Jeffco Animal Shelter hasn't the staff, the premises nor the heart to round 'em all up so anyone keeping chickens and rabbits tends to shoot on sight. Borscht was way too civilized to be let loose. I couldn't keep him, could I?

I'd never, ever had a pet. For all of my childhood in the basement of that house on Ladbroke Hill in London, the Missus upstairs had had little dogs. At first woolly white mops and then short-haired terriers. It had been the upstairs children's job to walk 'em. I'd hear barking through the ceiling and remember my Mum wrinkling her nose whenever she had to clean up their pee or vomit.

When I left home to be a working girl no pets had been allowed in the flat I rented with three of my classmates from Moneypenny's Secretarial College. We wouldn't have had a clue how to care for 'em, and as we lived on baked beans and fish and chips we wouldn't have been able to feed 'em, anyway.

Once I'd gotten to America, to Chicago, I'd been so busy working at the office all day and playing in the city all night that the thought of getting either beast or bird never entered my head. Not even when I had my kids and was a stay-at-home Mom. They were critters enough.

It was when I started cleaning homes on the West Coast that I met pets. Most dogs liked me, while the cats ignored me. The fish did their thing in exotic aquariums and the birds sang and fluttered in their cages. On one of my first interviews up here I'd encountered a pair of monkeys roaming free. New rule: I don't clean monkey messes.

The closest I've gotten to having a pet has been Clay's next door neighbor's handsome marmalade cat, named after Mr. Johanssen's favorite president. When my kids and I stayed over with Clay we'd often see Ronnie out on Mr J's stoop or hunting in the park. After Clay left his cottage to me and I moved in, Ronnie had promptly sauntered over to the porch and cleaned himself. Even though I've never fed him he'll occasionally rub against my legs. It's my Man he likes and when we're sitting on the porch Ronnie will come through the hedge, leap onto George's lap and contentedly purr away.

Now I was thinking of taking on my very own dog. Borrowed to be sure, although I had a feeling he wasn't registering on either Renee or Claire's radar.

While he looked a lot better, I worried about the after-affects of being cooped-up at least since Friday, given Claire's news about not being able to contact her parents. I knew exactly who to call.

"Wally, it's your loyalest customer. What're your rules about dogs in your cars?"

"Yo there, girlie. What cars? I got only wrecks." The man was in a good mood. No matter their age, every woman's a "girlie." I kinda like it.

"I just inherited a black Lab. Oldish. Been without water and food for—"

"Inside or out?"

"In a storage close. At least a couple of days."

"People like that should be shot!"

"Yeah, well, his master's dead and no one else is around."

"You bring him right over." Being retired military, Wally's used to giving orders.

"How do I get him into my beat... er... wreck?"

"'Load up!' usually works."

"In the back seat?"

"Sure, girlie. He drinking?"

"Gallons."

"Labs like water. Where are you?"

"Discovery Bay."

"Run him on the beach there?"

"Not yet. Won't he besmirch the upholstery with all that sand and salt water?"

"Don't you talk to me like that! Girlies oughta have protection."

"Any hints about training him to mind me?"

"They're easier than people. Feed him. Take him with everywhere and talk like you're the boss. He'll bide you. Oh, yeah, don't beat on him for nothing, no time, no how! You got that?"

"Yessir! What could he possibly do to make me hit him? He's not a puppy."

"He quiet around new people?"

"Don't really know. I've only known him for... once a week for... well, years."

"Trouble if he gets in bed with you?" I winced at the thought of Borscht stretched out on my brand new queen size.

"Ow, yeah! Got a man who fills that spot more nights than not."

"They'll have to get to know each other real slow

like. He still got his balls?"

"'Course he does! That's repulsive. Do guys really do that?" Wally's laugh roared in my ear.

"I mean the dog, girlie. What's he called?"

"Borscht. I'll go see." I bent over where my pal was dozing and stroked his ribs. Got his tickle spot on the first shot. He stretched out and jiggled.

"Nope, no balls."

"Say his name again?"

"Borscht."

"That Mr. Mel's Lab?"

"Yeah, you know him?"

"Doctored him a time or two."

"Can you change a dog's name?"

"If it's close to his old one." I could almost hear Wally's gears shifting. "Porsche!" He hollered.

"Like the car? Why's that different from soup?"

"Gotta have the same sorta sound."

"Well, it's classier and I guess dogs aren't picky about consonants."

"Say what? Girlie, you get him here ASAP." And he disconnected.

That's when I heard my music. Had it been playing all this time? I hadn't heard a note. I set my smoke in the ashtray Claire had made years ago, tiptoed into the kitchen and shut it off. With her on my mind, I went over to the wall phone, hit 69, got her voice mail and left my number. Then grabbed my boombox and slunk off to stow it in my beater. I sure wasn't going to be doing any cleaning here today, perhaps never again, and I was itching to leave this sad mess.

I took a beach towel out of the trunk, threw it over the back seat and called newly-named Porsche. He got up, teetered a bit then trotted over.

"Load up!" Without hesitation he leapt in, turned

around and settled across the entire sagging seat.

And then Deputy Haffey was coming along the breezeway, talking into his radio.

"Can I let the maid go?" He listened to the squawking. Maid indeed! "Detective's coming right up and then you can go home. We know where you live if we need you again."

"I'm not a maid, copper. Hasn't Lois told you, we're chars? Charles Dickens wrote about us. Anyway," I could see he was unimpressed. "I'm taking the dog over to Wally's Doggie Heaven for a check-up. I have another house to clean in…" I checked my watch on my shirt. "Yikes! Can I get my tools from the dumb waiter by the kitchen?"

"Sorry. Sealing the place up now. They'll be safe."

I was unconvinced. "That's a Dyson in there. I need… how're you going to lock up when you leave?"

"You have the keys?"

"Yeah, they're keycards. Do I have to give 'em to you?" He stepped away to talk into his radio. More squelching and squawking. I wondered how they ever got anything right, I couldn't make head nor tail of the noise.

"You do." He said stretching out his hand.

"Well I don't like it at all." I growled as I laid 'em on his gloved palm.

"No offense meant, ma'am." He made a fake smile.

"I'll get over it, deputy." I made my smile the same caliber.

We stood there awkwardly until Bill Westin came striding along the breezeway and Deputy Haffey left to string yellow plastic ribbons around the portico columns.

I was desperate for a dose of java and to be gone, so I wasn't thrilled when Bill Westin invited me to settle in Mel's chairs.

"Now, Sally, tell me how you found the vic... Mr. Birnbaum."

Two cigarettes and a lot of questions later he let me go. I bolted for my beater and snoozing Porsche.

At the wide open main gate a garbage truck was gobbling its breakfast from the Dumpsters. I waited, wondering if I'd ever be coming back here again and how Claire was soon going to be in a world of hurt.

Chapter 4

SCREAMING BLOODY MURDER

ON THE WAY TO PORT HADLOCK and Wally's Doggie Heaven, I was sucking up my much-anticipated brew from Melanie's Mocha Hut at Four Corners when my cellphone chirped.

"How're you handling it, hon?" George growled.

"I'm okay. Sad."

"How long had you known him?"

"Hang on a bit." I dropped the phone on the passenger seat so I could pull off busy Airport Way and stop in a turnout. It's The Law, you know: no cellphones while driving.

"I'm back," I said into my Man's ear. "Eight years ago, in Oakland."

"A good man?"

"I thought so." Said I, swallowing a lump.

"Don't mean to be... er... cold but you need to do a Sally Sees."

"A what?"

"Well, the way you describe your jobs, I've always

thought of 'em as Sally Sees."

Really? Was I detecting a note of hesitancy in my usually forthright fellow?

"Is that bad or good?" I wondered as a loaded gravel truck roared by towing its little piggie in a cloud of dust and chips.

"Er, good, I guess. You just have to remember what all you saw when you got there."

"Bill Westin's already asked me that."

"I know, but Detective Smith's the lead on the case, and I'm pretty sure he'll want to hear it from you directly. Gotta go, hon. See you for dinner?"

"Yes, please. Love you." I murmured, suddenly loathe to disconnect.

"Back at ya!" And he was gone.

GETTING BACK ONTO THE HIGHWAY and up to **speed,** I thought about what else I could have seen that might point to how Mel had died.

Ever since I started cleaning his dream house I've begun at the top floor bedroom suites. Initially I opened all the doors and windows to lessen the pong of new paint and carpets. Now I do it just to let the air out. Today had been so different.

I'd peeked into the guest rooms just in case, even though they haven't been used since Renee's iron curtain came down. Normally I start by stripping the bed and bathroom linens and drop 'em down the chute to the laundry hamper two floors below. Then I get fresh ones from the hall closet I restocked the week before. Not this morning!

For one thing the door to Renee's room had been shut. Usually she leaves it wide open, unlike her daughter. I'd felt compelled to knock and when I went in what hit me at once was the stale reek of cigarettes. Now you've got to understand that since she quit, Renee's been one mean anti-smoker. She and the rest of the State.

Her four poster bed with its pink canopy and swags was a wreck. The matching sheets and comforter rumpled, with pillows on the floor.

All the dainty dusky pink runners had been skewed out of their spots and across one was a trail of dark, dried blotches.

The pile of ashes in the fireplace, debris on its hearth, empty wood box and brass kindling scuttle told me she'd had a cozy time.

The coffee table was cluttered with half-filled wine glasses, empty bottles and a microwave dish with two forks in it. Stubbed into the desiccated leftover lasagna were cigarette butts, lipstick on a lot of 'em. Two milkshake spoons lay on crumpled pink paper napkins beside a cardboard strawberry ice cream tub in its pool of dried melt and condensation.

My need to investigate had overcome my urge to clean and I'd hung a left to the rose pink bathroom. What a mess there too! Towels tossed all over, the mat ruckled up beside the throne which had its seat up and yellow stains on its pink porcelain. In the pink trash bin was a wad of red-tinged tissues and a disposable razor. The mirror, pink marble counter and sinks had splatters all over.

Beyond, the walk-in closet, lit by the skylights that run on either side of the peaked roof, was empty. Before Renee started staying over in Seattle it used to be full of shoes and suits, dresses and trousers, blouses and sweaters. Now there was just one junky gym shoe in a corner and another half-hidden under a pink blouse puddled on the floor. All the drawers in the bureau were open and empty except for the lavender sachets I'd made. The jewelry chest on top was open with only a solitary earring and a broken tennis bracelet inside.

I'd tiptoed between the few barren hangers to the back where a lone, empty muslin bag dangled beside the wide-open safe. If the place been burgled wouldn't the alarm be screaming bloody murder? Wouldn't Security Jerry have mentioned that?

Back at the hallway door I'd taken one last scan of Renee's domain ending up at the sliding door to the balcony. There the garden loungers were pushed back against the glass with the green plastic table tilted against one. Renee hadn't wanted a railing to get in the way of the marvelous view so she'd had cedar planter boxes built at the edge and filled 'em with miniature azaleas. Something had looked off. Way too twitchy by then I hadn't gone to look. Wish I had now.

There's one place in Renee's suite I don't look at, or clean. It's her glory wall where her framed newspaper clippings and glossy publicity photos shout about the events she puts on. Posing with Seattle's movers and shakers, she's always in the company of the tall, blond impresario Alan Hatton.

I'd checked Claire's suite too cuz the last time I'd cleaned it, before she told me to quit as she was now a grown-up, it had been a mess.

I was impressed by how neat and tidy is was, with the moss green comforter and pillows on her bed perfectly undisturbed.

Her study desk was immaculate, her computer covered and all her dolls, horses and books carefully arranged. Nothing out of place, no clothes to be seen.

I trotted over to the bathroom door and pushed it wide. It's decorated in a tropical theme and except for one yellow towel folded differently on its rack, it looked good although the green tiles around the coral throne were lackluster and the shower door was opaque with scum.

I remember something in her trash bin catching my eye. A used pregnancy detection kit. Under it was the tester, with a positive reading. That was a shock.

Before I left her rooms I checked the door to her private covered deck and the staircase down to the drive. It was locked.

Back in the kitchen I stopped for a drink from my water bottle. The view through the serving counter to the dining room had drawn me to the wall of windows where I'd been mesmerized by the blue, green and purple vision. That's when I'd seen the cats stalking down to the bottom of the garden.

By then Borscht's barking had become a croak, so I'd scampered down that horrible spiral staircase to the utility room. I spend as little time there as possible since the remodeling cuz it's a dank dungeon lit by buzzing fluorescent lights. Today it too had been mess. What had got my goat right off, was the filthy marks on the folding table.

Now you've got to see this thing! Early on I'd been folding their laundry on a couple of card tables I'd found in storage. They weren't the steadiest and when they wobbled, all I'd done would take a tumble. I'd been swearing up a storm when Mel sauntered in after Borscht who'd bounded over for a look-see.

While I don't know what he's like as a husband and father he's always been a gent with me. He'd taken the time to pick things up and then asked what I wanted. So I told him. And wouldn't you know it, he'd grabbed a paper bag from the recycle box, took out his pen and wrote and sketched like mad.

Five Mondays later he'd had it built and installed,

and did he ever get it right! Except I hadn't envisioned something the size of a swing set. It had all the bells and whistles I'd asked for, in shiny stainless steel.

For some reason Borscht had quit barking so I'd looked around. There'd been streaks of dirt in the sink and my shoes squished on the wet carpet under it. There'd been their "eco-green" granulated soap spilt over the washer, and the door to the dryer was open with some cigarette filters buried in a wad of lint and a clot of scent-free dryer sheets in the barrel.

On the shelves above, six of Mel's white and black towels had been folded differently from the ones underneath, from the way I fold 'em.

What else? Oh yeah, the hose to that idiotic central vacuum system hadn't been retracted, just tossed over the laundry hamper. I hate that vacuum and the first and last time I'd used it was years ago after Renee threw a fit. I have another client with a similar system and I don't like it, either.

I'd been expecting Borscht to be in Mel's den so when he started whimpering behind the storage room door I'd pulled it open, releasing both the dog and a vile pong. He'd stood there shivering and panting, head, ears and tail hung low. I coaxed him out, and when I pulled the light chain, saw the source of the smell. Back in a corner against the far wall, Borscht had had to do his business.

The embarrassed old dog had staggered under the folding table to Mel's door. With my third cardkey I'd unlocked it and let him into the closet. Following him through the racks of everso neat clothes I'd seen dried mud smears on Mel's favorite black suede jacket and on three in a row of dry cleaner plastic bags.

THE DEAD HUSBAND

The black and white bathroom had been bad, too. Shower door scummy and a ring of grit, Madrona berries mixed with conifer needles over the bung hole grate. The throne cover was down, the checkered floor tiles smudged with clots of black carpet fibers everywhere. The wall of mirrors had smears of dried condensation and the marble counter and sink and the chrome faucets were all dull.

His bedroom, though, had been neat, ready for the night with the domino comforter folded back over the chrome foot rest. The black satin linens and pillows were undisturbed except for an indentation on the side facing a set of chrome shelves and Mel's *Playboy* magazines in their protective collector boxes with the year and title embossed in gold. I've looked at 'em and they start way back to the very first edition, before I got to America. Three on the bottom shelf had been put back in the wrong order.

The walls of Mel's lair are covered with photos of every sunset you could hope to see. He's won contests and some have been made into postcards which you can buy all over town. One graced the front cover of a Washington DOT map for a year.

When Borscht woofed, I'd gone through the living area, where the supplies for the woodstove and the entertainment center were as neat as usual.

Beyond the vast black sectional sofa Mel had looted during his exodus from upstairs is his office and computer carrel. When I'd asked him why he worked with his back to the view, he'd said he'd never get anything done if he faced it and besides he wanted the people he conference-called to see it. That's why he has web cams among the framed photos of Claire on the shelf over his humongous flat screen monitors, all four of which had been asleep. He never turns off his PCs and has a series of batteries under the desk for backup.

I'd checked the side door, his front door. It had been unlocked. Mel would never have left it unarmed. In the corner under his coats on the mat all his shoes had been jumbled out of their pairs.

Porsche had drunk his bowl dry, then wanted out. When I pulled at the sliding glass door it had been locked. The dog tottered out under the deck where he sniffed around, then he'd followed his nose out to the terrace and taken off down the hill.

I'd been all set to follow him when I bumped into Mel's HD camcorder on its tripod. It's what he records his sunsets with. It had been open and empty.

I don't know why I went over to Mel's computer and gave the mouse a nudge. One of the monitors came to life showing a sunset fringed by icons. In the tray a slew of files were open, and the icon for incoming mail was blinking.

Then the howling had started. I'd never ever heard Borscht make that sound before.

I'd stepped out onto the patio and into that mud puddle. The barbecue deck juts out so far that not even a westerly wind brings rain in. The hose, left in a contorted pile, told me how the puddle had got there. Mel always rewinds it on its reel after watering the honeysuckle he's trained to climb the posts from their barrels. They're for the Hummingbirds, long gone by now to their southern wintering grounds.

When I'd gotten to the edge of the patio and looked down at the bottom of the garden, there was Mel's dog pawing at something white.

Chapter 5
LIKE A FOUR ALARM

SATISFIED I'D REMEMBERED all I could as I drove along Airport Way, I went back to sucking up my latte while newly-named Porsche sniffed the stories whizzing by my beater's window. So when a memory of my kids' Dad popped up it blind-sided me.

I met Dwayne Emil Osterman at a fundraiser for the local Boys & Girls Club. I'd been a secretary in a Chicago bank, and had just become a newly-minted Citizen. He'd been the life of the party with a can of beer and a smoke in hand, laughing blue eyes, corny jokes and sexy teasing. He'd reminded me of a photo I'd seen while studying for my citizenship of a young General Eisenhower.

When he asked me out, my biological clock went off like a four alarm, and I convinced myself I had, at long last, found L-O-V-E. Then he invited me to move in to his third floor walk-up apartment off Clark Street and it was a thrill a minute, mostly in bed, until I got knocked-up. Oops!

Even though *La Chapelle*, the little cervical cap I'd

bought when I was bunking with my London flatmates, had been getting a workout I must have forgotten to put it in cuz I was everso surprised when my period stopped, all of a sudden. So I took myself to the Emma Goldman Clinic and was chuffed when I gave Dwayne the news and he said he was glad. So I convinced myself—I was good at that back then—that what we had was as real as any marriage. At the end of my fifth month, I quit my job at the bank and started feathering my nest.

Giving birth had been a fright! Still, it was soon forgotten as I cared for our little daughter June, my Mum's name, with all her fingers and toes and head of astonishing yellow curls. Dwayne turned out to be a Doting Dad and much better at parenting than me, truth be told. That's when he disclosed he was the oldest of five kids: three sisters and a brother.

While I was still nursing, Dwayne wanted some loving and another of his wrigglers made contact. This time he was not so amused and whatever had been between us evaporated. He started sleeping on the couch and leaving real early for work.

Most days he'd come back right after June's morning feed and take her off, returning for the midday milking and leave again. In a daze of loneliness, I shopped, did the housework and was often napping when he brought her back. In my sixth month, when June was already eating solids, my milk dried up and I'd wake to hear them playing in the bath, and him telling her stories as he put her to bed.

Cooper had popped out like the proverbial bun. After taking me in a cab to the hospital in a cab, Wayne whisked June off with him then stayed away the whole time, saying he had to take care of our daughter. Two days later, I staggered up the three flights with my son in my arms to find no one home. It all went downhill from there.

Dwayne gave me a hard time about the name I'd put on the birth certificate. He'd wanted to honor his grandfather, Emil. I'd chosen the name of the only man in my life who'd been close to a father.

Mr. Cooper (I never knew his first name) had been at my first typing lesson at Moneypenny's Secretarial College. Mrs. Nettles had us new girls stand behind our chairs while she introduced this scrawny, bald WWI Veteran with a horribly mangled face and empty sunken eye sockets. He'd sat at one of the manual typewriters while Mrs N read a business letter out of a book. He typed away like a Sten gun, sending the bell on his machine ringing madly. After she looked over his efforts, she waved the page at us.

"Nary an error for Mr. Cooper!" She'd warbled gleefully. "Now imagine what you girls with good, strong eyes could do!"

When I found I had a feel for machines it gave me an excuse to be in Mr. Cooper's company, and once he'd gotten used to me he was quite easy to talk to. He lived in a couple of rooms in the basement of the college where his newfangled transistor radio was always playing. In his workshop he'd teach me how to keep the office machines working. We'd talk about the news or a program, and I'd tell him about my Mum and Pa and my studies.

When I asked about his blindness, he told me he'd been bicycling somewhere near Amiens in France, taking a message from one officer to another when a Hun's shell landed too close. After three years he was discharged from hospital into the care of his sister Gertie. Their pater having died in the Boer War and their mater succumbing to the Influenza Epidemic.

Gertie had been a secretary in the War Office, eventually marrying her boss, Will Moneypenny. They'd never had children and after Will pranged the Alvis into a cow barn in the summer of 1929, she'd started her school, and taught her blind brother to type. I hadn't been able to suppress my giggle when I heard her name, and it was the first time I ever saw Mr C smile.

When I graduated and was ready set out into the working world with my brand new skills, the hardest person to say goodbye to had been Mr C. In that first year away from my Mum and the home I'd always known, he'd taught me so much about taking care of business, of making the best out of the worst. He'd been awfully shy when I'd hugged him farewell.

How I got to America involves my first American friend, Jake, who I also met at Moneypenny's, however, that story will have to wait.

So there I was in Chicago, with two buns out of the oven and three flights of stairs to herd them, their stuff, the shopping and the laundry up and down. I was a beast of burden with no energy for Dwayne.

He chose June's fifth birthday to break the news that he'd rediscovered Jesus and was going home to Oregon. It took a few heart beats for me to realize I wasn't included in his plans, nor were our children. He said I reminded him of his "profligate ways" and out of the blue attacked me for not having "an ounce of faith." And besides, I couldn't walk down the aisle a virgin, could I?

I'd sat at our kitchen table with the kids romping around with the new toys he'd just given 'em, staring at my hands while a high little voice screamed in my head: "You knew I was, the first time. You even said you thought it kinda cute! Me being so old and all."

THE DEAD HUSBAND

A month later he was gone, just like that! And I was all alone with my chickadees. At first I hadn't done so well. It took getting on Welfare and months of mental health therapy to coax me out of my misery. There was nothing I could do about June mourning for her Daddy cuz he'd always been the "good" parent. After I put 'em down for the night, I'd listen to her tell her brother all sorts of grand stories about her everso wonderful Daddy.

The exact moment I became fixated on going west I will never forget: standing in the produce section of a supermarket in the dead of winter, drooling over all the veggies and fruits from California I couldn't afford, while green snot ran out of my kids' noses. The *Sunset* magazines in the mental health clinic's waiting room with their photos of sunlit cities and countryside had sung the rest of that siren song.

My moving sale netted more than enough to buy Greyhound tickets, and the three of us were entranced as we rolled across America following the sun. It was a splendid way to take a rest although I smoked too much to quell my hunger and drank tea and soup so my kids had enough to eat at the depot cafes. Even so, I was revived when we stumbled out into sunny Oakland's bus terminal three days later.

Attached by a dog leash to my kids and dragging my cabin trunk with all our worldly possessions, we made it to a nearby motel. We ate porridge for breakfast and Top Ramen for supper and loverly fresh food all day long as we explored this bright new world by the bay. The green snot, by the way, cleared up before we reached Reno.

With money running out I had a chat with Mrs. Balko, the motel owner and proposed that I clean her units. I'd seen her crew's handiwork and knew I could do it better, and faster. I sailed through her training, thanks to all those years at my Mum's side. I liked the sameness of the rooms even if I wasn't that keen on the decor. And besides, we lived rent-free with all the hot water we wanted, a color telly and access to the laundry room. I was a happy, busy bee with money in my pocket.

It was Mrs B who turned me on to the Ahimsa Food Co-op and I never went back to a supermarket. I bought the co-op's cookbook, sharp knives, a cutting board, wok and steamer pot and our efficiency kitchen was filled with good eats. And I signed June and Cooper up for the co-op's alternative school, which they loved.

In no time I'd saved up enough to take those Human Potential seminars I'd seen flyers for pinned to the co-op's bulletin board, and that's where I met the Birnbaums.

Turns out they were founding members of Ahimsa and were taking a refresher course. They invited me to come play in their hot tub and at their Bridge tournaments. One afternoon as I was washing dishes, Renee asked if I'd clean for them. I enjoyed the winding bus ride into the Piedmont Hills overlooking the bay and their wood and glass house, built in the '30s, was an easy clean. That's where I first met young Borscht, now old Porsche.

A happy year later at the motel, I opened the door to a unit to find a gent sitting by the window with a three-ring binder on his lap. He was small and tidy with lively grey eyes. I apologized and was about to back out when he beckoned me in.

"Where are you from?" He'd said in his own slightly accented voice. When I told him, he waved me to the other chair and then recounted how his father, a

Polish aviator who'd flown with the RAF in the Battle of Britain, got to America.

By the time the cleaning crew caught up with me he'd missed his courses at the conference he was attending. Turns out Clayton ("Please call me Clay") Truman Zumbach was a doctor in a little town in the Pacific Northwest, wherever that was.

When I set out to pick up my kids from school that afternoon, Clay was basking in the courtyard. Said he loved kids and asked if he could he tag along. On the way back he treated us to supper at a McDonald's. June and Coop were thrilled cuz I never took 'em there. Have to say, I couldn't get enough of the French fries.

I'd been one happy woman when I finally rolled into bed that day. I'd liked the man's energy and he'd liked mine, and my kids.

The seminars had been teaching me about accepting the hand I'd been dealt so I was quite prepared to stay single until my kids were grown and flown. Now a new door had opened and behind it was this gentle soul.

After Clay came back from his conference the next day he again took us out to eat although I insisted we go to the restaurant run by the Ahimsa Co-op. Supper and a walk became our day's end ritual. Then he'd sit with me in the courtyard after I'd put the kids to bed. I'd been glad he wasn't a drinker, so over many a pot of tea, we shared our stories.

Too soon he was packing to go back to his life and as sorry to leave as I was to see him go. He called every Friday evening all through May and June before inviting us to come live in Port Townsend. He sent maps and brochures of where he lived and I began to plan. When I gave notice, both Mrs B and the

Birnbaums were quite disgruntled.

Once again I stowed my family's possessions in my cabin trunk (and a suitcase on wheels for my kitchenware), bought train tickets to Seattle and watched sunny, arid California turn into misty, forested mountains. Clay was waiting at the station with a rented minivan. Said he'd never owned a car and wasn't about to start now. He drove us to the ferry dock and as we chugged across sparkling Puget Sound took us up to the cafeteria for snacks. Then he herded us out to the sundeck where seagulls flew along beside us, and we watched the city skyline and the Cascade mountains grow smaller while the foothills of the Olympic came closer. Soon we were driving through more green trees than I'd ever seen.

He settled us in his sweet rental, a '50s three bedroom ranch house which fit my family perfectly. Only then did he mention that his practice manager was retiring in October, so with nary a twinge I went back into office work, although it did occur to me that perhaps Clay's ulterior motive had been to replace the venerable Mrs. Pilzer. Anyway, he quite made up for it with his affectionate attention and those would be the happiest of my mothering years.

Until June entered tenth grade with Coop a year behind and they got into intractable moods, and started campaigning to go live with their Dad. Finally, after a pincer assault that lasted an entire week over how I knew zip about cosmetics and clothes, music and boys (or girls for that matter); how they hated my dumb accent and having an immigrant for a mother cuz I didn't know squat about American school life, my apron strings snapped and I called their father.

He surprised me again by agreeing to finish raising 'em. After school let out he drove up from Eugene, without his wife and offspring. June filled me in on a Labor Day call about how Theresa was a stay-at-home mom with six kids, the oldest being eleven-year old Emil.

Dwayne had sat in his Suburban as our kids stowed their stuff, and with not a word or look at me even when I handed him their folder of papers, drove off. June and Coop were so busy drooling over their Daddy they hadn't looked back. Which was good cuz I was a puddle.

Dear Clay, knowing how that separation was going to pole-ax me, closed his practice and rented an RV to go cherry picking. That week in the hot Yakima Plateau had been glorious. When I said it was like a honeymoon he'd responded by taking me to bed in the middle of the afternoon. We had such fun playing house in that shipshape little nest on wheels, eating ourselves silly on cherries and giggling over the aftermath as we took frantic turns on the throne. We'd driven through some grand countryside, eaten at charming cafés and walked miles in the hot air that smelt of sage and hay.

Tired and content, he'd dropped me off Sunday evening. I hadn't thought twice about it because we often spent nights apart; it was the nature of our relationship and I respected that. I'd simply unpacked, rolled into bed and was out like a light.

I slept through my alarm the next morning, which gave me no time to get emotional about my empty nest. I'd dashed off to open Clay's practice, picking up the messages and mail from the answering service across the road and signing in his patients. As I waited for him to arrive I sorted the mail. When he hadn't appeared after ten minutes I called his home. The phone rang and rang.

Thirty minutes later, full of dread, I shooed his patients out, put the phone over to the answering service, locked up and ran the half mile down the hill to Clay's home.

He was in his sunroom on the chaise longue wrapped in one of my quilts. He'd always loved to watch the sunrise over the Cascades.

I sat beside him, remembering this good man who'd worked his healing ways on my sore and lonely heart. I'd loved his voice and stories.

In the kitchen, I called 911 and picked up one of his office pads lying on the counter. Clipped to it was a business card for a Steven Milnik, Esquire. My friend and lover, whom everyone said was a fine physician, had known something was up cuz he'd scrawled in more than usual untidy writing a note telling me to contact this lawyer. He'd even thanked me for my kindness.

THE PTPD OFFICER WHO KNOCKED at Clay's front door was Bill Westin. He lived down the road from Clay's practice, and with his wife, Marilyn, had brought his three little ones in for shots and colds.

"Hello, Bill, what do we do now?"

"Morning, Sa... Ms Collier. Sorry to be here like this. We're going to miss him. Would you step out so the medics can come in?"

He'd taken my elbow to steady me as I wobbled down to the steps. Then the fire station ambulance backed up the cul-de-sac and soon the EMTS were pulling out the gurney, putting cases on top and rolling toward us. I nodded to Jenny and Paul as they passed by and went inside.

Clay used to give annual physicals to many of the police, fire fighters and first responders. Paul was a

THE DEAD HUSBAND

volunteer and Jenny, like me, was on the logistics crew at the Annual Sandcastling Festival.

Bill Westin took notes when I told him what I'd found, and then a spiffy two-tone blue convertible slid into the spot by Mr. Johanssen's picket gate.

"That's Doc Nelson's '51 Chevy Coupe," Bill cooed. "He's our part-time coroner."

"'Morning, folks." The newcomer doffed his Panama hat as he entered Clay's home.

Bill and I waited in silence until the EMTs came out with Clay's mortal remains in a body bag. They stowed it into the back, climbed aboard and left.

Then Doc Nelson ambled down the path to us, lighting up a smoke.

"How did he..." I tried to ask.

"In his sleep, my dear," he patted my arm. "I'll know more when I cu—do the autopsy."

I watched him head back to his car. That's when a black SUV turned into my narrow street. It stopped beside the coupe and a huge chap got out. The two men shook hands and talked. Soon, slim and dapper Doc Nelson got into his car, pulled into the turnaround and waited for the SUV to park, before leaving, with Bill Westin's eyes glued all over it.

The new chap got out again and strode toward us. He was fitted out in a rumpled gray suit, blue shirt and thin blue tie. I had to look up into the sky to see his tanned and worn face with an old scar along his left jaw. His scalp gleamed under his buzz cut and when he took off his sunglasses, his pale blue eyes under their thick, gray brows were taking in everything. He smelt of oranges.

"'Morning, Officer Westin." The big one rumbled.

"Captain." Bill Westin responded touching the brim of his cover, and for all I knew he disappeared cuz those blue eyes turned on me.

"I'm George Tullock." He stuck out his huge hand, marvelously engulfing mine. "You must be Sally. Lost a good dinner buddy after he met you. Never saw him happier, though. Thought you could use some help."

When the tears started I got my hand back with a folded white cotton handkerchief. When I couldn't stop the wail he folded me into his chest.

It was George who took me to see Steven Milnik in the Proxall Building on Taylor Street. There I learnt my dear friend, having no living relatives, had left me his home, his two rental properties and several thousands of dollars. Clay's investment portfolio and practice were bequeathed to the University of Washington's Medical School.

When I'd stopped crying, Steve asked if, when he'd found an alumnus from the U-Dub to take over Clay's practice, I'd help the new doc settle in. I did, although my heart wasn't in it.

I moved into Clay's cottage and handed over the keys of his sweet rental to a high school teacher with her disabled husband and three kids. In the other, larger one across the lagoon, a hospital nurse already lived with her four kids and her mother.

That autumn when I was moping about having nothing to do and no one to do it with, both George and Steve, on separate occasions, asked if I was going to keep this up for the rest of my life. I knew what I didn't want to do: go back into another office.

So with Clay's seed money, George to bounce my ideas off and Steve's legal direction, I went into the cleaning trade.

Chapter 6

WALLY'S WRECKS

TURNING OFF AIRPORT WAY, Porsche and me zipped past the Jeffco library and on to the four-way stop signs of downtown Port Hadlock.

Security Jerry's office is in the strip mall on one of the corners where a beauty salon, movie rental shop and tax preparer hang their shingles. I crossed the intersection and headed into regrowth forest and Wally's forty acre wrecking yard.

I'd met him at the Chimacum Valley flea market. It starts in a field after the spring hay bales have been hauled off and closes when the wet season comes. It's been doing so since the '60s, and it's huge. People come from the I-5 corridor, Idaho, Oregon and British Columbia to wander around eating goodies and looking at vintage collectibles from the farming and logging industries.

The kids and I had taken the bus going to the Bainbridge Island ferry and when I found a stall of fabulous fabrics under a red, white and blue awning, knowing how I'd be there "forever," they'd peeled off to find friends.

The patriotic awning was Wally's fifth wheel Doggie Heaven. He parks it in the field all summer and sells everything you'd ever need for your companions. He also sells the German Shepherd puppies he breeds, and cars he restores.

Sitting in the shade at an exquisitely restored treadle sewing machine was one of the few black woman I'd seen in the crowd. Dressed in a colorful robe that covered her from neck to feet, the only parts of her I could see were her elegant hands and braided hair, gathered together in a rope down her back, jingling with white beads. Her face had no makeup and was dominated by brown laughing eyes under severely plucked brows. Her voice had a rich accent I hadn't known I missed. Pure Southside Chicago.

"I'm Della. How they call you?"

"Sally Collier."

She did a double-take when I opened my mouth.

"What kind of an accent is that?"

"English. What do you call your dress?"

"A *dashiki*. My youngest, Rosa, brought all this material back from Southern Africa. Our graduation gift, seeing as how her Pop's been giving her cars since she got a license." Della loved to laugh.

I'd been wondering who bought her green and yellow, red and black fabrics out here in the middle of denim and plaid redneck, lumberjack and country music land when a bevy of summer-tanned girls came prancing along in cowgirl boots, tank tops and everso tight hot pants. Their blonde and brunette corn-rowed hair gleamed with bouncing beads.

Once the maidens had giggled off, Della invited me to sit and take a load off. Soon we were sharing children news. She showed me photos of two daughters and three sons all following in their father's footsteps with careers in the military. I showed her grade snapshots of June and Cooper.

Then Wally stepped down from his trailer with a furry puppy curled up in his arm. He was a massive man encased in immaculate navy coveralls, with a head of close-cropped hair and a neatly clipped beard and moustache. All white against copper skin.

He opened the top of a wire cage set in the dry grass and gently lowered the pup in in with its sleeping litter mates. Then he settled himself on a wooden crate and lit a smoke.

Husband and wife were high school sweethearts from long ago Maxwell Street. Until he retired as Chief of the naval auto pool two winters ago, they'd lived in Bremerton for fifteen years. We shared memories of the Windy City and then Della told him to show me his wrecks. And yeah, that's what she called 'em.

One was a scarlet '70 Pinto. He took me for a spin around the back end of the field and I promptly fell in love with that sassy little automatic, even if I could see the ground through some rust holes. She rode sweet and had a working radio and heater. I wrote a deposit check, then went in search of my kids. On the bus home I thought through my finances.

Then June and Coop went into hyper-drive and as I contended with being a dumber than usual parent and running Clay's practice I kept reminding myself I'd lived quite well so far without any car, so how would one help.

After the kids had gone and Clay died, and my finances took a giant step up, I remembered the scarlet Pinto, and wondered if Wally still had it.

"'Course I do!" He rumbled. "You put good money

down, didn't you? Check didn't bounce, did it?"

"Honey?" Wise woman Della soothed her husband. "Seeing how she knows nothing 'bout 'em, why don't you teach her, like you did the kids? Then you can lease it to her."

Every chance I got I took the bus to Wally's lot so I could drive the Pinto around. That's where I met his giant German Shepherd guard dogs: Martin, Luther and wait for it... King. Wally bred King with a couple of pretty females he called... well, I'll leave that up to your imagination.

I studied the state motor vehicle code book and after Wally squeezed himself into the passenger seat and I did all he commanded as he made me practice parking, he opined I was ready for my test. He came with me to the DMV where I passed on the first go.

Whenever I could, I drove off to explore the neck of the woods Clay had brought me to until I'd done the entire circuit of the Olympic Peninsula. Once I even drove over the Hood Canal and Agate Passage bridges to load up on the ferry. After an hour on Seattle's crowded hills I'd turned tail, got lost trying to get back to the ferry dock and had a good cry as we chugged over the Sound. I'll take loaded logging trucks on switchback roads, any day of the week.

Then a bunch of safety laws went into effect and the lack of seatbelts doomed my adored Pinto. Wally graduated me to his newer, "safer" cars none of which had half the character so I didn't bother learning their brands. They were just Detroit beaters.

Wally took care of everything and if anything did go wrong or I got a flat, he'd come out in his tow truck. If he couldn't fix it on the spot he'd take me back to his yard and set me up with another. I'd also turned my Gals onto him.

Wally knew about two things very, very well: cars and dogs. Well, maybe three: women. And no, I don't clean his home. Wouldn't dare given he has one of the best wives a man could pray for.

WITH PORSCHE VETTED, I spent a small fortune on his needs, including a BEWARE OF DOG sign, then headed on home.

I parked at the sidewalk to let Porsche through the gate into my sunny garden. With gusto, he set about marking his new domain. I got his leash out of the Doggie Heaven plastic bag, sat on the porch steps, lit a smoke and watched him explore.

He scooted after his nose with much huffing and sneezing. I loved how his skin would rumple forward when he suddenly stopped at a smell, and his rear legs would lift off the ground. It didn't take him long to get where I didn't want him to pee.

Over by the hollyhocks, gulping in the smells from the compost bin he suddenly got lost and looked around perplexed. I called and he trotted over, licked my hand and sat down in front of me, cocking his head as if to say: "What's next?" I stroked his black head, calling him silly names. He'd take his big brown eyes off me, scan the garden, prick his ears when the surf thundered at the base of the cliff, then look back at me, sniff and lick my cheek.

Time to show him my neighborhood.

Old Mr. Johanssen was out clipping his roses. Ronnie was sleeping in a chair on the stoop. Porsche pushed his nose through Mr J's gate and huffed, his tail all a-wag. Ronnie's ears twitched, his tail flicked and then he was on the steps, marmalade fur standing out all over. He padded toward us, and then, about three feet away, sat and started cleaning himself. Porsche went down with his ears up and tail whipping. I could almost hear him ask "Wanna play?"

"Nice looking dog. Not a barker, I hope. Can't abide barkers," My neighbor said as he emerged from behind his roses.

"Not usually, Mr J. Does Ronnie like dogs?"

He eyed his cat. "Don't look bothered to me. You like these roses? They're for the wife." Clara's seventy-nine. Last spring she lost her footing in their kitchen and broke her hip. She's recovering at the Kah-Tai convalescent center.

Ronnie eased up real close to Porsche's nose and batted it. My dog gave a soft woof and leapt to his feet. Ronnie sat back and grinned.

I said goodbye and with a quiet "Heel!" Porsche came close to my leg, and we crossed the road into Chetzemoka Park. When I looked back, Ronnie was slipping between the gate slats.

Although I could have, I didn't let Porsche off the leash cuz I wanted to know how he'd do in a public place. With no kids about at this time of day we walked undisturbed past the gazebo where people get married and bands play during festivals, and on through the everso tall Spruces.

Ronnie didn't follow us when we left the park and began striding along Jackson Street for a turn around the presidential blocks before heading east for home.

Porsche trotted placidly on a short leash until we scared up a cat. Almost every house in town has at least one. Unlike Ronnie, they scattered at the sight my big, silent companion. Just a tug and a click of my tongue, as Wally taught me, got his attention.

By the time we were on the homestretch we were in fine harmony.

Chapter 7

GRAND TOUR

WHILE PORSCHE DOVE into the rhodies against the chainlink fence by the road, I hauled in his stuff. On my last trip I carried in his bedding. Hadn't sprung for a wicker basket with a cedar chip pillow although I had bought a bed ring for him to snuggle into. He was still outside, grunting and rubbing himself on the branches of the wind-stunted Red Cedar in the far corner of the garden.

I decided his bed would be under the end of the dining table facing the front door. Clay's maternal grandfather had bought this beauty by mail from Sears Roebuck back in the '20s. I'd found the invoice tucked away in Clay's files. $65.26 including shipping from Chicago. The estate appraiser Steve hired told me it was worth upwards of five grand now, and the six original chairs added another three.

I set Porsche's treats and feed under the kitchen counter and filled his new bowls. I liked how his nails clicked on the lino as he came to see what I was doing. He sniffed at the dry food and took off on the

Grand Tour of his new digs.

He was unimpressed by my spare bedroom. Clay's when he was growing up. It's now my office where my business machines roost like hens on an Ikea shelf unit. The closet is stocked with the tools of my trade.

Porsche trotted off to inspect the loo in the hallway. There are skylights in every room so they're brightly lit, when the sun shines.

Then he found my bedroom and sniffed long at my queensize. I've changed everything in here, putting down carpet and bringing in the first new bed I'd ever owned. Over it hangs my Mum's best quilt made from scraps of fabrics you can't find anymore. At the fleamarket I got a couple of end tables and school chairs. Half the closet is a built-in bureau. Out the window are Mr J's rhodies. All I do in here is sleep and dress, except when George stays over.

I growled when Porsche's haunches started bunching up, as if to leap on the comforter. He flinched and cast me a humble look. I said "No!" firmly and he trotted into the bathroom to nose at the throne and peer into the extravagant shower stall Clay'd installed. Porsche sniffed at the trash basket and laundry hamper, retraced his steps and headed into the kitchen, poking his nose into the utility room leading to the carport.

Then the French doors on the east wall beckoned and he explored the sunroom with its thermal panes, tiled floor and potted plants. Here's where Clay had gone to sleep forever, watching that glorious view. I read in here so there's a bookshelf and lamp by the couch. I'll have to set a bed here for my new pal.

Porsche asked to have the sliding glass door opened and stepped down into the little paved patio with its hurricane fence at the cliff edge. You can hear the surf real well out here. Under the deep eave is the grill George bought, where I cook what he hunts up, come rain, fog or shine. You can't get to the garden from here, so Porsche climbed back inside and headed for the sitting room.

He sniffed long at our double recliner facing the vestibule wall where the LCD screen George gave me last Christmas hangs above the entertainment machines. A card table's in the corner beside the bay windows that look out on the park. On it is a huge lazy-Susan I pleaded to buy from the Golden Gate restaurant and on top is a white board. It's for my jiggies. They give me a sense of accomplishment and soothe my nerves. I'm halfway through a 2500 piece vision of Crater Lake. A place I so want to see.

Porsche padded off into the dining room. It's the biggest room and a bit dark so on the far wall I put up a tall mirror to reflect the skylight and the front door. On the inner wall, beyond the wood box and stove stands a buffet with the same provenance as the table. It's where I display my family photos, all the earlier ones in black and white. There's my Mum with Auntie May posing on the front steps of the house I called home all my childhood. They're in matching summer frocks, white sandals and tightly curled hair. I'm between 'em holding on to their hands: a chubby toddler in a smocked dress of the same fabric, white socks and black buckled shoes.

My Mum had been the live-in help for the family in their house at the top of Ladbroke Hill in West Kensington. She wasn't a servant; it wasn't proper to call people that anymore. Auntie May, our only living relative, used to grumble that my Mum was "the dog's body" cuz she did everything for the Missus, the Mister and their six children. The two girls were adopted, unrelated war orphans from the then Czechoslovakia. The sons looked so much like their father we called 'em the Four Musketeers.

My Mum's stories were all about how she grew up at the bottom of that hill where Auntie May still lived in one of the two bedroom row houses built a century before for factory workers. My Mum left school when she was twelve cuz Auntie May, who'd married my Pa's older brother, was the Missus' mother's lady's maid and got my Mum the laundry girl position. As my Auntie May would remind me when I got all "princessy" about working with my Mum, when they'd been young, during The Depression, if someone offered you a job you took it and was grateful, no matter how old you were.

Then there's the formal portrait of my handsome Pa, Jimbo Collier, in his Merchant Navy uniform taken when he was seventeen. He'd been my Mum's childhood sweetheart and on her sixteenth birthday she'd married him. He'd also quit school to work for his Pa delivering coal. My Mum would look so young and dreamy when she told me about their courting. Of how they came straight from the registrar's office to set up house in the basement rooms the Missus had had converted into a flat.

Before The War really started (everyone said those words as if they were in capital letters, the same way as they spoke of The King) my Pa signed up. When I was ten months old his ship, in convoy bringing supplies from Canada was sunk by a pack of German U-boats. I spent my childhood staring at that photo in its place of honor on the mantel above the coal fireplace.

My Mum and me shared the chilly dark bedroom, sleeping on her full size wedding bed. Our dank

THE DEAD HUSBAND   57

bathroom across the entry hall had a tub, sink, throne and a pathetic one bar electric heater. At the end of the corridor beyond the water heater and baggage room was the coal cellar, which I knew well cuz I spent many a night there snuggled in in one of my Mum's quilts during air raids. The Missus and Mister were there too. Their kids were with the grandparents by the sea.

The first job my Mum set me to was cleaning all the fireplaces and dumping the ashes on the midden in the little back garden. Then I laid crumpled up newspaper and clinkers. By the light of a weak bulb, I had to refill the brass scuttles (my first polishing task) from that coal cellar into which my Pa's Pa poured sacks from his barrow. When I was seven, my Mum told me he wouldn't be delivering anymore cuz he'd died of lung disease. She never talked about her own family so I badgered my Auntie May into telling me what happened.

"A bomb blew half the row to pieces. Your Ma's Pa and Ma, your Pa's Ma and my hubby, home on leave, were buried in the shelter. Your Granpa lived 'cause he was night watchman at the factory I worked the night shift two streets over. There, you satisfied now?"

The summer I graduated from school with my GCE "O" levels, the Missus came down to tell us that the Mister was retiring and they were selling the house. She had tears in her eyes as she gave my Mum an envelope and a black jewelry box from a shop on Bond Street. Inside the thick envelope was a note of thanks, a two hundred-pound postal order and letters of reference for both of us.

In the box, laid out on blue velvet, was a set of earrings and a necklace of tiny, pretty pearls. My

Mum never wore jewelry besides her engagement and wedding rings, and as Andrea, my best school chum, had given me a pair of earrings she'd found at the Portobello Market and chivvied me into letting one of her aunts pierce my ears, my Mum gave me the box. When I put those little pearls on, I felt everso posh.

That evening my Mum announced she'd decided to move in with Auntie May. She took Pa's photo down, turned the clamps, pulled off the backing and handed me my inheritance. Inside the post office savings book was my birth certificate and a faded, much-folded document about my Pa's death. Then I started to read the pages and pages of weekly deposits dating from five months before my birth, at home, so the certificate informed me.

"I never wanted for nought but your Pa." My Mum said as she handed me the Missus' money order. "It's not much, dearie, but it'll give you a start."

I looked at the last total, thinking it was a lot. I showed her the one large deposit early in The War.

"What's this one, Mum?" She peered at it and sighed, wiping her eyes.

"That's your Pa's death compensation." Thank you, Pa! "What'll you do?" She asked, resting her cheek on her palm as she leaned on the arm of her chair. She looked nackered.

"Are you all right, Mum?"

"Just tired, dearie. Not looking forward to the move. Where will you go?"

"Thought I'd look along the High Street. Drop in at that job agency the school told us about."

My Mum hadn't wanted me in the way as she packed up her life, so I put my things in an old suitcase the family didn't use anymore and set it beside our front door, the one I'd come in and out of every day of my life.

The next morning all decked–out in my best bib and tucker, hand-me-downs from one of the upstairs girls which my Mum had altered, I was too excited to eat anything except dry bread and a cuppa. With the loverly handbag the Missus gave me for my birthday tucked under my arm, I set out to see what kind of work the Blakely Placement Agency had for me.

When I read the application form the receptionist handed over, my hopes were dashed as I couldn't check off anything in the office skills sections.

I instantly liked the heavyset lady dressed all in black who ushered me into her office and gestured for me to sit in front of her everso neat desk with a bouquet of bronze mums in a brown glass vase. Under her forearms, on a big white blotting pad were my application and GCE certificate.

"What are you looking for, Miss Collier?" She asked in a kind, crisp voice.

"A good job that'll show me something of the world, before I settle down."

"Mother hinting about grandchildren, is she?" When she asked that her smile was everso sad, and I guessed that the framed photos on the bookcase behind her, of two chaps in army uniforms, one much older than the other, both with the same eyebrows, nose and chin, meant Mrs. Blakely was not only a war widow, she'd lost her son.

"I know an excellent secretarial college less than a mile up the High Street. It will do for you very well, I think." She picked up her phone and asked to be connected to a number.

"Ah, Moneypenny, 'tis I. Yes, it definitely is. I have a young woman in my office in need of training. Do you have any openings? Please repeat that? Why, yes.

No, not at all. Would you? Splendid! I will send her along momentarily. Thank you, my dear." When she hung up her smile was pure glee. "You are in luck, my dear, a new term is to start in a fortnight."

On the back of one of her business cards she began writing with her fountain pen in the greenest ink I'd ever seen.

"Make your way to this address." She blotted the card and handed it to me. "Present this and the rest will be up to you. When you obtain your diplomas, I will find you a good position."

With her card tucked into the palm of my glove I set off for Moneypenny's Secretarial College which throbbed with voices, clatter and tinkling bells. The receptionist, a girl much like me, had a brass nameplate on her blouse that read Hyde-Smith, took Mrs. Blakely's card and lifted a telephone to her ear. I watched her hesitate over a box of blinking lights and black buttons before pressing one.

Out of the door across the office sprinted, and that's the only way to describe how she moved, the tallest, gauntest and most brightly dressed woman. Under her long mauve cardigan, her sky blue blouse was dazzling. She wore pigeon gray trousers and strode on gray suede lace-ups, with glossy, wood Cuban heels.

It was her hair, though, that had me gawking. Wavy on top, it was clipped as short as a man's at the sides and back and was also mauve, though the roots were pure white. She wore not a dab of makeup and her white eyebrows, like angel wings, flew all over her forehead. Her welcoming grin turned a lipless mouth into a fence of long, creamy teeth.

She raised part of the counter, waved me through and swept me into her office where she pointed to a chair on the nearside of a desk.

"Do sit!" She loped around the expanse of wood and settled in her red leather chair. "So you're Blakey's latest find, what?" She peered over her glasses resting halfway down her nose, framed in the same blue as her blouse. Her eyes were huge and the color of her cardigan. Everything about her was long, especially her neck and fingers.

"Just a sec!" She grabbed one of her two phones that was ringing, "Moneypenny! What? Yes, just now. Absolutely! Tata!" She rubbed her hands together. "The esteemed Mrs B wanting to know if you'd made it." She leaned backwards, grabbed the edge of her desk and pulled herself forward into the leg well.

"So, you want to be a secretary!" She pronounced it "secritry." All I could think of was that I should have asked to use the loo as soon as I got there.

"I was, once upon a time." She went on, smoothing the edge of her purple blotter with those long, suntanned fingers. "Back in the dark ages. Dreary little jobs till I got the position that suited. At the War Department, of all places. Married my boss. Which I do not recommend, by the by!" Her eyebrows flapped as she glared at me. "Should have lasted till our dotage, except he pranged the Avis and left me in widow weeds. Didn't have any offspring, couldn't go back to those smelly offices so I started this school. Long before The War."

She looked around her office, bright from the sun shining in the tall window off the High Street. There on the sill had been another bouquet of mums, only purple. All the mauve-hued walls were hung with certificates, calendars, blackboards and framed photos of groups of girls. Behind her was a huge color photograph of The Queen in her coronation robes.

"We pride ourselves in teaching our girls skills they'll use for the rest of their lives." She drummed her fingers on her desk, then looked up at me. "So they can earn their keep and keep out of trouble, what!" She winked, and I giggled. "You know the world's your oyster when you're a secretary!"

I reached up and touched the necklace the Missus had given my Mum.

"Now," she said getting serious. "What do you want to learn?"

"Typing. Shorthand. Telephones—"

"Ah, the works!" She sized me up.

"Yes, Mrs. Money—"

"Crikey, girl, plain Moneypenny will suit. And you will be..." She glanced down at a leather bound note book beside her. "Collier? What a sturdy name! 'Spect we'll shorten it to Collie. Will that... bother you?" She cocked her head, making a long face.

"Yes," I snapped out of it. "No, I mean..."

"You'll get used to it!" She snorted. "And a sight more before I'm through with you! Now, let's talk filthy lucre."

As she wrote, hugely in purple ink, in that notebook I listened to her totting-up the cost, and clutched my handbag, almost hearing the coins in my Mum's post office savings book clinking out of it.

"Can I earn some of my way?" I asked after a deep breath. "I'm a good scullery girl. And I do laundry and clean. Here, I've got a reference."

"Can you? I expect so." Moneypenny took the letter. "May you is another matter, what?" She scanned what the Missus had written then handed it back, "Excellent recommendation, by the by. Most girls don't want to see the inside of a kitchen, let alone pick up a broom. Ha!" She looked at me again, tapping the end of her fountain pen against her chin. "Tell you what, Collie! Eat and be merry till this lot's gone. Then we'll put you to work." She pushed herself away from her desk and stood up. "Care for the Grand Tour?"

I followed her to the maze of doors on the ground floor which, one by one, she opened to give me glimpses of groups of girls and their teachers. Then she herded me up the worn marble staircase.

"It's Finals fortnight." She spoke over her shoulder as she pranced upwards, never touching the banister. "By the end of next week they'll be off to the four corners. Silly saying really, don't you think?" The skylight high in the roof lit up her wink. We got to the landing. "Then it's quiet as a church till the new girls arrive. If you truly care to work off some of the cost we'll have plenty to do before term starts. Come, let's see which room you'll be in."

On the landing she inspected a blackboard on the wall lit by a lamp and covered with names in boxes.

"Ah yes, thought so. You'll be in Victoria with Jake. When she's gone, it'll be… Chitterjee from New Delhi. Daughter of one of my first pupils. I'll be picking her up at Heathrow when I send Jake back to America. You'll like Jake." She wrote my surname in chalk in the empty spot.

"Come!" She ordered as she clapped the dust off her fingers and headed for the next flight. "Up in the gods here." I was panting when she loped around the landing to the next flight and trotted on up, under the skylight. She opened the closest door with its portrait of the Old Queen as a young woman on it.

"You'll meet Jake tonight. That's Ruth Esther Jacoby to her parents. She's a lively one. Motor mouth, she calls herself. Apt sobriquet. Works in her father's bank in Chicago."

The Victoria room was about the size of my Mum's sitting room, with a window at the far end and twin beds sticking out from opposite walls each with a worn rug beside it. One was covered by a drab blanket and had a pair of bright green plastic slippers set right where you'd need 'em. On the other the mattress was rolled up beside a pillow and a folded khaki wool blanket. The quilt my Mum and I'd finished that summer would brighten up the place.

"You won't have much privacy, you know." Moneypenny eyed me.

"I don't now. I... my Mum and I share."

"Do you now..." She said quietly looking around the room. "Then this won't be new to you. That's good 'cause some of my girls get ticked-off at first. 'Why did Daddy pay for this...' What's Jake's word?" She frowned at the ceiling. "Ah yes, dump! I tell 'em it's shades of things to come for the working girl. Bed-sitters, you know!" When she saw I didn't, she shuddered. "You will! They're a fate worse than goal."

When we were back on the ground floor, Moneypenny took me out to the portico. She sat down on a park bench and brought a slim gold case and lighter out of her cardigan pocket.

"Best pop on home and get your things." She blew out smoke. "Be back by seven. Every working woman deserves a good dinner after a long day at the office. No grub if you're late!"

I put out my hand and she looked at it.

"Did I mention I play tennis?" She grinned. "It's been a jolly good summer, don't you think? What!" Her grip was fierce and I had to laugh.

I was still giggling as I loped home over the hill, thinking about the first night I'd be spending away from my Mum.

When I burst through our front door bearing a bunch of purple mums, my Mum was napping in the sitting room in her armchair. I made a pot of tea, laid the tray and put the flowers in the pretty chipped vase she couldn't throw away.

"Mum," I said loudly, setting the tray on the card table. "Tea time."

My Mum wiped her face with her hands, then saw the mums. "How lovely, dearie."

I gave her a cuppa just the way she liked it and sat down on my chair.

"I got into a school on the High Street. I'm going to be a secretary."

"That's nice, dearie, when do you start?"

All of a sudden I noticed how worn and cracked my Mum's hands were with blue, ropey veins on their backs. And the yellow cast to the rings under her eyes, her hollow cheeks. And so skinny. Seemed like this year she'd aged a hundred.

"Are you ill, Mum?"

"Nought that a good rest won't cure." She murmured into her cup.

"You won't get that at Auntie May's."

"Oh yes I will!" She flashed a warning look at me. "She's had a char come in for years, don't you know. Does the laundry too. Your auntie just wants the company." She stifled a yawn and finished her tea. "I'll be a lady of leisure, you'll see! Finish those quilts. For the little ones." She made her faded blue eyes wide with hints.

I wasn't thinking of husbands and babies so I stayed on a safer subject.

"Then it's all right if I go?"

"Why ever not? Nought's here for you."

"I'm going to..." I hesitated wondering how to say it. I decided to stay simple. "I've got to live-in there."

"You do?" My Mum looked surprised. "You'll stay in touch, then? Visit?"

"Bank on it, Mum. I'm going to miss you bad."

"Oh, you'll forget your old Mum out there in the big world. But you be careful, dearie, you don't know a thing about... I wish your Pa were..." She dabbed at her eyes with her faded apron. I hadn't seen her sew a new one in years.

"I bet he's up there watching us right now, Mum." I patted her hand, and she shrank away. For an instant I'd forgotten how she didn't take to touching.

"When will you go?" Suddenly she coughed, clearing her throat.

"Now." I said, feeling everso mean. I wondered if she knew she was wringing her hands.

"Now?" She whispered, blinking slowly as she stared at the unlit fireplace.

"As soon as I start earning, I'll bring you money." I sat up straight and poured us another cuppa.

"I'm not worried about that, dearie, I've my pension." My Mum pulled herself upright and accepted the fresh cuppa. "Don't you bother yourself about me. You'll need every penny out there on your own. Now, tell me what this school's like?"

IT WAS AN ADVENTURE, and on the buffet in my dining room clear on the other side of the world is my graduating class photo. I'm clustered with my soon-to-be flatmates and in back of us twelve girls stands Moneypenny and Mrs. Dell, the housekeeper. On either side of 'em are the other mistresses, and yup, that's what we called 'em! If Mrs. Blakely hadn't been visiting that day and hadn't tucked herself in at the

THE DEAD HUSBAND 67

end of the row, I'd never have gotten an image of her.

In another frame I set a couple of menus and the ticket of my emigration cruise around a Polaroid shot I'd paid a returning college student all of five dollars to take of me leaning over the rail of the old Italian rust bucket, the *Castel Felice*. It's my first color photo and in dawn's early light, I'm pointing to the Statue of Liberty, with the New York skyline beyond.

In a frame showing my Naturalization Certificate, I've got a couple of Polaroids from my Chicago years. One Jake's mom took when we were dressed as witches, scaring neighborhood kids on their porch during my first American Halloween, and the other's of the Jacobys and me at my Swearing In Ceremony.

Then there are my kids' school portraits ending with the graduation ones they sent from Oregon.

Hung on the wall is a yard wide panorama of shots I took of the Snake River on the Lewis and Clark Trail, on that cherry picking trip with Clay.

Haven't gotten any pictures of my Man yet.

Tucked in a corner is the industrial sewing machine I bought at the fleamarket from a retired theatrical seamstress who'd hauled it all the way from Broadway some thirty years before after she retired from PT's drama school. I'd also bought her wooden spool rack, ironing board and tailors hams for pressing bodice darts and shoulders. I put up lamps and a shelf for my Mum's sewing basket.

I'm a quilter from way back when I helped my Mum with hers. All done by hand during those long ago coal-heated London winters. I hear from my old school chum Andrea since it's been banned, the city's now cleaner than before Charles Dickens' time.

I stow my fabrics in two steamer trunks: the one I've lugged along for most of my life. The other Clay's father brought with him after VE Day. As he told it, his Dad met an American bomber pilot who'd told him to present himself at Boeing in Seattle, as a test pilot. There he found his friend who'd taken him sightseeing on the Olympic Peninsula and they'd stopped in Port Townsend, still an undeveloped little port back then. He'd seen this lot for sale and bought it. When he married his friend's sister, her family helped him build. Clay was their only child.

I also got him to tell me how he met his wife, Eleanor Jane. They'd been freshmen at the U-Dub and "had" to get married. While visiting his parents here she'd miscarried. Back then there was no hospital here and no supply of Rh negative blood, so she and the baby died. Years later, after Clay set up his practice and bought property (the rental I moved into when I first got here) his parents retired to Florida where, two years before I met him, they'd died in a nursing home, within days of each other.

After Clay moved into his parents' cottage he hadn't wanted to haul in wood for the stove and as he had no one at home to keep the place warm while he worked long hours, he had baseboard heaters installed with a central thermostat. One of the first things I did was have Al, the chimney sweep, take a look at that wood stove. He showed me how inefficient it was so I bought one of his floor demos with a loverly window. Now I can watch the flames as I did with the coal fire in my Mum's sitting room.

Porsche clicked over to his water bowl, lapped up half of it and sniffed at his chow again. I wondered when he'd start eating. I called him to his bed. He circled around inside his bed ring, flopped down, heaved a sigh and closed his eyes. He'd maneuvered around my home just fine.

Chapter 8

SAL'S GALS

BEFORE I TOOK OFF for my next job I got a cuppa and went into my office to check in with my Gals. I have eight now, cleaning everything from timeshares to restaurants, motels to offices and homes of all shapes and sizes all over the Quimper and Miller peninsulas and as far east as Shine and Port Ludlow by the Hood Canal Bridge.

After I left Dr. Berghoff settling in with Clay's patients, I'd canvassed likely places around town, showing Mrs. Balko's letter of reference from the Oakland motel, and had been hired lickety-split. Seems good chars were hard to come by up here. Before I knew it all my nights were filled with cleaning taverns and restaurants, and I was sleeping away most of my mornings. So I placed flyers around for day work which netted Mrs. Wallen. She turned me on to a couple who were doctors and the Sizkorski home. Soon I was booked solid, 24/7, and I was getting inquiries all the time.

One day I asked Mrs W, in my leaving note, what

I should do, given I had no more hours in my life to work. She called me a couple of evenings later and invited me over for a talk. And no, I couldn't use her house to train prospective chars: it would drive their security company nuts, and their already high insurance into the stratosphere.

Mrs W sat me at her dining table under the blazing chandelier and set before me a glossy mauve and teal folder. Inside was a perfectly presented business plan together with a list of proposed company names and employer rules, hiring and firing policies, getting a bookkeeper, bonded and insured, et cetera, et cetera, et cetera. She even had a classified ad all ready to run in *The Leader*, Port Townsend's weekly rag. One of her company names had been Sal's Gals.

Then she'd suggested I contact her friends, the Hudson-Polks. She'd already spoken to them and they'd be thrilled to have their home cleaned in exchange for using it as my training premises.

The first week I ran my ad I got five applicants right out of high school. Rejected every one of 'em. Why? They'd chewed gum, came dressed up in sexy outfits, sported lashings of makeup, silly hair-dos and hadn't listened to a word I'd said.

By the time the older women started coming out of the woodwork I'd gotten good at my spiel about how to clean our clients' homes, not their messes. Something I learnt at Mrs B's motel: never touch clients' personal stuff! Which means they have to be trained to pick it up before I get there. Why? I'm a char, not a maid.

I also talk about how Sal's Gals prides themselves on being neatly dressed, punctual in both coming or going and never bringing anyone with, for any reason. Nor were they to give out exact locations to their

THE DEAD HUSBAND

family and friends, just a street or neighborhood name. To always be alert for unusual patterns in the owners' housekeeping; answer their notes briefly and politely and notice when supplies were needed or anything new happened such as phone calls, loiterers outside, package deliveries.

Opening every window and door that will, is the first thing I teach. You'd be surprised how novel an idea that is. I blather on about how it lets the home breathe; getting rid of all the snaggly emotions, rinsing the place with fresh air.

In the beginning, my crew was not impressed by my company's name. In my former life as a secretary in Chicago at my American friend, Jake's father's bank the matronly office manager, Molly Markowitz, had collectively called all us office workers her "gals." I'd liked her firm and concerned control of us industrious, if immature stenographers, typists, file clerks, copy machinists and telephone operators.

And thus Sal's Gals are:

Joanne the Magnificent, a logging widow born and raised in PT, older than me by maybe a decade. Having just survived a bout with cancer which she doesn't talk about, she's handed off her pet and childless homes among us and has taken over running our company. Her daughter and two sons, long flown from the coop are, from the photos on her fridge, producing quite a tribe. She lives with her cats out on Vista Place overlooking PT Bay and Indian Island. She favors sweat suits.

Ethel the Ready's a transplant from San Diego and a longtime divorcee, about my age. Her two kids are in the military. One on her third tour in Iraq, the other's at the Pentagon. Ethel has a full head of red hair and a mouth and mind that'll surprise you. She has a degree in French Literature: don't ask, I don't know. What I do know is she has highbrow taste in furniture and can spot the provenance of a piece at fifty paces. I've seen her do it. And she swears loudly, in French. She'll clean anything that doesn't move and works seven days a week so she can take off for France every winter.

Wonder Woman Annie has a BA in PhysEd and used to be a high school basketball coach. Heading toward forty and topping six foot, she's our self-defense coach. At one time or t'other, most of us have had to use what she's taught especially when the males of the house are home. As one husband put it, there's something real sexy about Annie's butt when she's bending over the dishwasher. For a while he couldn't indulge in any connubiality nor smile without breaking open his split lip. Annie's a Vegan and into Yoga, and prefers older homes with mazes of rooms stuffed with clutter. She's buying and renovating a Victorian on Jefferson Street with...

Lois the Blueswoman. She's my age, short and not at all sweet. She's dating the aforementioned deputy sheriff and works only motels and taverns. She brought two of each with her when she joined. Also from Chicago, she sings at the Wise Fools West most weekends and still knows many of the Blues singers, enticing 'em out here for the annual festival. Clean and sober for twelve years, though she still smokes, she's big on the perils of booze and drugs.

Joy the Babe lives on a classic wooden sailboat at Point Hudson with her husband, a sail maker. She's stacked like Jane Russell, walks like John Wayne and talks like him on helium. She prefers condominiums and timeshares and brought six with her: four in Glen Cove and one a piece on Marrowstone Island

and along Dabob Bay. After the New Year, when her units are mostly vacant she sails around the South Seas and we all pick up her slack. By spring she's ready to be back on terra firma.

Shy Sandra from South Dakota just turned thirty and lives alone in a charming cottage out by Fort Worden. She works only two full days cuz she's our CPA and tax preparer. She even cleans like one, counting everything each time. That's how she discovered a burglar had been through one of her homes. She called the wife and then the police who let slip that just about every house in the neighborhood had been hit over the past year.

As the primary suspect, there'd been so much mayhem in her life she'd gone to the mental health clinic (for which Sal's Gals paid) and brought its cleaning needs to us. When Sandra had seen the monogrammed forks and spoons at a garage sale in North Beach, she'd made a citizen's arrest of the cutlery-knappers.

Zany Zoe was a music major at Ann Arbor U, Michigan. At twenty-eight she's our youngest. She sings like Doris Day and knows every song from every classic American musical. While attending Centrum's music festival at Fort Worden she'd fallen in love with the town and joined a commune in the Hippy Hollow. She's also into Yoga and prefers homes with children.

And then there's our floater Judith, of age indeterminable. She has a doctorate in Women's Studies and two passions: Internet research and gardening though she's a good char. She takes up our slack whenever we have to be someplace else. Because of her we've all graduated to PDAs in which we store our clients' data.

Yes, our business maintains an impeccable

reputation and makes quite a nice profit, thank you very much!

So you see, my Gals are all amply qualified. None knew each other before they answered my ad. Oh, and we get together and stay over at each others' homes once a month to talk shop.

I DIDN'T GET THE IDEA to clean with a spiritual bent from my Mum. She never spoke about religion and I learnt not to raise the subject. On Sundays, I'd listen to the bells chime in the church steeple at the top of the hill and wonder why we never went there. Whenever a religious service came on the wireless she'd turn it off. I did ask my Auntie May about it once. She'd actually gotten red in the face and snapped about "ruddy rubbish!"

It's not that my Mum didn't clean that home well, she did. It's just that she didn't do it with a light heart, have fun. Oh, quit sniggering! Of course you can have fun cleaning house. What's the first thing little girls play at?

Years later, Richard, my Chicago therapist turned out to be a bit of a prophet. You see, Dwayne's Parthian shot that I didn't have an ounce of faith cut deep. Richard said I'd find my faith, and I did, in Berkeley in an enchanting Tibetan Buddhist temple. One of the things I'd loved to do there was sweep the steps and garden inside the cedar fence, listening to the wind chimes and the chanting, high on wafting incense, on the energy in that enclave. So cleanliness and godliness became entwined and the places I clean become holy. I'm known to say that chars need to walk lightly, sing praises and carry a good broom. Of course these days, we tote vacuum cleaners.

I'm not preachy about it, mind you. When a

THE DEAD HUSBAND 75

prospective client leaves a message on my business voice mail it's usually something along the lines of: "Hello, my name is Jane Doe and I was just over at Mary Goodwife's. When I told her how good her home looked she told me about your company. Could you add mine? It desperately needs it. Oh, and I have a business office that could do with some TLC. Here's my cellphone number. Leave word and I'll get right back. The best time to reach me is between seven and eight in the morning or after nine at night."

Just to surprise her I'll call on the dot of seven. We'll do a bit of a schedule jig until we can come up with a time for me to look her over. Oops, Freudian slip there! Most times I'll know before I go, usually cuz she'll balk at our rates, or I can't get a word in edgeways. Only once have I been wrong and that was cuz the home owner had just come off a business jaunt to the Far East with a bad case of jet lag and still flying at 500 mph.

SO, ALL MY GALS WERE ABOUT their ordinary Mondays and all was right with their worlds. I sat staring out the window wondering why I hadn't mentioned my strange morning, and why I was still cleaning for the Birnbaums. I knew I hadn't wanted to hand it off to anyone. I'd had feelings for Renee. When she'd taken that job with the entrepreneur Alan Hatton a couple of years after they moved up here, things sort of faded between us. As I figured it, she'd started out commuting, then staying over. Had she also taken to what was in his fly?

For years now whenever I came to clean, the house would be desolate with Mel holed-up in his den and Claire at school.

Once, when I was almost done and before Mel had

returned from walking the dog, Renee'd whirled in leaving a limo purring outside. Just here to grab some clothes, check on hubby, leave a message for the kid and then she was off again, no doubt, to another great gala. Where once she'd been a down-home kind of wife and mom comfy in jeans, t-shirts and domesticity, she'd transformed into a fashion plate in fancy suits, styled hair, expensive perfumes and jewelry.

Just last month I'd been thinking it was time to let this job go. Renee'd already left, if I read the cards right. And Claire? I hadn't seen her since her graduation.

What had really bothered me though, was that positive pregnancy test kit.

DONE WITH MY CALLS, I was in need of another cuppa before loading up Porsche and setting out for my afternoon job. The Hudson-Polks' is a three storey, six bedroom, four bathroom home up on Morgan Hill. I love cleaning it. It has a welcoming, much lived-in feel. They're a twice-married couple with eight teenagers between 'em. Four of each gender with two adopted: a girl from India and a boy from Romania. Every one of 'em musicians and their home's a clutter of instruments. The Missus has a passion for cut flowers so Judith works the garden and leaves bouquets in the mud room.

Breaking my own rule I took my cuppa to my end of the recliner just to catch my breath, and promptly conked out.

Chapter 9

BANGING THE HUSBAND

PORSCHE, BARKING UP A STORM, blew me out of my nap. I peeked out my bay window to see a Jeffco sheriff's cruiser parked outside where two deputies were settling their covers on their heads. Soon they were knocking.

"I'm putting the dog in the back!" I called through the mottled glass diamond in my front door. I hustled my growling canine into the sunroom and after making sure the door to the patio was open, and he had water out there, pulled the door shut.

Deputy Banner, the shorter, older copper who often wins the annual Kinetic Sculpture race, was grinning when I opened my door.

"Hyah, Sal... er... Ms Collier, Sheriff Morrow asks if you'd come to the office."

"Why?"

"Didn't say, ma'am," said gruff-voiced Deputy Ramirez. I'd never met him before. You have to realize we're a sparsely settled county and, as George has explained, the departments of those who Serve and

Protect, funded by our taxes, frequently intermingle. Clay having left me a nice stash and me running my own business, I now know something of taxes.

"You like dogs?" I asked. They both shook their heads. "Gotta settle mine down." I shut 'em out and ran to set Porsche free from the little patio. Back on his bed, he looked up at me, ears perked, a huge question on his face.

"Guard the house!" I ordered in my best bossy voice. I took off my uniform which I hadn't realized I'd slept in and threw it in the hamper, dressed in a sweat suit and made sure I had my wallet and keys, and left. Most of the time I don't lock my door, and now with Porsche on guard, I figured it was even safer. The idea flitted through my head that I'd better put up that BEWARE OF DOG sign I'd just gotten from Wally's Doggie Heaven.

As we drove in silence up Sims Way, I suddenly realized where I wasn't. I speed dialed Judith, catching her as she was leaving for some gardening.

"Got a problem, Jude. Sorry to dump it on you so late, can you cover the Hudson-Polks?"

"That's cool, Sal-da-Gal, always liked their place. When was I supposed to be there?"

I looked at my watch, "Thirty-five minutes ago."

"Sleeping on the job, Boss? Have you called their security? Give me their code." I recited the numbers.

"You really can do it?"

"Sure, nothing in the Keene's yard can't wait."

"I'll call security right now. Thanks a bunch."

"No prob, is why I'm da floater."

Once upon a time, just about every home we worked had no security other than locked doors. In this post-9/11 new normal, with meth labs and illegal aliens on the rise in our neck of the woods a whole new industry has sprung up. We're all still getting used to the protocols, codes and alarms, however, only the primary cleaner can register a change of circumstances with their homes' security company. There are now two companies in Jeffco: the aforementioned Jerry in Port Hadlock and the upstart GuardWell here in town. Marci took my new information on the first go.

The ride to the new Justice Center building in Port Hadlock took less than ten minutes, probably cuz the lights were flashing on the cruiser. Then Banner and Ramirez got me through the metal detectors and inspection, and turned me over to Deputy Markham, a woman I'd met at PT's Blues Festival, and hadn't known was a cop. She was perhaps a little younger than me and looked smart in her uniform. I liked the way she strode about in her black sport shoes, glad the department hadn't hobbled her in high heels and a silly skirt. Perhaps she'd broken the sartorial ceiling.

I looked around. No Renee. No Claire.

Markham did know something. Seems Mrs. Birnbaum, when she'd phoned in, had said I'd been banging her husband for years. The deputy had the decency to grimace as she ushered me into an interview room. Just before she closed the door, George came striding up.

"Let me speak with her for a moment, Deputy."

"All yours, Captain."

George waved me into the room and to a chair on the far side of the table. He sat opposite me, with a wide mirror behind him.

"What're you doing here?" I whispered.

"I work here, remember?"

"Should you be talking to me?"

"I can poke my nose any place I want." George huffed, and patted my hand. "It's just an interview, hon. With Smith, the lead detective. Remember? We'll talk more after dinner."

"What if they don't let me out?"

"They will."

"Then why am I here?"

"Because of the wife's accusation."

"They found her?"

"Not yet. Were you banging him?"

"No! Why would I? I've got you."

"That's what I told 'em."

"What did they say?"

"Ever hear of adultery?"

"Jeez, George, that's crude."

"So's murder, Sally."

I sat back in the chair and blew out a breath. "Well, I didn't do it. No motive. And from what I saw he'd been dead long before I showed up."

"That's the key. You not being there since what... last Monday?. The security tapes'll verify that, right?" He got to his feet. "So where were you last night?"

"Home alone, as you well know. Oh yeah, Joy dropped by for an hour. Then I moped around cuz my main squeeze was catching zzzs elsewhere."

"Gotta go, sweet pea." He made ready to leave.

"You'll bring the meat?" Reluctant to see him go.

"Don't I always?" He made a huge wink.

It's true, without George I'd be one scrawny vegetarian, mostly cuz I know nothing about meat. He, on the other hand, is a throwback to the Noble Hunter, bringing me succulent steaks and ribs. He just doesn't cook any of it, which leaves me sweating over his propane grill while he unwinds in the sunroom with a diet Pepsi and a smoke. I keep him up at night, as payback.

I watched him walk across the bull pen. He's a big man. Owns three shabby gray suits, a drawer full of blue shirts neatly encased in plastic from the cleaners, and two blue ties. I gave him a colorful one, once. He grunted a thanks, and wears it to work for the Holidays, just to humor me. He also owns three pairs of brown shoes as glossy as horse chestnuts.

"Don't have to bother deciding what to wear if it's all the same." He'd growled when I commented on his wardrobe. Images of a fussing wife popped into my head, so I shut up.

What I like most about George Harold Tullock is his constancy. Not that he's predictable or dull, so much as he doesn't go in for surprises. What you see is what you get. What you don't see under his jacket, unless it's a hot day, are his weapon and badge.

What he wears on his days off are blue plaid shirts, stretch blue jeans, and WalMart sport shoes, like mine, only four sizes bigger. He doesn't wear green. Says there's too much all around and he doesn't want to blend in. As if he could!

Every morning, rain or shine, before he breaks his fast at the Salal Café, he walks the four blocks from his apartment building on the bluff above the sports field to the only barber in town for a shave and shine.

During those first inquisitive months when we started keeping company, George told me that after Vietnam his priorities changed. He decided his body was as important as the auto he bought out of the dealership every September. He favors black SUVs.

"Must I remind you," I'd snipped when I first saw him in it, "these are the most coveted by chop shops?"

"Actually, they're not. Besides, no one would dare

steal from a cop!" He grinned out of his window.

"How many miles to the gallon does it get?" I peered in at the airliner wannabe dashboard.

"Enough for my comfort and joy." He patted my shoulder.

"George! It's... embarrassing." I hadn't realized how close we were, close enough for kissing.

"Yeah, but it drives like a dream. Let me show you." And he did, out along SR20, effortlessly over Eaglemont Hill to the bottom of Discovery Bay, and then south on Highway 101 beside the Hood Canal, through forest and settlements with those haunting water views, while we listened to Ray Lynch's *Deep Breakfast*. That's another thing I like about him: he loves wordless music.

When we got to the junction for Olympia, the state capital, he asked if I had to go home. When I said I didn't, he turned southwest through the Willapa Hills, ending at Long Beach in the late afternoon. We found the manager of a condo who rented us a ground floor unit, and told us the best place to eat was at the tavern. After a scrumptious surf and turf dinner we wrapped up in the comforters off the two queensize beds, and sat on the balcony to watch the sun sink into the Pacific Ocean. Lying separately in those beds with the constant rumble of the sea, I'd hardly slept a wink. George, naturally, had conked out the moment his head hit the pillow.

He says it's all in the details, and if you've got the money why not spend it? I'm still getting used to having it.

WHEN I FIRST GOT HERE, I was eager to learn all I could about Port Townsend, so I hung out in the museum and noticed the names of the pioneers were mostly northern European. In the past thirty years that's changed and there're little pockets of people from all over our global village. There've been Chinese and Mexican eateries since the early 1900s, and now we've added Thai, Vietnamese, Italian and Indian, from India, to the mix. If you want American Indian cuisine, you have to go to the various Nations around here, like the Makah of Neah Bay.

So it wasn't exactly a surprise when I noticed one morning as I met George coming from his shave and shine, that his barber was Asian. We ate at the Salal, in silence as usual, then as strolled along the pier for our postprandial smoke, I asked George about him. He told me he'd gotten Ma Che Sam and his pregnant wife out before Saigon fell and sponsored them in the Bay Area. Years later when he had to take early medical retirement from the Berkeley PD, Ma Che Sam had followed his War Brother north and bought the last barber shop in town. His wife opened the Hole-In-The-Wall restaurant for the generation of Viet Vets who live around here.

George exudes… well, what? It's not a testosterone thing. More a presence. Women watch him as we walk by. Men step around him, and me being a runt, I like that he can look over most people's heads, and gladly trot in his wake through crowds. His deep bass laugh turns heads, and I like that I can make him laugh. I can also make him do other things that're best left in the bedroom.

STILL WAITING IN THE SHERIFF'S interview room, I felt the need for a pee, so I leant out the door and got Deputy Markham's attention. She escorted me down the corridor and left me to do my business.

"Do you know how much longer I've got to hang

around?" I asked her when I was done.

"I'll find out, ma'am." She moved off into the maze of desks. Then she went into an office and returned with a couple of men, wearing exactly the same outfits as George.

And there was Detective Westin again. His partner I'd met years ago in an altercation with a stoned patient at Clay's practice. The fellow had been ranting on about herbs and hemlock, and wouldn't let go of the bust of the legendary Hippocrates Clay kept in the waiting room. I'd been giggling when I dialed 911. PTPD Officer Smith had not been amused. Perhaps it had been his first case of bust-knapping. He's a skinny, short chap with a slicked-down head of ginger hair and a scrappy cant to his jaw. Behind him, tall Bill Westin loomed like a heron.

When Smith caught me studying him, he scowled. His partner, on the other hand, grinned in that fresh-faced way I remembered.

"Hello again, Ms Collier."

"Why'm I here?"

Smith cleared his throat, put a little tape recorder on the table and turned it on. He spoke into it about the date and who was there.

"Miss Collier, I'm going to read you your ri—"

"You're kidding!" I shrieked, bolting to my feet.

"Sal, it's okay, just a formality." Westin said to calm me down.

Smith, not a bit perturbed, proceeded to read me my rights and then got down to business.

"Mrs. Birnbaum says you were... romantically involved with her husband. Care to fill us in?"

"You've seen her?"

"She called," Westin supplied, even as Smith glared at him, "Said she's coming over fro—"

"What can you tell us?" Smith interrupted in his no-nonsense tone.

"Mel and I were not doing anything. That's Renee's guilty conscience. If he slept around maybe she wouldn't feel so... you know. A couple of months after she got that job in Seattle, she asked if I'd do her a favor," I used my fingers for quotation marks. "Would I sleep with Mel? Actually, the way she put it was service him. He was so lonely and she knew he liked me and well, it'd all be between friends, right? I figured she'd just seen a rerun of *The Big Chill* so I told her to piss off. Thought she'd gotten over it."

"Never saw that one," mused Westin.

"You should. It's the breakout movie of so ma—"

"Did that change your... relationship?" Smith growled, keeping us on track.

"For a while. She got frosty and Mel was embarrassed."

Smith glanced down at his notebook.

"Know anything about drugs in the house?"

This I didn't like. "Why? Did you find some?"

His chin stuck out. "You tell me."

"Two, three years ago, I got there a bit early. She used to drive home and be there... anyway, I'd gone upstairs to start with her rooms and I... she was in her bathroom, leaning over something on her counter. I could hear her... er... sniffing? She saw me in the mirror and slammed the door. We never spoke about it. Other than that, no. They're more into wine." I'd hauled plenty of empties to the recycle bin.

"Tell us how you found Mr. Birnbaum." Smith's hard voice brought me back to the sad present.

And so I did, again. Several minutes into it, Westin's cellphone must have vibrated cuz he got up pulling it out of its holster, and left. When he didn't come back, Smith finished the interview, and then told me to wait while he got my statement typed up, so I could sign it. I stared at the NO SMOKING sign and almost dozed off in that airless room. George was nowhere to be seen. Deputy Markham was on the phone. When Smith came back, I read and signed the paper and then he escorted me out a rear door to where the same who driven me there deputies waited.

"I could take the bus. Save some tax dollars." I quipped as I got in.

"Is all right, ma'am. We brung you, we takes ya back." Ramirez drawled.

AS SOON AS I STEPPED through my front door, Porsche greeted me with much sniffing, licking and bumping my legs. I kissed his brow, scratched his back and called him silly names. Then it was time to go shopping.

I was turning into the co-op's parking lot when my cellphone chirped. It was my main squeeze. Well, actually, my only squeeze.

"I've got the steaks."

"I've got the dog."

"The what?"

"One of those four-legged, woofy things."

"Really! When did you acquire same?"

"After I found the dead husband. Renee would've had him put down, and he's got a few good years left."

"Like someone else you know? What's he called?"

Here we go again. "Um... it used to be Borscht and now it's Porsche." I eased into a parking spot.

"Will he take my place in your bed?"

"No way, big fella!"

Chapter 10

HOW DID IT GO?

NOW, GEORGE AND I were sitting in my sunroom devouring the steaks I'd grilled as we watched the light show over the water. Like a sphinx, Porsche lay by the door to the patio, licking his chops.

We'd already chomped down the rabbit food, as George calls my salads. There are no cobs of sweet corn with lashings of butter, no potato salad in mayo.

Funny thing, that first meeting between the de-balled one and my Man. Porsche wasn't yet sure of his place in my cave so when we heard the utility room door open, he'd only lifted his head and ears, at the ready to pounce from his bed. When George came in carrying his briefcase and a package wrapt in butcher paper, Porsche's nose went on alert and he thumped his tail on the floor.

"George, I'd like you to meet Porsche." I ducked down under the table and brought him out. "And you, Doggy-do, meet my Man. He's the biggest puppy around so when he barks, we jump. Okay?" Porsche licked my hand, which was of no interest as I'd just finished fixing salad.

George handed me the paper packet, put his briefcase on the table, took out his travel case with his insulin and ice pack and gave that to me too. Then he got down on the floor in front of Porsche's bed, bent his legs in a facsimile of a lotus position and offered his hands. By the time I returned from seasoning the meat, the two were nuzzling. If George had had a tail, it would've been wagging as hard as Porsche's. So much for male rivalry.

"It'd be different if he wasn't cut." George had a goofy look on his face, "I'd have to show him who's the alpha male. It's the rule of the pack, and we're the humans so we're the boss all the time." George just kept stroking Porsche until he was an ecstatic puddle on his blankets. I knew the feeling.

"Had a dog in a previous life?"

"Yup," my Man nodded, lifting Porsche's head and kissing his nose, "Sue didn't like him. Too dirty. Got Ruggles in the divorce. He was the kids' dog really. After they left and the house sold, I moved into an apartment complex near the station. Got real busy at work and had no time for him. Blame myself for him losing interest, for dying in his bed a few months later." He got to his feet slowly. "Not allowed pets now." Porsche followed him into the kitchen. "Gotta take my blood. I'm starved." He brought his kit to the dining table and went through the ritual. "Seventy-four. I need fuel."

IT'S NOT SIMPLE DATING A DIABETIC. Without warning, an evening at the cinema can turn into a bad horror flick; a quiet drive into a gut-wrenching obstacle course. There've been times when, deep in a heavenly spooning snooze, I've woken to George shaking me. He'll say he can't see much of anything, then settled in our recliner he'll chew his special tablets and take his blood count and eat something. After that, he'll go back to sleep right there under a quilt, and be exhausted in the morning.

The first time I witnessed a crash we were driving through the rainforest toward Elkorn Lake near Dosewallips. He'd pulled over into a turnout, put his Escalade in park and wiped his face with his hands.

"Damn, I'm crashing." He'd mumbled as he fumbled at the latch on the overhead compartment.

"What do you need?"

"Tablets, up here."

I punched a couple out of their plastic pouches and he popped one into his mouth.

"God, that's sweet!" He grimaced as he chewed. I helped him around to the passenger seat and then got behind the steering wheel. While he used his monitor, I studied the dashboard. When I looked up at the windshield, I could barely see over the wheel. Or reach the pedals. I pulled and pressed a few knobs before I got adjusted.

George's blood sugar count was 47. He chewed another tablet.

"That'll keep me till we get back to civilization and food." He moved the passenger seat back and closed his eyes.

As ready as I'd ever be, I put the urban tank into gear and hit the accelerator. Bad move! The pedal responded to a feather's touch and so did the brakes. With room still to spare in the turnout, I let the car idle while I revved up my nerve. Then I practiced until I got the hang of it, put on the turn signal, and did a perfect U-ee.

What a ride! In comparison, my old beater was like a horse-drawn wagon, without any springs. And yeah,

I've been on one: a hay ride somewhere in Illinois, during my first Midwest autumn.

George napped all the way home, waking only as we cruised through Chimacum Valley.

"Let's go to the Golden Gate," he said, as we crested Sims Way overlooking PT. I caught his grin out of the corner of my eye. "No, my faint-hearted wench," he crooned, patting my shoulder, "the Chinese place at Point Hudson."

My anxiety level plummeted. I made it to the parking lot without hitting a thing and parked the mighty machine far from other cars, then let my heart slow down.

George took his blood again, worried about how much insulin to take and gave himself a shot. Once we'd walked across the windswept parking lot, he stumbled on the steps and gripped my arm. After a pit stop at the restrooms, I led him to a booth. Waiting for our dinner, he admitted he'd had no feeling in his feet for years, and now his fingers were going numb.

The condemned man ate hearty, and I lost my appetite. It was the first time I paid.

I got the SUV into his slot in the apartment garage and walked him to the elevator. Holding the door open, he assured me he was okay and said I should go on home.

I'd sat at my computer and searched the Internet to learn all I could about diabetes, and find recipes. Then I went through my kitchen like a dose of salts.

Once in a while a sinking feeling will pole-ax me when I think about how numbered George's years are. It's different from the occasional realization that any one can kick the bucket at any time. He's more philosophical about it. Says he's had a good life, fathered enough children, worked at something that interested him, read a ton of good books and found a good woman to love and be loved by.

"HOW DID IT GO?" He asked as he let Porsche lick our plates and then gave 'em to me to wash. Porsche immediately went to his dish of dry food, settled down in front of it and started munching.

"Gotta get the juices flowing," George watched the guzzling hound. "He'll probably eat most of it now. Maybe some more later. You got water for him outside?" When I shook my head, he bent down to a bottom shelf and liberated a crockery bowl I hadn't used in ages. "This okay?"

George bore the bowl out the front door. Porsche stopped chewing to look after him. Then he scrambled to his feet and trotted outside. I refilled the plastic gallon jug with rinse water I keep in the hall toilet for power outages. Then I knocked the bung hole strainer dregs into the compost bucket and followed my males. I emptied the bucket in the wire yurt and checked the fertilizer tea reservoir.

George was in his chair on the porch, Porsche beside him. The tops of the Spruces in the park blazed with the last of the sun.

I dragged the hose over to the yurt and gave it a drenching. Then I started on my flower beds. Porsche came over to see what I was doing and huffed away when I sent the spray at him. With the last of my flowers sucking up their supper, I went inside for a couple of shawls. George wrapped one around his shoulders, offering me a lit smoke when I sat down. Contented, we watched Porsche pad through the dampness, following his nose.

"So, how did it go?" George asked again.

"We didn't spend much time on the banging part. Mostly they wanted to know how I'd come upon the scene, and if I'd seen any drugs there."

"So, tell me how you found him... Mel."

LATER, AS GEORGE WATCHED the Shuttle arrive at the International Space Station on the NASA channel while I cut out material for the comforters I was starting for Joy. That had been her news when she'd popped by yesterday evening. She had a brace of buns in the oven, three months along. She'd positively glowed.

George roused up, refreshed his water mug and called Porsche. I listened to him chatter about vitamins and treats, and being a good old dog. I straightened up from my cutting to watch. It must have been a trick of the light cuz I could've sworn I saw a young man in uniform talking to an eager puppy. Then the spell broke, and my dog settled down at his bowl and started chomping again while my Man got his insulin. He sat in our recliner, tested, filled his injector, pulled his shirt out of his pants and stuck himself in the belly.

After I returned the kit to the fridge, I snuggled my arms around him.

"Time to call it a day, hon. I'm beat."

"You staying?"

"Figured you could use the company."

"Appreciate that. Want a shower?"

"Nope!" He leaned back into my chest. "Just you."

ONE OF THE FIRST THINGS I DID after Dwayne left, was get a tubal ligation, at the time a thoroughly new procedure for which Welfare was willing to pay. After the Ob/Gyn's lecture about how it was irreversible,

I'd still said yes. And hadn't changed my mind when the doc said I had to read and sign his two page disclaimer form. Otherwise he wouldn't touch me. It declared that I wouldn't hold him responsible if the procedure failed. In other words, should I get knocked-up again I couldn't sue him for shoddy surgery. He'd been the third doc I'd seen: the others wouldn't do it cuz I was: a) too young. I was then twenty-eight with two buns already out of the oven, and b) would likely change my mind when I met the man of my dreams. I'd signed.

Back in London, when I started at Moneypenny's Secretarial College and Jake, my American roommate was showing me the night life, she'd spoken about sex. How she got down to brass tacks fast was what I'd liked so much about her. As we dressed to go out she showed me a pink plastic case, rather like a powder compact only bigger. In it lay a strange pink rubbery thing that looked like half a deflated balloon, with a lip. I got my first lesson in contraception.

When I graduated, a year after Jake had gone back to America and in which we'd exchanged monthly letters, I moved into a flat with classmates: Staffy, Bubba and Conny. We were all virgins intent on changing that status, and deathly scared of getting pregnant. In those days you had to have your doctor write a prescription for birth control no matter your age, especially if you were unmarried.

On my walk home from work. Yeah, Mrs Blakely had indeed found me a perfect position as export secretary at a 200 year-old distillery in Earls Court. Anyway, I'd drop in at the tobacconist for smokes. Yeah, I'd started. Liked the flavor, the company during breaks, and how it calmed my nerves.

Next to the tobacconist was the laundrette we

used. I ended up working there on weekends (and doing my wash for free) when I was saving to emigrate. On the other side was a narrow little shop with discreet signs in its window. It took ages to screw up my courage to open its door.

Inside, everything was painted red with floor to ceiling drawers labeled in all kinds of languages. Behind the glass counter a hairy gent sat reading. That's all I remember: long gray beard, long gray moustache, long gray plait, and a red shirt with short sleeves showing blue tattoos of wings and things. He sat not looking at me until I managed to ask about contraceptives. Then he nodded, put his paperback book away and lifted a worn catalogue onto the counter, turning it so I could read. As I looked at the pages, he gave me a dignified and, given the subject matter, modest introduction to his world of sexual paraphernalia, as he called it.

I left with burning cheeks, a little red box tucked into my pocket, and a whole quid lighter. *La Chapelle* was a pink rubber cervical cap. On the inside of the lid, in French and English, were instructions on how to use and care for it. My flatmates were thrilled.

We were still untrammeled when we disbanded a couple of years later, though we'd thrown weekly parties and groped a lot of boys who couldn't be coaxed over that invisible line. Of all the wonders I met after crossing The Pond, the strangest was the fending off of single and married men alike, all eager to be the first. By then though, I wasn't looking for mere deflowering, I wanted to fall in love!

Chapter 11

BUT ME NO BUTTS

SOMETHING HAD BEEN BOTHERING ME all night. It made me leap out of bed before my alarm rang, leaving George snoring on his own.

Then I nearly collided with a silently prancing black shadow with eyes like shiny buttons, a long pink tongue and grinning white teeth. That's right, I no longer lived alone! I wrapt up in the mauve robe George had given me and barefooted it to open the front door. Out zoomed my Dog.

Marine mist lay low over everything today making the tops of the Spruces in Chetzemoka Park float eerily. There was a quietness and a shine to the world. The sweet scent of the yellow tea roses blooming in their pot beside the porch filled my nose.

I turned the coffee pot on on the way back to my bedroom, grabbed a set of sweats from my chair and headed for the shower.

With the sunroom being socked-in solid and the world ending at the chain link fence, I carried my cuppa and smokes out to the porch. As I lit up, I suddenly remembered the filters I'd retrieved from near Mel's body.

I hadn't, had I? Oh, no! I stubbed out my smoke in the ashtray Cooper had made for me, and ran to the bathroom, flipping open the hamper lid and dug out the uniform I'd tossed in yesterday. Sure enough, in a pocket was the baggie with the butts. Dorals.

George is a tad testy when he doesn't get his eight hours. Since I'd gotten out of bed, he'd rolled clear over to my side. I gently stroked his back.

"Good morning, big fella. Time to rise and shine."

"I'll give you till noon to stop that." Came a muffled mutter. He stretched and groaned. I learnt early on in our sleeping together that if I didn't wake him slowly and gently, his warrior hardwiring would have him rising out of bed at full throttle.

"Well, is it shining?" He growled into the pillows.

"No, it's foggy." I stroked him some more.

"What's up?" He rolled over.

"We have a problem, Houston." He pulled his hands out from under the bedding and rubbed his face. Then glowered up at me.

"Uh-uh." He threw off the covers, swung his legs over the side and sat up. George changed my life a lot. I now sleep like him, buck-ass naked, as he calls it. He rubbed his head, and scratched his jaw. I felt a sudden urge to roll him back into the warmth and forget everything. "Can it wait till I shit'n'shower?" His eyes looked just like Porsche's, mournful and wary.

"Sure, big fella." Then I opened my hand and showed him the baggie.

"Yeah, so?" He looked sleepily at 'em.

"See those ones? They're not mine. I... um... found 'em, you know... yesterday beside Mel."

"You're kidding!" He kept blinking at the baggie. "You come across a real live dead body and then you actually... oh-oh!" My thoughts exactly.

"I was wearing work gloves if that helps. What do we do?" He stood up and stretched his fine naked bod. From his towering height he bent a fierce look upon me.

"What do you mean "we"? Let me wash up and then we're going in for some serious back-pedaling." He headed for the bathroom and in the door jamb turned to me. "Ever been in jail?"

"George! That's not funny!"

"Not meant to be, Sally. Let me think." And with that he closed the door.

So much for cleaning today. I left the baggie on the counter beside his coffee mug and sweeteners and went into my office for a look at my calendar.

Well, whaddya know, it's my day off! In all the kerfuffle I'd forgotten that Tuesdays I didn't do anyone's home anymore. All my Gals were committed though. So why was today's box blank? What did I usually do on Tuesdays? I checked my voice mail. Nothing. So I called Joanne.

"What do I usually do today, O Mighty Business Manager?" One of the reasons I like George so much is he's of the same generation as Joanne, except she talks in questions.

"And is it a good morning for you, Boss? Don't you usually do the lady of leisure thing... like sleep in?" The butterflies in my tummy wanted out. I heard the shower start up.

"Joanne, I've got a problem. The Birnbaums. The husband. I found him dead at the bottom of the garden yesterday."

" You mean dead dead?"

"What other kind is there?" I hiccuped a giggle.

"So you called the cops, right?"

"Absolutely. Immediately."

"And?"

I dry-mouth swallowed. "You know how I dispose of my ciggie butts..."

"Yeah?"

"Well.. I... oh, Joanne, I'm in such trouble!"

"What've butts got to do with it?"

"There were two near... Mel." Joanne's silence was deafening.

"And you picked 'em up?" She shouted.

"Yeah." I squeaked.

"Are you a dumb Brit or what?" She was guffawing. "Did you give 'em to the cops?"

"Everything was so crazy and I was worried about Borscht."

"Say again?"

"That's what they call their dog. I call him Porsche now."

"You do?"

"Brought him home cuz I was sure the wife'd him put down. I couldn't let that happen. He's really a great dog. He was barking and barking. He found..." I felt I might start blubbering.

"The body... and?" Her drawl brought me back.

"I don't remember doing it. It's like... an unconscious thing."

"Don't I know it! Seen you do it all the time. So?"

"At some point I must've picked 'em up."

"You got your captain with you?"

"In the shower."

"Why aren't you with him? Forget I said that! Anyway he'll know what to do. Think you'll go to jail?"

"That's what he said!"

"George'll steer you clear." She was laughing again. "Anything I can do?"

"Just keep things running. I might be out of circulation for a bit."

"You'll be sprung by the weekend, right? You're the Hostess with the Mostess, remember?"

"That's what I'm supposed to do today, shit!"

"Don't talk dirty to me or I'll take Irish Spring to you. Why don't I have everyone over here instead?"

Back in my chair on the porch, I shivered as I sipped my cold tea. George ambled out with his jacket on and coffee in hand. Porsche came over from his morning patrol and the two males bonded some more.

Then George brought out his notebook and pen plus the butt baggie. I'd not seen his professional manner before and couldn't get the image of his handcuffs out of my mind.

"Now, Ms Collier, tell me exactly what you remember about these cigarette filters. Where you found them, why you picked them up and what you did with them."

THAT DONE, it was time for his shave and shine, and some fuel. What I eat for breakfast George won't touch. Once a week I cook up a big pot of lentil stew. After I brown garlic, onion and lentils in olive oil with a bay leaf and a dash of Italian seasonings, I add water and chopped veggies. Once it comes to a boil, I let it simmer until the crispy side of done. Then I dump in a tin each of beef stew and tomatoes. They're the only tinned foods I can swallow. I got the basic recipe from the Ahimsa Co-op except theirs was totally vegan. Most mornings I zap a bowl in the microwave and suck it down. With my Man around, it's off to the Salal.

While Porsche was under the rhodies doing his morning dump, George dallied in the dining room.

"Got a spare blanket?"

"What for?"

"Don't know when you'll be back. He'll be cooped up here. Can't let him out alone in the yard yet. He's powerful enough to jump your fence and run off."

"Really?" George nodded seriously. I pondered the inside of his new Escalade seriously.

I dug into Clay's father's cabin trunk and came up with an electric blanket I'd pulled the wiring out of in readiness for filling a quilt. George took it and disappeared through the utility room. Porsche came inside grinning.

"Guess you're coming with, Doggy-do." I told the curious canine. "Remember to slobber with gratitude, okay? This is a major privilege."

"You still got the Birnbaum keys?" George asked on his return.

I shook my head. "Deputy Haffey took 'em all."

He nodded, and then gestured to the dog.

"Porsche, come!" And away they went. I gathered up the insulin ice pack, threw on my windbreaker, made sure I had my wallet and keys and followed.

It's a tight squeeze to get into the SUV beside my beater. Porsche was already sitting on the blanket in the back and my Man was behind the steering wheel with the motor purring.

George opened his briefcase and put the butt baggie with his report taped to it inside. I leaned over to stow the insulin in the cooler that's plugged into a power socket. We buckled up and he backed out.

While George was in with Ma Che Sam, I leashed Porsche up and took him for a quickie along the waterfront. He found lots of loverly new smells and I practiced heeling and stopping. Now, when did I put a handful of treats in my windbreaker pocket?

All squeaky clean and smelling yummy George emerged as I was settling Porsche in the back. We hopped in and found a parking space along Water Street near the Salal where we slid into our corner table and slurped coffee while Mindy, our waitperson of many years, scribbled our orders which she knew by heart. Soon she came bearing platters.

"Eat hearty." George said as I was about to dig in. "Your next meal could be prison chow."

The hiccup of fear surprised me and I had to put my fork down. George passed over his impeccable cotton hanky without looking up from his plate. I snuffled into it. When I offered it back, he declined. We resumed our silently ate meal.

On the way out to the Justice Center, we smoked and George called ahead. When we got there he drove around and around the parking lot.

"What are you looking for? There's a spot... and there..." I peered at him as he swung around yet another row of cars. I love watching him drive. He's so competent and graceful. His loverly hands that turn me to mush, handle the wheel as if born to it. He says he's been driving since he was twelve. He wears no wedding ring. On his left wrist is his expandable Timex and on his right is his medic alert bracelet. Sometimes, when I'm staring at him dreamily as we're cruising along he'll take his left hand off the wheel, point his index finger and "pow" me. Naturally I melt at the way he grins and winks.

"Shade." He growled. "Can't leave a dog in a car in the sun." Outside the fog was indeed burning off.

Finally the Great Lot Hunter found what he was looking for and backed in. He turned around in his seat and eyed the situation, then fiddled with a couple of knobs on his window consul and the rear vents opened.

"Guard the car!" George ordered and our black dog huffed and settled down like a sphinx.

Walking into the station beside the Chief of Detectives got me a very different reception. After the metal detectors and scanning wands a deputy ushered us into Sheriff Morrow's office where George introduced me, and we all sat down.

"This is evidence from the Birnbaum place." George opened his briefcase and handed over the baggie and his report.

Sheriff Morrow read it, then glanced at me.

"For the record," George said in his stern cop voice, "Ms Collier's an upstanding citizen, gainfully employed even if she is a dumb civilian who's tampered with a crime scene."

"That she has, Captain. Think she'll need a lawyer?" Without waiting for an answer, Sheriff Morrow pressed a button on his phone unit. "Please ask the detectives working the Birnbaum case to come in. And Doc Nelson, if he can spare the time." Then he read the report some more. "We'll wait for them so you won't have to repeat how you come to have these in your possession."

Chapter 12

IS THAT A CRIME?

BY THE LOOKS ON THEIR FACES, Smith and Westin had less polite names to call me after they'd read George's report.

Never had I wanted to hang onto his hand more than I did in that office, facing those policemen. I kept reminding myself that I was totally innocent, and anyway it would embarrass the hell out of him.

Smith stalked out to send the butts for analysis as Deputy Farias, who had shown us in, offered around a plastic basket of water bottles. Behind him Doc Nelson came in with something in his hand. He pulled the cap off it, and advanced on me, saying, "We need a swab."

I offered my mouth. That done, I took a water bottle, cracked the lid and drank. The Doc gave my DNA to the deputy, then settled in a chair.

"Did Claire ever come home yesterday?" I asked Westin. He glanced at George who nodded.

"No, and neither did her mother," he answered opening his notebook. "She made that one call from her cellphone. Could have been anywhere. We've got someone backtracking cell towers."

"I got a call from her." I volunteered.

"Mrs. Birnbaum? Why would she call you?" Westin asked.

"No, Claire. She phoned home just after I got there. Wanted to know if I'd seen her parents." Westin was writing, so I slowed down, "Said she'd been out at Lake Quinault all week, closing a camp. She's at her father's parents. In Sequim."

"They're retired?"

"'S'pect so. Never met 'em."

Westin looked up from his pad. "How long did you say you've cleaned for the Birnbaums?"

"Up here? About four years."

"What do you know of the wife's family?"

"She's from back east, too. One weekend early on, they invited me to come over and play—"

"Play?" Sheriff Morrow echoed.

"Yeah. They used to be Bridge addicts. Put on weekend tournaments. Four or five tables. Husbands and wives, kids in the rec room and hot tub. Lots of food and wine. We'd sleep over and break up after Sunday brunch." I coasted off into memories.

"And?" George prompted me by laying his hand on my arm.

"Er, yeah... um... one time Renee had a new Bruce Springsteen playing, really loud. She was a bit tiddly and bragged how he was the one homeboy who'd made it big. Wonder if Mel was a homeboy, too?"

"Asbury Park. New Jersey." I hadn't heard Smith come back in. He was nodding. "I'm a fan." He made a face at Westin's snigger.

"She always beat around the bush like this, Captain?" Sheriff Morrow leaned back in his chair, pursing his lips, his eyes twinkling.

"Yup!" My Man's freshly-shaved face reddened.

"Do you know Mrs. Birnbaum's maiden name?" Smith asked. I shook my head. Then a memory flashed.

"Wait... it's... um... the same letters. Renee R..." I closed my eyes. "Do you have their daughter's full name?" Smith looked over Westin's shoulder as he flipped through his notebook.

"Yeah," Westin said when he found it, "Claire Rainey Birnbaum. Just graduated high school."

"That's it! When I met her Renee'd printed all three on her name tag."

"Where was that?" Sheriff Morrow asked.

"At a Human Potential seminar in the Oakland Red Lion. We did the exercises together and when I said something about Bridge, Mel invited me over that weekend. I was washing dishes, I like doing that in other people's kitchens, and Renee asked if I'd be interested in cleaning for them. I was looking for work so I said yes. It was fun back then. She liked being home though she'd leave most days to work at their food co-op. We'd all sit in the kitchen and talk about things before I got to work. When they moved up here they tried Bridge again, except Poker's more the game. And then..." I hesitated cuz I was getting into very private stuff here. "They had a falling out. Renee got that job over in Seattle and Mel moved downstairs, and... I never saw her much after that. In the beginning she'd leave notes on the kitchen counter, along with my money." I remembered the look of the kitchen when I got inside. "It wasn't there! And Mel's espresso machine was cold."

"Unusual?"

"Very!" I turned to Westin. "Did you look in all the rooms?"

"Why?" Westin gulped.

"Did you find the pregnancy test kit in the daughter's bathroom?"

There was silence.

"Oh, come on!" I chided. "It was positive. What if it wasn't Claire's? Can you test it for DNA?"

"Sure," Doc Nelson drawled. "Whose else would it be?" His keen blue eyes sized me up.

"Renee's!"

"The wife?" Smith snapped. "Isn't she too old—"

"Not by a mile! She was only seventeen when she had Claire." Suddenly, very clearly I saw Mel and Renee as a couple. "You know how most married people are glad to tell you how they met? With them, their story was of how they ran off to the West Coast before she started showing. They both used to say that drive was the happiest time of their lives, sleeping and screwing their way across America in his Econoline. She was a high school senior. He'd just started college. Said the van broke down in a McD's parking lot in Oakland, so they decided that was where they were meant to be."

"What did they do for money?" Westin asked.

"Started the food co-op. Up here I used to see stuff in the trash, from big name companies." Nothing more was coming.

"Do you know how Mrs. Birnbaum got that job with Hatton?" George steered me in another direction.

"Only what she told me, when we were still speaking. Said she'd been over in the city with a couple of girlfriends, and no, I don't know who they were. They'd gone to the opening of something... AIDS? A hospice? Anyway, she said she'd seen some things she could've done better. Found out who'd put it on and impressed him with her ideas. She started driving over there, a lot. I don't know when she began staying over cuz I'm there only once a week. For a couple of years her bed was always slept in, though for how many nights I wouldn't know. Then it wasn't used at all. Yesterday was the first time it had been used since Claire's graduation."

"Do you know if Mrs. Birnbaum ever went back east?" George kept on.

"I bet never."

"Why?" Sheriff Morrow jumped in.

"Er... once we were sharing parent stories and I was surprised at how... well, spiteful she was about her parents never having seen their only grandchild."

George touched my arm again. "What else do you remember?"

I closed my eyes and let the memories flow by.

"Things changed after Renee quit smoking and kicked Mel downstairs. When she got that job, Claire and her Dad kinda limped along with their lives."

"Do you know if Mrs. Birnbaum owns a car?" Smith asked.

"Sure, a Mustang. Hang on a bit! Sometime back, maybe early August, Mel said something about how she'd just bought a new Beamer."

"And?" George murmured.

"He was mad cuz she'd traded-in that red Mustang. Said it was a classic." I jerked up, "Claire has her Dad's Cherokee. Here, I've got her cellphone number." As I brought it up on my phone, Westin scribbled it down. "Mel was furious that Monday, smoking in the kitchen, swearing up a storm. All the dishes were in pieces on the floor." I squirmed remembering his rage. "He was so apologetic, you know, about the mess."

"First time you'd seen him angry?" Smith asked.

I nodded.

"Maybe he didn't get over it." Westin mused.

"Maybe more than just dishes were tossed this time!" Smith added.

"The kitchen would've told me that."

"You didn't see a dead body in the yard for what, almost an hour!" He countered.

"You can't see the bottom of the garden from any of the windows!" I leaned back in my chair. "How did he get buried then cuz Renee sure wouldn't have gone out in all that mud."

"What do you know about Alan Hatton?" That was George changing the subject.

"Only what I've seen in the papers, and on Renee's glory wall."

"Do you know if Mrs. Birnbaum and he were... intimate?" That was Smith.

"I've no proof, just suspicions."

"What kind?"

"Mel—"

"Ah, the dead husband." The way he said it made me blush.

"Yeah! They had loved each other back then, you could see it! She'd been a happy housewife until she got that job and started... well, ignoring her family, and her roses."

"Her roses?" Smith sneered.

"Who did the cooking then?" George said to curb my retort.

"I wondered about that. They never replaced the broken dishes, just paper and microwave ones, or takeout. There was always a cookie pan, for croissants. Mel loved those, ate 'em all the time. And he never went up to the top floor anymore. Haven't found anything of his in her rooms in years."

"Like what?" Smith prodded.

"Undies? Socks. C-condoms in the bathroom. That sort of thing."

"Undies, eh?" Smith chewed his cheek.

"You know what I mean!" I eyed him. "Did you notice his *Playboys*?"

"What about 'em?" Smith scowled.

"There was something wrong and I couldn't..." I saw them again in my mind's eye. "The boxes on the bottom were put back differently."

"You see a lot of pornography cleaning houses?" Doc Nelson sounded interested.

"Some. Most folks kinda hide it in their bedside tables or under the bed. Don't go prying, mind you. If it's sort of out there for anyone to see, well, sometimes I look at it, if it's a new issue."

"Really?" Smith smirked.

"Yeah, is that a crime?" I felt my face flaming again.

"No it's not, Ms Collier." Even though Sheriff Morrow's voice soothed my hackles, I still glared at Smith. The other men cleared their throats and shifted about.

"How come you're so observant, Ms Collier?" Sheriff Morrow rubbed his jaw.

"I take my work seriously. Had a good teacher, back in the Old Country. My Mum. She'd say a family'd be surprised at what their char sees."

"Char?" Westin screwed up his face.

"Yeah, charwoman. You know Charles Dickens wrote about us. My Mum wasn't a char really cuz she lived-in. Anyway, she taught me a family's home will tell you a lot about how they're getting along. That's why I've been bothered about Claire's room."

"What about the daughter's room?" George said

leaning forward, quelling Smith's reaction with a shake of his head.

"It was tidy."

"Tidy?" Smith seethed.

"You have teenagers?"

"Not married!" He sneered. No surprise there!

Sheriff Morrow leaned back, rubbing his jaw. He was doing a lot of that. "I do, three of 'em. Please, Ms Collier, tell us about teenagers and their rooms."

"First of all, they're never tidy, right?" Morrow smiled and nodded. "So when I saw Claire's bed all made up with not a wrinkle, that got my attention. And her windows and blinds were closed. She's a fresh air freak. And her clothes were picked up, every one of them. That's scary! The bathroom was empty of her everyday stuff. It smelt stale too, as if it'd been closed up for days. When she called, she said she'd been gone a week. Still, it was all way too tidy."

"What would make a teenager clean her room?" Sheriff Morrow asked.

"Worry, rejection, a family fight." A years-old memory suddenly surfaced. "Wwhen her Mom kicked her Dad out and I'd still been cleaning Claire's room, she told me she'd stayed out of the line of fire by tidying her stuff. I bet there was a fight Friday night!"

`None of the men looked convinced, and I knew I couldn't explain what women do when they're angry or frightened. I'd done it enough times myself.

"Back to the butts." That was Smith. "Does Mrs. Birnbaum smoke?"

"No way! After she quit she was super-anti. I... well... I thought it hypocritical. Snorting stuff and guzzling wine and then nagging Mel about him smoking. Wasn't like he puffed away day and night. And he did it outside."

THE DEAD HUSBAND 111

"Does the daughter smoke?"

"She didn't the last time she was home when I was there, back during spring break. She came out for a chat with me and her Dad, and we lit up. Actually, she's about as snarky as her mom about it."

"Snarky?" That was Westin.

"Bitchy!"

"Right."

George nudged me. "What about Borscht the Porsche?" My heart sank, and I pleaded with my eyes. He frowned.

"Um... Captain Tullock's reminding me I've got to tell you about the Birnbaums' dog—"

"Which you took home because there was no one to care for him and you didn't want him sent to the Humane Society where he might be put down, him being so old and all." My Man finished for me.

"Dog?" Westin was flicking through the pages of his notebook again. "Here it is. Old black Lab."

"He was barking and barking when I got there. He never does that. Then I found him shut up in the storage closet behind the utility room. That was deliberate. He'd been there for days and had to piss and poop in a corner. He wanted in Mel's apartment. Drank his water bowl dry, poor thing. Then he wanted out into the garden."

"Yard." Smith snapped.

"Yeah, and I suppose you do yardening!" I shot back. I turned to Sheriff Morrow. "I followed him down the slope. I'm sure he could tell us wh—"

"Ah, jeez, why don't we just hire the local pet psychic!" Smith was again chomping on his cheek.

Sheriff Morrow sat up, looking to Doc Nelson.

"How's the autopsy coming along, Jim?"

"Waiting on toxicology, of course. Time of death is

seventy-two hours before we found him plus or minus twelve. Skull's crushed in the rear ant—" He glanced at me. "Contusions and bruising to the throat and shoulders. Both clavicles broken, fractured left—"

"How could all that happen?" George quietly broke into the Doc's inventory.

"If the subject had been in a culvert, I'd have said he'd been a victim of a hit-and-run. But because of where he was found, so far the injuries indicate a fall, say of thirty or so feet."

"Then how did he get to the bottom of the garden?" I blurted out.

"Couldn't say. What I can tell you is there's mud under the nails consistent with the location, as well as in the nasal cavities, mouth, windpipe and lungs. Though severely injured, Mr. Birnbaum was very much alive when he was buried."

Chapter 13

SEE SALLY SEE

"THEN WHY DID HE DIE?" I wailed.

"I've got more to do," Doc Nelson brushed off the knees of his trousers. "But I'd say from a combination of hypothermia and... bleeding in the brain."

We were all silent, digesting his news.

"Captain," Sheriff Morrow cleared his throat. "Isn't it time we let Ms Collier off the hook?"

"Well, now..." George stroked his chin and I could have whacked him.

"Ms Collier," Sheriff Morrow leaned toward me over his desk, "We found other Doral filters in the dirt beside the... Mr. Birnbaum. The chain of evidence is secure." He got to his feet. "So, gentlemen, what are we going to do with this civilian?"

I couldn't help clutching at George's hand.

"Give her a citation!" Westin chortled hiding behind his pad.

"Put her in county for a week!" Smith chimed in, rather seriously.

"What if we thanked her and sent her on her way?" George said as he stood up. Everyone else did too.

"Better yet, detectives, why don't you take Ms Collier out to the Birnbaums' house and have her show you what she saw? Then we'll let her get on with her life."

And that's what they did. Out in the sunny parking lot George and I loaded up as Porsche panted in greeting. We followed Smith and Westin in their black sedan out to Airport Way, where they turned on their lights and sped twenty miles above the speed limit all the way to Four Corners.

Then I was back at Bluff Haven, on a foggy, damp day. No view of the water or mountains this time. Smith inserted a keycard and the gate rolled open. He repeated it at the Birnbaums' drive. George slowly maneuvered his SUV around Renee's roses, and stopped beside the garage.

"I'm not coming in, hon." He patted my shoulder. "Give 'em a thorough Sally Sees, okay? I'm taking Porsche down to the beach. He's freaking out." I listened to the snuffling in the back where our dog was on his feet, nose to a vent, hackles stiff, ears laid down, tail low.

"Wish he could talk." I leant my cheek on George's shoulder. "Thanks for your shield. Hope I didn't embarrass you."

He kissed the top of my head.

"No more than usual, hon." He chuckled. "Go show 'em!"

I felt deeply uncomfortable entering that empty house. No Mel, no Renee, no Claire anymore. An entire family wiped away.

Yellow tape sagged around the portico columns. Smith was about to put a keycard in the front door.

"I always go in through the kitchen." I called to them from Mel's Chat Pad. Westin stooped under the tape and trotted toward me with Smith sulking behind. George's Escalade purred off into the fog.

Westin offered me a pair of gloves.

"No thanks, I'm allergic to the powder."

"Then don't touch anything, okay?" Smith ordered as he slipped the keycard into the slot beside the door and stood aside for me to lead the way.

I dashed to the security pad before I realized it was still de-activated. No blinking light. The monitor above was dark.

"That's damn careless," I growled. "Leaving their security off like that. There're a lot of valuables here and with everyone knowing no one's home, it'd be easy pickings."

Smith read Jerry's security company name off the alarm and tapped it into his cellphone.

"Okay." I took a deep breath and looked around. "What's all this then?" I barked, pointing to the black dust and smears that covered everything.

"Fingerprinting," Westin murmured. "Wait while I get this thing working." He was fiddling with a tiny tape recorder. I held my peace until he'd clicked it on and spoke into it with the date, time and our names. Then he nodded at me.

"Right then." I closed my eyes, at first to block out the mess and then to bring up what I'd come upon yesterday morning. The urge to wipe everything clean was worse than a nicotine fit.

"First thing wrong was Mel wasn't waiting for me." I pointed to the Gaggia machine. "Then that was cold." I trod carefully over to the dumb waiter door. There was powder on the handle. "When can I have my tools back?"

"I'll let you know as soon as possible." Westin murmured.

I took a deep breath, crossed into the foyer and

started up the main staircase. Why was there no dust on the banisters?

"There's a guest powder room and coat closet underneath." Smith and Westin followed me up, their shoes squeaking on the wood. Unlike yesterday, everything was dim under the fog-drenched skylights.

"Those doors are guest rooms with a bathroom in between. Haven't been used for a couple of years." I walked along the hallway, telling them what I'd seen and the layout. Arriving at Renee's suite I stopped."She used to leave her door wide open, yesterday it was shut." I led the detectives in. "What you can't see and I can still smell is the cigarette smoke. Remember, Renee hates 'em."

No powder smudges up here either.

"See the bed? All this summer, it's been the way I left it." I pointed at the floor runners. "See those stains? Wine, maybe. The coffee table and the meal on it? The fireplace? Then there's the bathroom." I walked into it. "Mess here too. See the trash and razor? Maybe someone who's used to electric ones?"

I pointed to the closet, and they filed into it.

"Look at the far end, see the safe?"

They squatted down beside it.

"No idea who has the combination, I certainly don't. If the place had been burgled, wouldn't it set off the alarm? It wasn't ringing when I got here. Have you gotten the gate discs from Jerry?"

They stood up, Smith's jaw was canted and Westin was squirming.

"In all the years I've cleaned in here the safe's never been visible, much less open. Tells me she was in a hurry, maybe not coming back."

"Please, Ms Collier," Smith had his hands on his hips pushing his jacket back and he was chewing his cheek again. "Just do what the Captain ordered."

I walked over to the sliding door to the balcony.

"Did you look out there?" That's when I saw cigarette butts in the planter under the azaleas. "Those might interest you."

Westin looked where I pointed and spoke into his recorder. Smith stood behind us jingling something.

I so wanted to get this over with. I turned back to the room, no longer able to avoid Renee's glory wall. "You'll see Alan Hatton in every one of those photos." I told Smith as he stood beside me, scanning each picture. A bubble of rage popped in my throat and I stepped out into the hall, over to Claire's door and went inside. Westin hurried after me.

"Here's the tidy teenager's room." I walked straight to the bathroom." See all the dried stuff on those tiles? The pregnancy test kit? Not much else besides that hand towel hanging there."

"What's wrong with it?" Westin asked quietly.

"See the nap?"

He inspected all the towels and nodded.

"You're going to see a lot of that when we get down to the laundry room. All this time, remember the dog was barking his head off." I squeezed by them and stomped back down to the kitchen and that horrible spiral staircase, making it to the floor just as it started vibrating as Smith and Westin descended.

"The reason you won't find my fingerprints anywhere is cuz I wear gloves, all the time. Now, to you this is just a laundry room. To me it's a mess." I pointed it all out to them and then went over to the storage room with the light still on. "Here's where I found the dog. Take a whiff in there." They both peered in. Smith coughed and retreated.

I set off for Mel's door. "He made a beeline for

here." I halted, "It's self-locking. I can't get in."

Smith took the three keycards from a pocket and fanned them out as if he was performing a magic trick. I pointed to the one to Mel's domain. As Smith pulled the door open, I had to remind myself no one in this house had any privacy anymore.

Westin gestured for me to go in and as I walked through the closet I pointed out the mud smudges on Mel's clothes. When we were in the bathroom, I showed them how filthy it was and watched the two chaps eye the place in awe.

"It is?" Westin murmured. To him, being married with kids, this must have looked spotless.

"Mel never leaves the toilet like that. See the smudges, the carpet fibers? Bend down, see those shiny tiles? That's where I cleaned last time. See all the smears? Someone wiped up. See how the towels are hung differently." I indicated the shower stall. "See the dirt around the bunghole?"

Then I walked out into the living rooms, their wall of windows dull from the fog.

"Wait, I've got to turn the tape." Westin was fiddling and walking. Smith stood behind the black sofa, scowling and chewing his cheek.

"Nothing much wrong here, if you don't count how neat the bed was after a night when Mel should've been sleeping in it, and that indentation where someone must have sat right in front of the *Playboys*." I peered at them. "Those three are in the wrong order." I saw Smith get it and kneel on one knee to pull out the leather bound boxes. Sure enough behind 'em was a safe, looking like a fuse box, except it had a tiny blinking red light. A memory surfaced. "Mel once told me you could program anything to tell you if someone had tried to get in."

THE DEAD HUSBAND   119

Smith set the boxes down against the wall.

"It's hard to see the vacuum stripes now." I said as I tiptoed across the carpet. "With no sunlight and me coming and going." I sighted along the black carpet. "See the difference in the pile? All the way back? Why are there no other shoe prints?"

"Damn!" Smith muttered, looking a bit sick as he slid the glass door open and waved me ahead onto the patio.

"Mel never leaves the hose like that and there was a puddle here." I headed out onto the terrace. There were muddy footprints all over it.

"It was spotless yesterday." I turned to look at the back of the house. Mel had always called it the front. Something was bothering me again.

Smith and Westin came out into the soft mist and stood beside me. I was not sure I had anything else for them.

And then, when I was scanning the upper floor I saw it. Over the edge of Renee's balcony, an azalea bush was hanging on for dear life.

"What do you see up there?" I whispered. Westin squinted up where I pointed.

"Well, look at that! Andy, we're going to have to get the tech team back out again!"

I didn't wait to see Smith's reaction. I sprinted across the terrace to the steps, taking 'em two at a time. Ran through the kitchen and over the glossy floor to the glass deck door off the dining room. I flipped the button, pushed it open and rushed to the white painted wrought iron railing, scanning the underside of Renee's balcony.

While Smith prowled around, Westin joined me.

"Bill, here!" For the second time Smith registered surprise. He showed his partner something on the underside of the railing. A scrap of white fabric stained brown lodged in a curlicue crevice.

I ran upstairs with Smith on my heels, issuing orders into his cellphone and Westin tagging along, urgently dictating into his recorder.

Out on Renee's balcony the damage was clearly visible, now we knew what to look for. Westin carefully leaned over the planter boxes and looked down. He raised the recorder.

"Damn! Got another tape?"

Smith dug into his pockets and came up with one. Westin ejected the used one, they both signed it and he stowed it away. As he clicked on the recorder, I pushed aside the lower branches of the evergreens.

"See the gold leaf filters? Those are Mel's Sobranies. See how one of 'em burnt itself out?" I peered closer. "All the others are Dorals."

Then something poked my ankle, just above my shoe. Part of the cedar box was dented in with splinters sticking out. I tapped Smith on the arm.

Figuring I was done, I left them busily detecting and ran downstairs, exiting by that front door I never use. There was the Escalade purring in the mist.

"Hold me!" I whimpered as I pulled open the door. George was out and had me in his arms in a flash. All I wanted was to burrow into him.

"What did you see?" He rumbled.

Before I could find my voice, Smith and Westin arrived on squeaking shoes.

"Doc Nelson was right, Captain. We've got a ton of new evidence."

Chapter 14

FROM FRIENDS TO LOVERS

GEORGE AND I WERE FRIENDS long before we were lovers. It took 5 months, 3 days, 22 hours and 49 minutes before we rolled into bed.

After that first meeting when I found Clay dead, we'd chatted on the phone in the evenings, sharing our stories. I'd tell him about my years in London and Chicago, my kids and quilts, and he'd share some of the funnier cases he'd worked. Said he didn't want to scare me just before I dozed off. Such a considerate chap! I never let on I only listened to his dreamy voice, snuggled under my Mum's quilt.

It was George who accompanied me to Clay's lawyer, Steven Milnick, Esquire, and helped me understand how my life was about to change.

Most Friday nights we'd meet for supper and a movie at the Rose Theater, stopping afterwards at any place open to talk about the state of the world and our community. Then we'd amble over to his apartment building where I'd leave him and Power Walk home up the hill.

When my favorite week rolled around, the Annual Blues Festival, even though I was mourning both my empty nest and Clay's departure from this world, I wasn't going to miss it. It reminded me of my friend Jake cuz she'd introduced me to the Blues when I was new to America and madly in love with everything. So George and I danced in every bar and pub, and walked home with our ears ringing, stone cold sober, drunk on how much we liked each other.

I even got him up on a July dawn when the tide was at its lowest to drive to the Fort Worden for the Sandcastling Exhibition I helped organize. By noon though, with the meds he was taking he couldn't stay in the bright sunshine and he'd taken off. For the first time in all the years I'd been part of the fun, missing my kids and without George, I'd been a bit bereft. I finally met up with him again at the Golden Gate, all sunburnt, sandy and majorly tired.

A while after Joanne, Ethel and Judith joined Sal's Gals and the business was humming along, George had to take some tests at the Veterans Administration Medical Center over in Seattle.

In preparation, he had to fast and take meds which kept him marooned on his loo. He wouldn't let me near him, telling me all the miserable details on the phone.

On test day, at five in the morning, I walked over to his place and met him in the garage. When he got into the Escalade's passenger seat, it dawned on me I was going to have to do the driving. I kept reminding myself I was in the best Detroit made and I'd be fine on the streets I'd fled before. We got there just as rush hour was clogging the streets, however it was a clear shot to the VAMC up on Beacon Hill with only one figure of eight to weave through. Found out that the Escalade's size intimidated most commuting sedans. Though a white knuckle passenger, George was a fine navigator.

Afterwards, we were the last to load on a pre-rush hour ferry and before we'd left the dock, George was snoring. He didn't wake once as I drove through the dusk, listening to music and finally enjoying the ride.

When we got home, all he wanted was his recliner. He staggered into his bedroom, stripped down to his t-shirt and shorts and shambled over to his Lazy-Boy. Groaning, he eased himself down, pulled the lever to raise his feet and stretched out. I covered him with his ratty old Afghan.

"Just need to sleep it off." My haggard friend murmured, and promptly did.

After all those months it was the first time I'd been up to his aerie, so I decided to explore his manly space, painted in that invisible sand color with beige wall-to-wall carpet.

Beside him on an unfinished pine table was a reading lamp and a couple of piles of books with markers sticking out of the top ones. Behind those were a jar of dry roasted peanuts, a test kit, a pack of smokes, a Zippo and an ashtray filled with sand. A cordless phone in its charger and a universal remote filled the rest of the surface. Underneath were boxes of injection supplies.

His huge LCD screen hung dead center on the opposite wall above a credenza with a DVD player, satellite receiver and Bose sound system. On the shelves were his music CDs and movie DVDs, and below that were neat rows of *Shotgun News*, *American Police Beat Magazine*, *Popular Science* and *Penthouse Letters*.

All his dining area had was shelves, half-filled with

science fiction and military memoirs. On the carpet were the sound system speakers and leaning against a wall five plaques with a shield and citation on each. Three windows gave a panorama of the sports field with its lights ablaze as a soccer game was in play. The lights of downtown to the west made the fog glow. To the east was Point Hudson. On a sunny day, the view of all the water, the islands and both mountain ranges would be spectacular.

When I took his insulin kit to the fridge in his utility kitchen I was impressed with the *Penthouse* calendar held in place by two well-endowed babe magnets. The month's blond had a smile on her flawless face and a come-hither look to her azure eyes. She was pouring her perfect bosom from a glossy black bustier. Notations on the days were about appointments and meetings. Inside were a couple of gallon water jugs, a half-full bottle of V8 juice, a case of diet Pepsi cans and a Pyrex bowl of apples. That was it. I stowed his travel kit beside the boxes of insulin in the door. When I put away the ice pack in his freezer I saw a solitary tub of sugar-free chocolate ice cream, and an ice maker tray.

I left the insulated case on the counter beside the stainless steel sink and a brand new draining rack with a glass turned upside down. Not a dish towel in sight, only a hanging paper towel roll. On the counter was a huddle of medicine and vitamin bottles.

I peeked into his cupboards. Another glass and two plates. The other side had microwave containers of baked beans, soups and chili, an opened slab of Hershey's dark chocolate, a box of WheatThins and a jar of crunchy peanut butter, half eaten.

When I went for a tinkle in his bathroom a fan hummed to life as I pressed the light switch. A set of

THE DEAD HUSBAND 125

white towels hung on the shower door, the mat over the top. His white robe dangled on the back of the door. Under his linen shelves was a clothes hamper.

On the counter he had a moustache mug with his toothbrush and paste, a box of tissues and a blue bottle of orange water that gave the whole place its pleasant scent.

Then I peered into his bedroom. His king size just about filled it and was covered with a comforter that looked like a castoff from a motel, like Mrs. Balko's. On his beside table he had another cordless phone in its charger, a lamp and a wind-up alarm clock.

An unfinished tallboy filled one side of his closet with his pocket stuff on the top. On the shelf above was a gun safe. Below hung his suits and tie rack and under those his shoes were neatly paired beside a black leather grip.

I kicked off my shoes, lay down on his bed and pulled the comforter over me.

"HEY, YOU HUNGRY?" I woke to George stroking my arm. "Got Golden Gate to deliver."

I wondered where I'd sit, not reckoning on the size of his leather recliner. We snuggled in to eat and watch the news. I didn't last long and woke to find myself wrapped around a dozing bear.

It was my dash for the loo that roused him. I stayed while he tested his blood and took his insulin. Then I kissed him good night and left.

As I walked home through the fog to my own bed, I wondered why it hadn't occurred to me to sleep over. Then I worried that if something went wrong the first I'd know about it would be someone at the Justice Center fielding his calls.

So on the last day of that vacation when we were

finishing breakfast at the Salal, the idea kinda just popped into my head. Yeah, right!

"Care to break in a brand-spanking-new bed with me?" I'd teased.

He looked up from leaving Mindy's tip and grinned. "Do I get to do the spanking?"

"Naughty, naughty!" I wagged a finger at him. "Only after the delivery chaps have gone. Gotta be back by..." I pulled up his sleeve. "Twenty minutes." That touch just about lit the two of us up like bonfires. We practically sprinted to his Escalade, racing it up the hill to my nest.

I'd already dismantled Clay's bed and Ethel had come and taken it home cuz she'd drooled over it, and the buffet, the dining table and chairs when I'd given her the tour. I'd been sleeping on an air mattress ever since. My new linens were washed and ready, along with the four new pillows and the huge down comforter and duvet I'd sprung for.

George and I'd sat out on my porch and smoked, jittery with anticipation. Half-an-hour after they said they'd be here, the furniture guys drove their van into my cul-de-sac and had a heck of a time parking.

At last they were gone, and once George had again assured me he'd fully recovered from the tests, I led him inside, locked the front door and turned on the dreamy *Hearts of Space* channel. Then we'd made the bed and lain on it, and done some loverly stuff. Thought I'd like his bod as much as his mind.

AT THE TIME, George had been divorced for almost two decades, living alone and content with his life.

I'd been unattached, without kids for almost a year. I'd settled into my very first home, started a company, and was also content with my life.

THE DEAD HUSBAND   127

I wasn't expecting this to change anything except maybe get rid of the itch that bugged me whenever I thought of George. Was I ever wrong!

The sex hadn't changed our friendship, we just made more time for it. Every day! For three months! We'd been like teenagers who'd never had a date in high school. Which was true for me and, after George told his stories, for him too.

It was a blood sugar crash at four in the morning at my place that scared us so much we decided we'd better grow up and slow down.

George had been so... well... absorbed that sometimes he'd missed testing or forgotten to bring along his insulin. And all that loverly sex had us eating... well... extravagantly.

I realized I'd have to be responsible too: about what and when we ate, and how much, and keep track, when we were together, of his meds and his gear and the monitor testing.

So we decided that during the week he'd go directly home from work and we'd talk hot and heavy on the phone. Then the weekends were ours except, of course, the last one of the month which was reserved for Sal's Gals.

I really liked seeing his casual clothes hanging in my closet and was quite sappy about laundering them. I liked seeing a pair of his shoes beside mine, too. I liked handling the books he left on the table by our recliner, and the bottle of his orange water on the counter in my bathroom.

George brought a pleasant scent to my home, companionship and a groundedness to my life.

NOW, AFTER BRINGING ME back from showing his detectives the Birnbaums' home, he let me and my dog out and with a toot of his horn drove off.

Porsche blessed our gate and when I let him into the garden, trotted around after his nose for a while and then made a beeline for his water bowl and lapped most of it up. Then he flopped down at the bottom of the porch steps.

There were three messages on my voice mail: Steve Milnik requesting I return his call. Joanne asking if I was still a free woman. Claire wanting to see me now cuz it was really, REALLY important.

Chapter 15

SILLY QUESTIONS

ALL THE YEARS I'D KNOWN Steven Milnik, Esquire, he'd never initiated a call. Susannah, his paralegal, put me through, pronto.

"What's up, Steve?"

"You're presence is required here Monday at ten for the reading of Melvin Aaron Birnbaum's will."

"Me?"

"Yes, you. Will you be here?"

"Of course."

"Good. I won't have to sic the Cop Shop on you."

"You'd do that?"

"Sure. Had you not called back."

"Okay, then I'll see you Monday."

"Consider yourself served. Oh, and Sally..."

"Yeah?"

"Be prepared, it's going to get uncomfortable."

"Thanks for the warning. So the wife's going to be there?"

"The widow, and yes, she's been notified. As well as some others."

"Jeez, Steve, wasn't Mel just a computer geek with

a good eye for sunsets?"

"Oh, no, my dear, he was far more than that!" He ended the call.

"Holy-moly," I muttered as I pressed Joanne's number. Getting her voice mail, I left word that as of this moment, on this day I was still a free woman.

Then I called Claire on the landline number she'd left. An elderly woman's voice answered.

"Mrs. Birnbaum?" I'd not spoken with Mel's mother before.

"Who is this?"

"It's Sally Collier. In Port Townsend. Claire left me a message."

"Sal-the-Gal? Who cleans my son's home? Forgive me, that's the only name my granddaughter uses. She's been so worried since she got here."

"When was that, Mrs. Birnbaum?"

"Why, right when *60 Minutes*. She hadn't eaten and... well, she had a lot of laundry to do. We stayed up quite late."

"Do you know where she'd been?"

"Oh yes! Out at the Lake Quinault camp. She's been going there every summer since, oh, eighth grade? You know, first as a camper and then a counselor. This year she was helping close it. Usually her parents drive her there and back. She said her father let her drive herself. Do you know where he is?"

"Mrs. Birnbaum," I sure didn't want to be the person to tell her. "I can't... may I speak with Claire?"

"She's right here."

Claire came on the line.

"Hyah, Sal, sorry 'bout that... I need to see you. Can we meet?"

"Sure. Shall I come there?"

"Don't do that! I've got wheels... Sal?"
"Yes, dear?"
"Is my Dad all right?" She whispered.
"No, my dear, he's not." How much should I say? "Where do you want to meet?"
"You know the boat launch at Gardiner?"
"Sure, what's there?"
"My favorite pee stop, otherwise nobody."
"And that's important?"
"Very. Sal, I really can't talk right now."
"Okay. I can start out in about fifteen minutes."
"Fine."
"I have somebody for you to see."
"Don't bring anyone else, Sal!"
"Why on earth not?"
"God, stop being so dumb! Just you or I don't come."
"Okay, Claire. See you in an hour."
"Who were you going to bring?"
"Not going to tell you now!" And I disconnected.

I knew I had to call someone on the case. The thought of telling either Smith or Westin made me feel like a traitor. I pressed my captain's office number.

"How can I help you, Ms Collier?" No lovey-dovey stuff on the recorded connection.

"I'm driving out to Gardiner to meet with Claire Birnbaum. Would you let the detectives know?"

"I will. Where in Gardiner?"

"The boat launch."

"Okay, you get there ASAP. Don't go over the limit. Then wait for the case detectives."

I took a leak, gathered my stuff, called Porsche and loaded him. After gassing up at the Shell station on Sims Way, we headed for SR20.

I was coming to the propane yard when my cellphone chirped. I pulled off into a turnout.

"I'm serious, hon, don't leave Gardiner. And don't let Claire. I'm siccing Smith and Westin on you in exactly ten minutes."

"We'll be waiting."

"I'm tied up with something here."

"And I'm with Porsche."

"That'll be good for her. How is she?"

"Bad. Mad. Asked if her father was all right."

"What did you say?"

"That he wasn't."

"You'll have to tell her he's dead but nothing more. Let my detectives do that."

"Any news of Renee?"

"None so far. Drive carefully."

WHEN I FIRST GOT TO PORT TOWNSEND on its little Quimper Peninsula on the hem of the great big Olympic Peninsula, I considered it a good omen that upon the largest tank at the supply station south of town was brightly painted Paradise Propane.

Then one lunchtime after I had wheels, I'd gotten caught in a rare traffic jam. My eyes eventually focused on the herd of cars I'd blundered into. I'd never seen so many realty signs in one place. Then I remembered reading in *The Leader's* obits that five children, all octogenarians, of the pioneer settlers had shucked this mortal coil within days of each other. Their homesteads, which inclued farm houses and barns, a dairy and meadows for cows, a blacksmith's corral and forge, vegetable fields and orchards were up for grabs. Within a year the cows vanished, the orchards were cut down, the fields plowed over for everso neat housing developments of neo-Victorian houses and their drawing board gardens.

In Clay's home, my home, the cook stove and water heater run on propane so I have my very own pet tank, about the size of a cow.

I knew things were changing in my neck of the woods when the delivery truck rolled up one day with a new sign on it: Suburban Propane. So who thought suburbia better than paradise?

CLAIRE WAS RIGHT THERE, coming out of the comfort station as I pulled into the parking lot at the Gardiner boat launch park on the west coast of Discovery Bay. I parked beside the Cherokee under the conifers and made a dash for some relief of my own. Then I let Porsche out.

"Borschty-poo!" Claire yelped, getting down on her blue-jean knees in the forest duff and hugging him. There ensued a burst of embarrassing baby talk. By the licking and tail wagging, I could see the dog remembered his pack mate.

I stood nearby, sniffing the damp scents and drinking in the loverly water scene as still as a mirror with wisps of mist rising over the far forested shore. Then I sat down on the picnic table bench.

"Claire, we've only got a few minutes before a couple of detectives get here."

"You told the cops where I was?" She whined, letting go her furry friend and rising. Porsche bounded off sniffing around and relieving himself.

"Had to. Been with 'em for hours. This is serious, Claire. They're going to want to talk to you."

"I knew it!" She buried her face in her hands, moaning. "I don't know anything. Really, I don't!"

"We don't have the time for this." I called Porsche to me and clicked the leash to his chain. He settled beside my legs. Claire blotted her eyes on the sleeves of her denim jacket.

"What's going on with your parents?"

"Mom came home Sunday night."

"Two days ago?"

"No!" She pouted impatiently. "Last week. I was all packed for camp. Had my bags in the Cherokee. Dad and me were in the kitchen, talking about the drive and eating croissants and hot chocky. Like we always do in the evenings. And she just walked in... with that asshole Alan!" She glared at me and wrapped her arms around herself. There were dark circles under her eyes. She wore no makeup and smelt of sweat and fear and... ahha! What I'd found in Claire's bathroom trash was definitely not hers.

"What happened?"

"Mom started yelling. Dumb stuff like how dare he smoke in the house. What did he think he was doing feeding me that crap. Stuff like that, you know? Dad lost it. I've never seen them fight like that, ever!" She rubbed her cheek. "Then asshole Alan said something like 'Hey man, cool ya jets.'" Her voice went down a register, then it flew upwards, "What a dork! I mean who talks like that? Anyway, Dad turned on him and they were all yelling at once, something about jealousy and old scores and... I never knew they knew him before."

"Before what?"

"Like from high school!" Her jaw jutted out and she stamped her foot.

"How did it end?"

"Don't know, I split. I mean I was already packed. With them all yelling who'd notice?"

"And you did?"

"Not right away. I..." She kicked up some duff and

sighed. "I wanted to know what it was about. I tried to calm them down, you know, like they used to when me and Donna and Britney fought." I had no idea who she was talking about and she could see that. "My best friends... when they stayed over."

"And?"

"It was like I was invisible. So I just went up to my room. Started tidying." Claire stopped kicking and suddenly grinned, tucking her hair behind her ears. "You looked in my room, didn't you?"

"I did."

"Bet it freaked you out!" She giggled and started pacing around, swinging her arms.

"It did!"

"You know, you can hear everything going on in the house through the heat vents. It went on forever. Don't know what time they quit cuz I fell asleep on the floor. Woke up when the front door slammed right under me. Then two car doors went bang, bang!" She mimed the sound. "And there was Mom's Beamer driving off." She hitched a buttock on the picnic table and swung a leg. "Dad called me to come on down. He looked so sad. Wouldn't talk about it. Had my coffee ready and a bag of croissants. Said I might as well start out as you could see the mountains already, so why wait? By the time I got to Sequim it'd be full light. Told me to use my credit card for gas in Forks, and then he... just stood there watching me leave. I didn't think anything of it. I mean, I'd be seeing him again in a week, right?"

"And you never heard from either again?"

She shook her head, hands now stuck in her jean pockets. "I called. Every chance I got. Left messages. You know, they're always telling me to be responsible. Why aren't they? So, how is Dad really?"

"Really?" I eyed her distraught face. "He's really dead. Down at the bottom of the garden."

Claire started gulping, then suddenly bent over and vomited. I handed her one of George's hankies I found in a pocket, and my water bottle.

"When?" She moaned, straightening up and sipping the water and sluicing it around in her mouth before spitting it out.

"Long before I got there, and he was all wet."

"Could it have been last week?" Claire peeked at me through her hair.

"Doubt it. Soon as I know, you will too."

"God, I'm going to miss him." Claire slid onto the picnic table bench.

"Me too." I murmured.

"Why you?" She wiped at her chin. "I heard Mom ask you that time. Why didn't you?"

"Your father was married!"

"So? People fuck around all the time? What was wrong with my Dad?"

"Not a thing. I just... don't mess with married men is all."

"You call what Mom and Dad had a marriage?"

"Well—"

"That dumb job!" She leapt to her feet and circled around the table. "Made Mom a bitch on wheels! And that asshole Alan! What does she see in him?"

"You think they're lovers?"

"Duh?" She snorted.

"Silly question."

"Double-duh!"

"Where will you live? Will you still go to college?"

Claire kicked at some cones. "I only applied cuz Dad wanted me to go to his precious alma mater. Said he wanted me to finish what he never did. I won't now."

"Why ever not?"

"What's the point? Anyway I've got... other plans."

"Hasn't your Dad already pai—what other plans?"

"Not going to tell!"

Porsche raised up and looked east along the highway, his ears pricked, nose twitching.

"Is Dad really dead?" Claire asked in a little girl voice. I nodded.

She raised her eyes up to the tall trees overhead. "The Gramps are going to be so sad," she whispered, heaving a huge sigh and then said quite calmly, "Suppose I'm going to have to live with them now. That's so dumb. Did you find him?

"Actually Porsche did."

"You changed his name!"

"Yeah. Never did like calling him a soup."

"You know how he got it?" She bent down and stroked his head. For a moment he basked under the caresses and then returned his attention to the highway. "Back when everything was all right," Claire continued. "You know, in California, Mom was making some borscht for the co-op and he got into the beet skins in the compost bucket. They must have been sweet cuz he just kept eating. He shat purple for days." She grabbed Porsche's ears and rocked his head. "Yes, you did, Borschty-poo." He backed into my legs.

"Dumb dog." The grieving girl pouted.

I caught a flash of a red light through the trees.

"They're almost here." I leaned over and held her wrist. "Listen, you've just told me your story. Now, when they get here you're going to have to tell it again. Probably—"

"The cops'll have to listen to me, won't they!" She

looked toward the highway. "Maybe they'll..." She shook my hand off and got up. I did too and sprinted for the Cherokee with Porsche snug at my side. Got there before she did, leant in and plucked the keys out of the ignition.

"Was that your pregnancy tester?"

"What? Where?" Claire gaped as she came up behind me. "No way! I don't do that icky stuff!"

"Yet." I murmured watching her frown, thinking.

"My Mom's pregnant? No fucking way!" A siren gave a warning whoop.

"Only that way, girl. Any idea where they went?"

"How would I know?" She scowled at me. "They never tell me anything! Why're you here, anyway? You're just the cleaning bitch."

"Excuse me?" I gawked at her mood change.

"You grown-ups think you know everything but you don't. Nothing!"

"You've totally lost me."

"Yeah, just bet I have! Why're you here?"

"You tell me!"

"Well, I don't need you. I'm eighteen. Go away!" She turned her back. "And take that dumb dog with you."

"Gladly, once the coppers get here."

Chapter 16

WHEN THEY WERE YOUNG

THE BLACK SEDAN that Detective Westin had gotten out of at Mel's home churned up dust as it came to a stop on the other side of my beater. Smith was out in a trice, striding toward us holding up his ID.

"Are you Claire Rainey Birnbaum? Detective Smith, Jefferson County. We'd like to talk to you in connection with your father's death. Would you show me some identification?"

Claire took her wallet from of her jacket pocket and held it open.

"Please take out your driver's license and hand it to me." As she was doing that he glanced over at me. "We meet again, Miss Collier." He looked down at what Claire had given him.

"Fancy meeting you here. Nice dog." Westin quipped as he arrived, closing his cellphone.

"Would you be willing to take us to your grandparents? Where do they live?" Smith was all efficiency.

"Sequim," Claire answered, taking a nonchalant

swig from my water bottle and then licking her lips. "Two-o-three John Wayne Lane. Do I get to ride with you guys?"

"No, Miss, we'll need you to drive yourself."

"Would you follow us, Ms Collier?" Westin said as he watched his partner at work. My instant reaction was: I'd rather not. Instead I held out the keys to the Cherokee.

"Would you mind stepping over this way?" Westin gestured toward the cars. I loaded Porsche into my beater en route.

"She was going to leave before we got here." Westin spoke quietly, standing half turned away from his partner and Claire.

"Why don't you ask her?"

"Wait here, would you?" He trotted back to where they were talking.

As Claire wound the two men around her little finger, I again pondered on the ways of American maidens. She didn't flirt, exactly, just presented her assets. Off came the denim jacket revealing an eye-catching bosom tightly wrapt in a loverly pink teddy top over a black bra. What a goddess!

While I had the feeling much of Claire's story was as true as she knew, the next time she told it she'd likely embellish it a bit, and if the temper that had snuck out was anything to go by, Smith and Westin were in for a performance.

It's not that I faulted her for being so mercurial, she was after all, only eighteen and had no idea what the hormones were doing to her, especially at this time in her month. I certainly hadn't. Except I knew Mel, unlike Renee, hadn't let their daughter grow up like a weed they couldn't get rid of.

My gut told me Claire knew where her mom had

gone, or thought she did. Perhaps she'd heard something she didn't realize was important. Would she tell the detectives? As I watched 'em, I wondered which would fall for her. My bet was on Smith. Westin, at least, was married with children. Claire's cynical retort echoed in my ears.

I pulled out a smoke and lit up. I so wanted to go home, brew a pot of tea and sit on my porch watching my dog enjoy my loverly garden. Then I wanted to take a long hot shower and wash this family right out of my hair.

When Westin came over, I knew I wasn't going to get off that easy.

"Miss Birnbaum has agreed to take us to her grandparents. Would you be willing to follow? I think she could use your... er... support." He hadn't witnessed her flying off the handle. "Oh yeah, we'll get an escort once we cross the county line."

I told Porsche he was a good dog when he licked my ear, and started up my beater. Smith loaded Claire into the Cherokee and took the passenger seat while Westin pointed his sedan out of the park and, ahead of a cluster of RVs, floored his accelerator. In seconds we were up to speed, cruising over the ridge still socked-in with marine mist.

Claire had no problem keeping up with Westin. My old beater was shaking, and I wasn't doing much better. I hate driving on someone's tail.

WE SPED AROUND THE BAY and as we crested Diamond Point a Clallam County cruiser with its lights flashing pulled out and took up the lead. We flew past lavender farms, through Blyn village, the Jamestown S'Klallam tribal center on Sequim Bay and then past the Seven Cedars Casino with its full parking lot.

After the exit to the John Wayne Marina the Clallam County copper veered off the highway and slowed down to enter Sequim.

It's now a retirement town on the fertile post-Ice Age delta of the Dungeness River where pioneer farmers used to unearth mastodon bones and turds. It has its own climate and during WWII, the USAF often flew from air bases to the Sequim Hole when the rest of the Northwest was socked-in.

We turned onto Brown Avenue and cut onto the Old Olympic Highway to where, just a decade ago, there'd been potato and corn fields.

Mel's parents lived in a ranch house with wide lawns all around where eastern Maples were dropping their scarlet leaves in perfect circles. I slid to a stop behind the Clallam County deputy as he parked on the road while Claire's convoy swooped up onto the two door garage apron.

Mel's father opened his front door and let us all into the living room where the cloud-dappled Olympic Mountains filled the picture window. Mrs. Birnbaum, in a purple mumu, stood gripping her walker with horribly twisted fingers, rings embedded in the flesh. I couldn't see a thing about her that reminded me of her son. Her faded blue eyes were on her only grandchild who skulked behind the detectives, hugging herself. Mrs. Birnbaum's wig of short curly hair the color of Claire's was slightly askew.

Mr. Birnbaum on the other hand, looked like Mel would have had he lived thirty more years. The same head of hair, only his was white and short. No beard or moustache. The same eyes, nose, even ears filled with old-fashioned hearing aids. I felt a sob catch in my chest. So sorry, Mel, so sorry.

THE DEAD HUSBAND

I stood inside the front door and witnessed Smith and Westin deliver the worst kind of news to parents.

Husband and wife sank into their recliners, grief and confusion crumbling their faces. An orange Pomeranian leapt up on Mrs. Birnbaum's lap and she stroked it with her left claw while her right one reached for her husband. With tears in his eyes, he patted his wife's hand with his own trembling one.

Claire slid onto the plastic covered couch, demurely pressing her hands between her knees, watching her grandparents.

I tuned 'em all out and took comfort in something familiar: checking out the home as if it was a prospective job. I always look at the floors first. They tell me volumes. Here the sky blue carpeting was soft and smooth with vacuum stripes in the low traffic areas. When I shuffled my feet I could smell a recent shampooing. There wasn't much furniture, just the couch and recliners with side tables and lamps. Recessed into all the walls were glass shelves filled with gilt edged cups and saucers and glass figurines, mostly unicorns.

Beside Mrs. Birnbaum was a fake fireplace with a dog basket and pillow. On the fake mantel were three cute pastel portraits of little red dogs.

On the wall facing the recliners, in back of Smith and Westin, hung a wide plasma screen tuned to a muted talk show.

Through the counter the dining room morphed into a white kitchen with blue trim. Glowing outside the wide window over the sink Steller's Blue Jays were attacking a feeder hung from the eave, sending seeds cascading. Beyond the sliding glass door a patio extended out to a gray cedar fence. I could just see the edge of a blue and white umbrella and the back of a blue garden chair.

I looked down the hallway where the dim white walls were crowded with framed photos. The nearest were sepia-toned studio portraits of two almost identical wedding couples: wives in white, lacey, post-Victorian dresses, with hands resting on husbands' shoulders. Under lace veils their thick and wavy dark hair cascaded around pretty, unsmiling faces. Both seated grooms wore neat dark suits, high white collars and black bow ties. Their faces with thick brows and neatly trimmed moustaches and beards, were rather jolly.

The next set of photos had the same couples standing behind little old ladies smothered in black. One had three towering young men lined up behind. The other had two demure maidens in 1920s frocks sitting at their grandmother's knee. No older man in either. Next were couples with infants. Then two, three and five kids. Now they were growing up and the mothers wore black with husbands absent. Then there were young men in uniforms and girls in '40s short-sleeved frocks and hair styles. One wore a white hospital coat in a tropical setting. Another, in coveralls, was stepping into an airplane cockpit.

As I sidled down the corridor I came upon a bare baby on his tummy on a fur rug. From there on, I watched Mel grow up before my eyes.

By the time I got to his full color prom shot with Renee hanging onto his arm, I was blotting tears on my sleeve. How bright and hopeful they'd been. Renee in her pink Jackie Kennedy dress, pink bow in her high bouffant blond hair and corsage on her wrist. Mel with his curly dark hair tamed and moustache trimmed, and a deer-in-the-headlights look. All decked out in a baby blue tux and ruffled shirt with a blue carnation in his lapel. I wondered if his shoes had been blue suede.

That's when I found the powder room and quickly relieved myself.

When I came back out I scanned the other side of the hall. Here was a gallery of enlarged snapshots of Mel and Renee and friends. One showed her in a booth in a gym with a basketball hoop high above and half of a school's name behind it. She was leaning toward Mel with her eyes closed. Both had their hands behind their backs. The sign above them read $1 A KISS. They were very young.

The next was of them in a group of lads and lasses sprawled on some grass amid piles of books. The girls were in blouses and skirts of all different lengths, some showing a lot of leg. The boys wore jeans, white t-shirts and all kinds of jackets, hair slicked back. Renee was leaning against Mel's chest. One long, blonde youth lay on his back on the other side of her with his arm over his face.

Now they were bundled up in puffy jackets and knitted hats grinning at the camera. Icicles dangled from Mel's moustache. The street behind was filled with snow covered cars.

Another photo had Mel and Renee leaning back-to-back in swim suits and sunglasses on a crowded beach with the same friends. One lad with a floppy hat on his head had his bare back to the camera. Was his hand touching Renee's foot?

Then, just the two of them beside a green Econoline van. The driver's door was open and Renee had a sandaled foot up on the running board. She was in gag-green hot pants, a pink and green striped tank top, a ponytail and sunglasses. Mel leaned on the steering wheel wearing a short-sleeved blue plaid shirt and sunglasses. His curly black hair, moustache and beard in full bloom. He was grinning toothily.

The last photo was of a summer backyard. I counted seven couples holding up glasses. There was Renee with her mouth open with Mel behind her. Next, was a Boss look-alike with an arm around a girl with a veil of long brown hair. And there in the back by the barbecue, not holding up anything nor smiling was a very young version of the chap in all those photos on Renee's glory wall. Alan Hatton.

So, that answered a huge question. They had indeed been from the same place and time.

WESTIN POKED his head into the hallway with a question on his face. I beckoned him over and showed him the photo. When he didn't got it I pointed to Hatton. Westin's eyebrows shot up.

"They go back a-ways, eh." He murmured.

Smith's voice was loud in that small house as he prompted Claire. I sidled back to the photos in which the young chap had shied from the camera, tapping my finger on each. Westin sidestepped with me.

"Where do you think they are?" he breathed

"Claire says she doesn't know."

"You believe her?"

I shrugged. "Think the Birnbaums knew the Raineys?" I caught his arm as he turned away. "Claire says the pregnancy kit's not hers and... well, I know it isn't."

"Really?" And he left me in that dim corridor.

Chapter 17

MY FIRST AMERICAN

I FINALLY DID GET THAT POT OF TEA on my porch though all my mind wanted to think about was Ruth Esther Jacoby, aka Jake. She got me to America by having her Pop offer me a job in his Chicago bank.

I met her at my first dinner at Moneypenny's Secretarial College and liked her instantly. She was everything I wasn't: funny, outgoing, a teaser with a mouth that never stopped. I thought her beautiful and sophisticated and loved listening to her strong accent. She had the widest blue eyes, black wing eyebrows and a mop of short curly black hair that made her look a little like a poodle.

"So, Collie, what're you in for?" She was shoveling in the cottage pie like she was starved. While everyone else was downing tea with milk and sugar, she drank water from a tall glass with ice cubes clinking away.

"The Works," I answered after swallowing. I wasn't used to talking while I ate. Jake had it down pat. She even put her elbows on the table. I was about to say something when I saw others doing it, so I shut up and watched, listened and learnt.

"Did that four years ago." Jake went back to attacking her food with her fork. "Moneypenny chauffeured Mom around while Pop was here with the Marshall Plan. You know, helping you guys pick up the pieces. Pop called it making a prosperous peace. Mom sent me here as a graduation present. Thought a year in London would round me off." She gulped down some water.

"Did you like it?"

She nodded. "Sure. Not as much as Chicago. You ever get there, Collie, I'll give you the tour. You know any places to dance and meet guys?"

"I've never been out at night."

That stopped her fork on its way to her mouth with another load.

"Say again?"

"I hav—"

"Heard you the first time! Where've you been? In a hole? You wanna come out with me after?"

"Tonight? Are we allowed?"

Jake put her fork down. I'd been noticing the strange way she used her cutlery.

"What?" She grinned. "Never seen an American eat before?" I felt my face flame. "God, Collie, you're such a virgin! 'Course we're allowed. Just gotta sign out on the board. Where we're going. Then we have to be back by midnight. Like Cinderella. You know who she was, right?"

I nodded and kept eating. For all the years I'd lived in West Kensington I knew next to nothing about the town itself and Jake decided, in the days she had left before flying home, to show me. That first evening she took me to two dives with live bands. One was an all-girl group dressed like weird creatures. The other was a foursome of long-haired lads.

Jake pulled me onto the floor and taught me how to dance. At some point she offered me a cigarette, a mild American menthol. She didn't try to ply me with booze. She didn't touched the stuff, only Coca-Cola.

At eleven-thirty she grabbed her denim jacket from the back of her chair, pulled out her wallet, and left a tenner tucked under her soda bottle.

"Curfew, my little innocent, let's split. We're not far but we're gonna have to shake a leg!" I followed her through the throng out into the cool night.

Jake strode along dodging around people, leaping across roads like she wore seven league boots. I trotted beside her with the music still ringing in my ears and the colors dazzling my eyes. I'd loved the energy in those dance clubs and knew I'd go back.

All the way she chatted on about the differences between America and England, the politics back home and why she'd come back to Moneypenny's for a tune up.

"Knew my speeds were way down. Got in some bad habits too. Been well worth the money, and the night life's great. Jeez, Collie, if I ever get you to Chicago, you're gonna have to hear the Blues!" We loped up Moneypenny's stairs with minutes to spare.

"Don't think anyone's ever been locked out." She panted as she pushed the door open. "Still, I hate being late!" She led the way down to the Commons in the basement where there were fridges with leftovers and fruit for snacks, tables and chairs and an electric kettle. "Come on, let's have talk before we crash."

Jake wanted to know all about me and I wanted to know about America. Long past my bedtime, I was dozing off when she shook me awake and chivvied me up to our room.

For all her constant motion, Jake never made a mess. She took her clothes off and just naturally put them in their place. And she wasn't the least bit shy about wandering around starkers, out to the loo or the showers, around our room. She even slept naked which shocked me as I wrestled into my nightie.

After she'd turned her bedside light out she called quietly, "Night, Collie. Nice meeting you."

"Me too, Jake. Thanks for a loverly time."

"You're welcome. Tomorrow I'm gonna take you..." I have no idea what she had in mind cuz on my first night away from my Mum, I was already dancing in my dreams. It wouldn't have surprised me if she'd spent the whole night talking cuz she woke me the next morning with her goading.

I'd never before thought of people as colors. In my eyes, my new friend was the vividest blue, like a peacock feather.

Jake had three more exams to take and then she was as free as a bird, eager to whisk me off on the Underground and buses to shop for things on her Mom's list. She also took me to museums and art galleries. Even a ride on a launch up the River Thames past Big Ben and the Houses of Parliament. I felt like a tourist in my own town. She took me up in a lift (she called it an elevator) to the top of a new skyscraper so I could see just how big London was.

"Chicago's got hundreds of these, you know." She bragged, as I stared at the panorama of the city I'd lived in. "Most are lakeside and downtown. Lake Michigan's probably bigger than all of England."

"Really?"

Jake laughed and swatted at my arm. "Yo, Collie, you'll see. Everything's bigger in America!"

She was so right.

THE DEAD HUSBAND

I WAS AWFULLY SAD TO SEE JAKE OFF at Heathrow amid hugs and promises to write to each other. Then, with tears in my eyes I'd trotted after Moneypenny to the luggage claim area and shrank in shyness when I saw her greet the vision in a red sari who was going to be my next roommate.

Chitters and I didn't hit it off at all. From a political family with oodles of money and servants, she was untidy and haughty. Jake would have called her a "godawful slob." My new roommate whined about everything and had a difficult time with her hair, which I admired so I had her sit on her chair and brushed and plaited the yard long black cascade. She once said, in a snit after I'd complained about her mess and her perfume ponging up the place, that if Daddy hadn't ordered her to get some skills she'd never have come here. She was already promised in marriage and couldn't understand what Mummy had seen in this dreadful little school.

I kept my nose to the grindstone determined to pass my courses with the highest degrees. And I did.

NOW, BACK IN MY OWN HOME, I took Porsche for a quick walk in the park, filled his water bowl and then took a shower and a nap.

Sometime later I awoke from a strange, desperate dream in which Mel was flying through the air with no head. Trees were moaning as they marched uphill and cigarette butts dotted about like tombstones. In my ear a dog was growling, and that wasn't part of my dream.

Porsche's hackles were up and between growls he was nudging me. He went silent when I rolled off the bed and bolted for the loo. I was pulling on a sweatsuit, when a pounding started on my front door.

Dreading another visit from the police, I hustled Porsche out to the sunroom. Then I tiptoed to the front door and locked it. On the other side of the distorted glass window, Renee was pacing. Out beyond my gate was a silver sedan and when smoke puffed out of the open window I realized there was someone inside.

The boards creaked and suddenly Renee was peering in my bay window. She didn't see me tucked into the dark. Again the boards creaked and she was rapping hard on my door. I wished George was here.

"I know you're in there, Sally! Your old heap's in the carport."

"What do you want?" I reluctantly called through the wood.

"You told me to come get the dumb dog."

"Did not! I told you I was taking him home."

"You gonna keep him?"

"Yeah, you never liked him."

"Dumb dirty thing!"

"So? You got a problem with me taking him?"

"Far from it! One less to suck off me."

"No one's ever sucked off you, Renee!"

"First Mel and then dear little Claire. God, I hated how needy they were!"

"Well, they don't need you anymore now. Your husband's dead and your daughter's off on her own life. What do you want to talk to me about?"

"Let me in! It's so dumb yelling like this through the door."

"From what I hear, you've been doing a lot of yelling lately." Now why was my heart pounding? Renee was a mere slip of thing and I was in pretty good shape. Right, and Mel's dead and buried at the bottom of his garden.

THE DEAD HUSBAND   153

I tiptoed to my office, plucked my cellphone from its charger and punched George's private number. Then I crept back to my hiding place.

"What is it, hon?"

"She's here," I whispered. "Pounding on my door."

"Who?"

"The wife!"

"Renee Rainey Birnbaum?"

"Yeah! Wait..." I took the phone from my ear so he could hear Renee yell.

"Where's Claire?"

"Don't tell her!" George ordered. "It'll take less than five minutes for a cruiser to get there. Stall! Don't hang up!"

I wondered where he was. Likely eating dinner someplace. Then my own guts gurgled. Tough luck, tummy, you'll have to wait this one out.

"What's it to you?" I finally yelled back.

"Just want her safe, Sal."

"They're on their way," George came back on, "Keep her talking. Ask if she knows anything about... her husband."

"You know how Mel died?" I obeyed.

"Your call's the first I heard about it."

"Sure it was." I muttered to George.

"Where's she been?" He prompted.

"Where've you been?"

"Over in the city." She was calming down a bit.

"With Hatton?"

"Yeah, so what?" Oops, her fire was back on high.

"Why did you tell the cops I was banging Mel?"

"Oh, Sal, I was frantic! Didn't know what I was saying. It just sort of slipped out."

"Sure it did." I breathed into the phone. Then I raised my voice, "Well, coppers take those sort of accusations seriously. I was really embarrassed."

"Hey, sorry 'bout that, I was scared." She thumped the door again.

"So, are you pregnant?" I blurted out before I'd thought it through.

"No, don't go there!" I was surprised by the urgency in my Man's voice.

Renee battered my home some more. "Sal, you open this fucking door right now! We've got to talk!"

"We're doing just fine like this. That was your husband I found at the bottom of the garden and I haven't heard one word of... well, remorse or—"

"You want grieving widow? The dumb prick wouldn't let me—" She kicked at my door again. "Fuck. Fuck!" Something clunked against the wood.

"Was that your pregnancy kit?"

"No, no!" George squawked in my ear.

"Yeah, so fucking what?"

"Hatton's?"

"What if it was?"

"What do you mean was?"

"Ever heard of abortion? Had one this morning. You think I want another dumb kid?"

"Then why's Mel dead?"

"Because... shit!" Now she was really punishing my door, and pushing and pulling at the handle. I touched the lock inside. "Open this fucking door, I really gotta talk to you!"

"Do not let her in." George had regained his usual basso profundo. "Where's Porsche?" I straightened my spine some.

"They're not going to come with sirens blaring, are they?" I whispered.

"Nope."

I sighed with relief. "He's hiding out in the

sunroom."

"Wise dog. God, I wish I was there! Keep her talking! Ask her—"

"Why do you want in? What do I matter?"

"Sal? Sal? Come on, open up, please." She was wheedling now. "Hey, we're old friends, right? Got a lot of history together. Let's talk, like we used to. You have no idea what I've been going through."

"We haven't talked in ages. Which reminds me, why did you tell me that fantasy about how you started working for Hatton when you've known him all your life?"

That made Renee go silent. Then she said, real quietly, "What're you talking about?"

"He's in all those photos hanging in Mel's parents' hallway. Looked like you were stringing both him and Mel along back then."

"We all did. Fucking musical couples. Didn't mean a thing."

"Yeah, right, I bet Hatton thought it did. He's never married, has he?"

"What matters is I make good money. You know, for my family."

"I bet they'd have preferred having you home. Anyway, you're wearing most of it. And that sedan must have cost a pretty penny."

"It's a Beamer, you dumb bitch. You've been in America what, thirty plus years and you still talk like a dumb Brit?" Now that was below the belt! Whenever I'm under stress or excited the Old Country tongue pops to the surface, thick as Sunday roast drippings on a doorstep of bread like the Missus used to feed my Mum and me on laundry day.

"Well, you ignorant Yank, you've been married for twenty and you can't raise a tear when your husband winds up dead!"

"You're nuts, you know that? You know how much I've paid you over the years? Must be thousands. If it hadn't been for me you'd never have gotten your dumb little business off the ground!"

"If it hadn't been for me, your home would still be a pigsty! I earned every penny, and then some!"

George had been silent on my cellphone so long I shook it and then whispered. "You still there?"

"Sure, hon. You're doing just fine. They're a block away. Keep her busy."

And then I heard the whoop and car doors slamming. I peeked out the window to see two huge, handsome coppers with their squad car snug beside Renee's Beamer.

She really started kicking my door then.

"Fucking bitch, you called the cops!"

"You're trespassing and harassing me."

"How near are they?" George murmured.

"Coming through the gate. Well, one is, the other's talking to Hatton."

"Do not open the door until he gets to her."

I waited in my corner until I heard new footsteps on my porch and Renee stopped hitting my home.

Chapter 18

KEEPING A CIVIL TONGUE

I OPENED MY DOOR at the officer's request and found him right beside Renee. When she came at me, fingers like talons, he grabbed her arms and pulled her back.

"Hold on, ma'am, you don't want to add assault to this citizen's complaint." I'd seen Officer Ferrell on patrol for years though had never spoken with him.

Renee's face was white with dark circles under her eyes. Her lower lip was swollen and her usually impeccable hair hung in stringy clumps. Her fancy teal green power suit was rumpled, and the front of her bronze blouse stained. A gold chain necklace had caught in her diamond earring, and she was clutching her purse like a football.

I don't know what made me look down, maybe it was her kicking at me with her bronze pumps, the toes the worse for wear from attacking my door. That's when I saw a dribble of blood running down the inside of her left calf. There were drops on my welcome mat.

"You're bleeding, Renee!" I pushed the mat to the side with my foot. And right on cue, the grieving widow collapsed, almost taking the officer down with her. He lowered her to the boards.

I bent to pick up her glossy purse. It was lumpy and heavy and partially open. When I peeked inside, there was a little snub-nosed shooter snuggled in a pair of pantyhose. I proffered the bag to Officer Ferrell, who shook his head at its contents then pulled a large plastic bag from a back pocket, and stuffed it inside.

"Ma'am? Why's she here?" I stood straight, and suddenly felt most of my strength ooze out my feet.

"She... her husband... I found him dead yesterday. I clean for them."

"Where's this?"

"Discovery Bay."

"Ma'am, you're going to have to stay right there until we can sort this out. Who're you talking to?" He nodded at the cellphone in my hand.

"Oh!" I raised it to my ear. "George? You still there?"

"Just crossing Blaine."

"Captain Tullock." I said as Officer Ferrell wrote in his notebook, the plastic bag with Renee's purse tucked in his armpit. We both turned to look out at the street when the ambulance gave its whoop, its lights flashing as it backed up to the squad car. Two first responders I didn't know came charging up my path. Ferrell stepped off the porch to let them get at the supine Renee.

"She's just had an abortion," I offered, as the female medic started taking Renee's vitals, speaking into the mike attached to her head.

And the rest was beyond me. I ran to let Porsche

out of the sunroom, then pulled one of the secretary chairs out from my jiggy table, rolled it to the door and sat down. My legs were shaking something fierce. Porsche stuck his head under my arm. I could see Mr J out on his stoop with Ronnie in his arms, watching the goings-on.

It was all over so quickly. Strapped onto the gurney, Renee gasped awake from the fumes of something the medic broke under her nose. She started cursing again as they trundled her down my path. Hatton, on his cellphone, had his back to his lover as they wheeled her by.

Relief flooded through me when George's SUV turned slowly into the crowded dead-end. He parked in front of Mr J's picket fence and when he got out, gave my neighbor a wave. He walked to where Hatton and the other officer stood watching the ambulance drive off to Jefferson Memorial on the other side of Kah-Tai Lagoon.

The three men, with George in the lead, started through my garden. When Hatton flicked a cigarette butt into my herb bed, I was glad I was too shaky to do something silly, like stuff the thing up his nose.

Up close, Hatton was taller than George and both coppers, though a lot skinnier. He had a deep tan I've only seen on people who sail a lot, or use tanning salons. His straight blond hair stuck up all over his head, and his five o'clock shadow was in full bloom. He too had rings under his grey eyes, and lines like corduroy across his forehead. His dark green suit was as rumpled as Renee's. His silver tie was undone ,and I caught the gleam of gold chains inside the open neck of his pale green shirt. When he pulled out a pack of Dorals from his shirt pocket and lit one, he used a silver butane lighter. He had gold rings on each pinkie and, of course, no wedding band.

George parked himself beside me with his hands on his hips, his jacket wide open showing his weapon in its holster and his shield clipped to his belt.

"I thought you were her friend." Hatton's voice grated in the sudden silence after the ambulance's wail diminished. He took another drag.

"I'm just the char. You've gotta be Alan Hatton."

"What if I am? She just wanted to talk. Find out if Claire's okay."

"With a gun in her purse?"

"She's had that for years. For protection."

"She know how to use it?" That was George.

"'Course. Got a concealed carry permit. Takes practice in the city."

"You carrying?" Ferrell asked.

Hatton shook his head and nodded to the Beamer "In the glove compartment." The other officer trotted back to the car.

"So, Ms Collier, what happened here?" George turned his eyes on me.

"I was napping when the dog woke me cuz someone was banging on my door. It was Renee, and she was yelling... so I locked it. Said she wanted me to let her in. I wouldn't, so we yelled some more."

"Why's she here?"

"I really don't know." I sighed.

Ferrell turned to George. "Who's handling the case, Captain?"

"Smith and Westin."

"They've interviewed Ms Collier." Not a question.

"Twice." I blurted out in a strange sort of brag.

"Twice?"

"First cuz I found the dead husband and after she called saying I was..." I couldn't go on.

THE DEAD HUSBAND

"Banging her husband, I believe is how Mrs. Birnbaum put it." George said quietly. The coppers exchanged looks.

"She was upset! Didn't mean it." Hatton had a whine in his voice. Ferrell ignored him.

"And the second?"

George flexed his knees. "Ms Collier inadvertently took something from the crime scene. She was returning it." Hatton took a step away. Ferrell reached out and stayed him with one of his hands. His right, cuz his pen was sticking out of his fingers. That's when I noticed he had latex gloves on.

"Don't go anywhere just yet, Mr. Hatton, let's get this report finished and then you're going to accompany us to the station."

"Why? I've got nothing to do with any of this."

"Then what were you doing in the driver seat of that car?"

"Won't say anything else till my lawyer gets here."

"Did you tell him to meet you at the station?" George growled, "Better call him back and do so."

With the ease of much practice, Hatton flipped open his cellphone and pressed a number. While he waited, he flicked another butt into my garden.

"You just stop that!" I was on my feet. "Can't you see the ashtray there?"

"Shut the fuck up! You've already caused enough trouble for one day."

"Officer," I seethed, "I think you should save those butts cuz I found a couple just like them where Mel... Mr. Birnbaum was buried."

As Ferrell let go of Hatton, George stepped in closer and pulled out a plastic evidence bag from his jacket pocket and handed it the officer, who trod on the live butt, then retrieved it.

"Don't forget the one in my herb bed." I pointed, glaring up at Hatton. Ferrell strode off.

George stood right in Hatton's personal space. Bulk versus height. I'd put my money on bulk every time. Then again, I'm biased.

"I'll be at the Cop Shop." Hatton spat into his phone, "Know where?" He grunted and snapped the phone shut, dropping it into his jacket pocket. "Damn cunts screw up everything!" He muttered, making a production of lighting another Doral and blowing the smoke out of the side of his mouth. Unable to hold George's gaze he looked away into my garden. I couldn't tell by the way George eyed him, whether he wanted to light one up too or lit into Hatton.

"Please keep a civil tongue." George countered as Ferrell came back with the other officer, his own evidence bag stashed under his arm.

"The detectives are on their way. Said to stay here." Finally I got to see his name plate. Officer Shier looked us all over and decided to stand on Hatton's other side. As he settled his belt, jiggling his handcuffs, George backed off. I sat down again and Porsche wedged himself between us. Our hands met as we stroked him.

"Will you register a complaint about Mrs. Birnbaum?" Ferrell asked me.

"Will it be against them both?"

SMITH AND WESTIN rolled into my road several tension-filled minutes later. I kept wondering if Hatton would bolt or do something equally idiotic like take a swing at the placid policemen, or me.

"Gotta stop meeting like this, Ms Collier." Westin grinned as he came up.

"Don't you have a life?" I teased right back.

"Marilyn's beginning to wonder who you are!"

Smith was eyeing Hatton with an odd look. Perhaps he was the first celeb he'd been up close to. Then he took control of the meeting out there on my porch as the trees in Chetzemoka Park caught the light of another setting sun. Westin took notes, and Ferrell checked his. And I, like the Cheshire Cat, became invisible.

I brought Porsche out into the garden, sniffing all the new trails, lit a smoke and warmed my back in the lowering light.

Soon the chaps on my porch had come to some decisions. George beckoned me over.

"Miss Collier," Officer Ferrell was closing up his notebook, "I'll have the papers drawn up. Please come by tomorrow and sign them."

"I will. You're not leaving his car here, are you?"

"No, ma'am, we'll have it towed," Ferrell said.

"Gotta go, hon, get some rest, you look bushed." George squeezed my arm. I leaned into him and could have gone to sleep right there in his huge safety. Instead I pulled away and watched him go.

With my front door firmly locked again, I cranked up the heat, turned on all my lights, closed my windows and drew the curtains. Then I punched on my music station, loudly.

Porsche curled in a ball in his bed. I nuked a bowl of lentil stew, grabbed a spoon and sank into my recliner feeling like I was in for a big cry.

AFTER COOPER WAS BORN, Dwayne closed down and went all cold. He began nagging on me about my looks, my care of the kids, the house, everything. Some nights he didn't come home at all, and those scared me. From the smell of his clothes I figured he was drinking and smoking a lot. Even so, the kids would climb all over him as he taught them to spell and count and played games until they were exhausted. With them, he had the kind of endless patience I envied.

He and I just quit being together, and I didn't know what was wrong, what was missing, just that my heart wasn't in it anymore. So I soldiered on, as my Auntie May would have said, smothered under the chores and everyday busy-ness.

Then suddenly June was ready for kindergarten and I had to learn how to swim in a whole new pool of rules and schedules. Dwayne registered Cooper at a Head Start daycare center, and after I dropped 'em both off, I'd simply sit in a park or wait at home, doing housework until it was time to pick 'em up. When the weather turned cold, I roamed around second-hand stores. Then I came across a jigsaw puzzle of the Houses of Parliament and Big Ben, and a flood of homesickness welled-up. I bought the puzzle and a battered card table and got addicted. Yet all the while I kept feeling there was something else I ought to be doing.

Sometime that year I noticed Dwayne's clothes had quit stinking and he wasn't smoking in at home anymore. When he told me he was going back to Oregon, the kids were frantic. I was frantic! He said he'd pay the rent for another three months by which time he expected me to have my shit together. He did, and I didn't.

Once he was gone, not being able to cry got me into such rages that I made our life hell, and my kids my enemy. All the time, mind you, mentally whipping myself for not being able to handle things on my own. Hadn't my Mum raised me all by herself? Not exactly.

THE DEAD HUSBAND

Auntie May dropped by everyday after work. The upstairs Missus did all the cooking cuz of the rationing and when that was over had kept on feeding us. My Mum only made tea, hot chocolate and toast. She let me follow her around while she cleaned, and my clothes had simply been added in on wash day.

At least I knew I didn't have the skills to be a parent, couldn't remember a thing my Mum had done. I was resenting my kids and slapping at them when they didn't get things right. And I was beginning to hate myself. Didn't help that the kids grieved for their Dad everyday, loudly.

On our route to school we passed a mental health clinic. One afternoon on our way home I walked right in and said I needed help.

The first thing I asked the therapist, after leaving June and Coop with their very own counselor, was if I had to sit in that horrible chair opposite his desk.

"Not at all!" Was Richard's surprised reply. I got off those scratchy cushions, went to a corner of his office, slid down the wall and wedged my bum into it. I made a beeline for that niche every time, for weeks.

Richard began peeling off the layers of how deprived had been my childhood: no father, no sisters, no brothers, no dolls, no pets... no body to care for.

When I whined that I felt like I wasn't doing anything, he suggested I get a journal and start writing a list on a fresh page each day of every single thing I did, no matter how trivial. That was an eye-opener. No wonder I was tired. He also suggested I get to the Emma Goldman Free Clinic for a check-up and ask about a tonic to boost my energy.

Another of his ideas was that I take my kids to the library, and start reading myself, paying particular attention to the Feminist literature then being published. That was mind-blowing!

When I mentioned how guilty I felt doing jiggies, he commented that maybe I was resting, thinking things through.

Then he asked if my Mum or Auntie May had ever cuddled or played with me, assuring me that there was no right or wrong answer and I wasn't being disloyal. That's when I remembered how my Mum hadn't taken to touching.

Like working those jiggies, the stuff that was making me crazy started falling into place.

The session Richard asked me if I ever cuddled my kids broke the dam and I bawled for all the years I'd deprived us all of such expressions of affection.

"There, that wasn't so bad, was it?" Richard said.

"Thought I'd never stop!" I hiccuped, clutching a wad of tissues I'd been plucking from the box on the coffee table.

And every time after I dropped the kids off with their counselor and got to Richard's office, I'd burst into tears. It took a couple of months to drain my reservoir and I felt a ton lighter for it.

By the end of that year, in which I'd walked my kids the fifteen blocks to and from school, the clinic and library, come rain or shine, I felt ready to get on with my life. By then, the call to go west was howling.

AND, having remembered all of that, instead of a big cry coming on, I simply conked out in my recliner.

Chapter 19

FINDING FAULT

I WOKE THE NEXT MORNING to a panting dog, a stifling home and a body as contorted as if I'd fallen asleep doing one of Annie's Yoga asanas.

My big black companion was making it very clear he wanted out, so I opened the front door. Grumpy and sweaty I hit the off button on my remote, silencing the music on the telly that sounded like someone gargling. I turned down the thermostat, scolding myself for spending more on electricity last night than all summer long, and as I went from room to room, clicking off lights, flinging up windows and opening doors my home exhaled with relief and sucked in cool fresh air.

Then I took a leak, jumped into a tank top and a fleece outfit (courtesy of one of my clients) and the shoes I keep only for Power Walking. Outside, I did my stretches while Porsche did his business. Then I grabbed his leash, hooked him up and we were off into a foggy dawn. I powered up Jackson and over the hill to Fort Worden with its long grade down Harbor Defense Way to the lighthouse, with Porsche trotting easily beside me.

    I discovered Power Walking in one of Clay's medical magazines and found it cleared out the cobwebs lickety-split. It's all in the rhythm. After a mile of steady striding and breathing, my circulation gets flushed and whatever's been bothering me rinses away. Then I enter the Here-and-Now Zone, the article mentioned. On a morning like this one, I was getting lighter by the step and breath. I pulled off my sweatshirt, tied it around my waist and went on in my tank top, the salty mist tingling my bare arms and shoulders, setting my nipples on alert. I love the smell and taste of dawn air, before the cars start farting. Such a loverly feeling: alive, strong and sexy!

    Then it's around Sunset Circle, back up the long grade, across the parade ground scuffing through the mounds of leaves, out of the park onto Cherry Street. Here, I had to slow down cuz Porsche got distracted by all the cats and dogs out and about. Up little P Street (it's only a hundred paces long) to Maple, across Morgan Hill, cutting over to Cosgrove on to Taft and home, forty-five minutes later.

    I was steaming as I did my cool down stretches. Porsche lapped up his water, then dashed off for the bushes. I went inside for a long drink of sweet well water, then stripped, got in the shower and inevitably started thinking about the Birnbaums.

IT WASN'T, I THOUGHT AS I DRIED OFF, that I faulted Renee for her tepid milk of motherly love. I too, had had little enough of that and my therapy had uncovered much of why I hadn't known how to demonstrate love. Going back with my therapist and retrieving those memories had been the uneasiest work I'd ever done.

THE DEAD HUSBAND

It wasn't that I faulted my Mum for a lack of anything, until I saw how other families did it. Jake's parents often touched each other, always held hands when they went out walking around their Near North block in Chicago. And both kissed their daughter. So, naturally, Jake was a kisser too, which had embarrassed me no end.

Then Richard guided me through my years with Dwayne. That had been horrible cuz I'd convinced myself we'd had a fine romance until Cooper was born. I'd squirmed and resisted as Richard took me down that memory lane. So unfair! There I was on the verge of feeling whole and happy for the first time in my life, and he had me digging up more uglies.

I soldiered on, and that wise therapist lanced a wound I hadn't known was festering and had me clean it out before setting me back on my feet and giving me tools to get on with my life.

"I'm going to California. The Bay Area." I announced one bright and shiny Spring day. Unable to sit still I was pacing about his office. "Can't take another winter here, nor another tin of food."

"Good for you!" He sat back in his armchair, steepling his fingers. "I recommend you look into the Human Potential Movement out there. Done some reading on it and a couple of my colleagues have taken their trainings. They say most are good but some are very dangerous, particularly for single mothers. If you find one that expects you to join 'em, move in... don't!"

He leaned forward and locked eyes with me. " I'm serious, Sally. They're cults and want you and your kids and your Welfare money, and they're hell to get out of." He flipped through a stack of magazines on his desk and handed me a *Psychology Today*. "This one's got a good article." He steepled his fingers again. "Now, I know what Dwayne said about you not having an ounce of faith bothers you, and for what it's worth, he's wrong. When you're settled, look around. Berkeley's quite a spiritual center. Maybe there'll be one for you." He rocked some more. "Back to those trainings. Find one that meets in a public place and lets you go home each day. They're pricey but the ones on the up-and-up don't want your life, nor all your money."

When I snorted, he nodded. "I have a feeling you're not going to be on Welfare much longer. You've grown a lot from when you first walked in, and I want you to know it's been my privilege to be a part of your healing. By the way, June and Cooper's counselor says they've also done well. Much more grounded. So, you've got some tools now, Sally, get out of here and use 'em!"

IT WASN'T THAT I FAULTED RENEE for kicking up her heels after all those years of domesticity and go galloping off to rub shoulders with Seattle's elite. What then, did I fault her for? For I surely did.

It came to me as I was combing out my wet hair, looking at myself in the mirror. I'd finally gotten to like my compact bod that was now in pretty good trim cuz of all my physical labor.

Neither Dwayne nor Clay had ever mentioned liking my looks. George, on the other hand, in between the sheets always has something nice to say.

That's another thing I got from those seminars: what I thought love was. It having less to do with the people I love than the love I allowed myself to feel. That no one else can make me feel loved if I didn't already love myself. So ever since, I've been my own best chum, and it works.

What I faulted Renee for was bad-mouthing her life. And her daughter was showing signs of becoming just like her. Everything was dumb or stupid.

I also faulted Renee for not taking responsibility for her actions. That was the foundation of those seminars we'd taken together. And the trainers had pummeled into our brains that as we'd already accepted the hands we'd been dealt, the quality of our lives was up to us to play the best we could with what we had. No excuses. No abuses. And no blaming anyone else, not even Satan or God.

The trainers would taunt us into re-wiring ourselves to take responsibility for our choices, to accept and apologize for our mistakes, and then learn from 'em. The metaphor they used was how we were so focused on our rearview mirrors that we were constantly crashing into our present, reacting so badly to circumstances that we kept on making the same lousy choices, so much so we couldn't begin to visualize a happy, productive future. It had all made a ton of sense at the time. I've come to realize that you had to have been there, in that energy zone, ready for the information and willing to change.

"Now that you know how fucked-up you are." My favorite trainer would roar into her head microphone. "What're you going to do with the rest of your life? I can't hear you!"

And we'd all squirm in our chairs as she recited our righteous reasons for why we kept wallowing in our predictable soap operas.

At first I hadn't understood any of it: why the tirades of foul language given at a mind-boggling pace? Then one evening, the way Pitman's shorthand had suddenly made sense after months of scribbling by rote, I got it. And couldn't stop laughing as I started seeing how I'd walked around a sad and pathetic victim of my sorry lot. O woe is me! Yeah, right! Suck it up and make changes.

I'd relished those trainings. In part because I'd been earning good money and was able to pay for 'em without batting an eye.

I'd walked right into that hotel ballroom where 99 others were gathered around a 100 chairs lined up, and then listened to people who were live wires, who drew me out of being a spectator in my own life. That was what I'd been looking for: laughter and tears, grimaces and gusto!

I learnt that the passive, proper manners I'd carried all my life had been throttling me. Those seminars showed me how to take my hands from around my own throat, open up my heart and do some lusty living.

My posture started mirroring the way I felt: shoulders uncurled, spine straightened and I began to look to the horizon, to my future. And they herded us out the door every night, just like Richard warned me they should, to go back into our lives and practice what we'd learnt.

I'd liked the way Mel had been laughing, right along with me, as was Renee on his other side. Those had been good times with my newfound friends.

PORSCHE'S GROWL raised the hairs on my arms. Not again! I'd just taken my cellphone out of its charger when a shadow flickered in the dining room mirror. My dog was on alert in his bed. In my wide open front door stood Alan Hatton.

I pressed George's number on speed dial and tucked the phone into my uniform pocket. Then I stepped into view.

"What are you doing here, Mister Hatton?" I said loudly as I walked to my door, remembering I hadn't been to the Cop Shop to sign that No Contact Order. "No, don't come in." With my energy, I pushed him back out onto the porch.

"Why're you screwing with Renee?" He countered.

"How is she today, Mister Hatton?"

"Fine, fine. A little hemorrhaging. They've stopped it. She's resting." He was taking long drags on his Doral, blowing the smoke out his nostrils.

"Is she conscious?"

"Oh yeah! Talking to her lawyer." He jingled something in his pant pocket.

"Why do you think I'm making it hard? I'm just the char, not important like you, Mister Hatton."

"Ha! She thinks you walk on water."

"Does she now?" Somehow I doubted gorgeous Renee had me on a pedestal.

"Sure, says you've got your own business. Make your own money. That sort of shit."

"Seems to me, she's doing very well for herself, working for you. How did you guys set that up?"

He made for George's chair. I waved him off.

"You're not staying, so don't sit. Actually, you've known each other since high school, haven't you?"

"More like fifth grade." He tossed his butt out into the garden. "That's not why I'm—"

"Carrying a torch for a married woman all these years? I'd have thought you'd want her husband out of the way long ago. Why now? What's changed?"

"You dumb... that's got nothing to do wi—" He loomed over me. Porsche rumbled in his throat.

"Don't you touch me, Mister Hatton." I stuck my hands on my hips, chin out, daring him.

"Think I care? We've got to talk—"

"That's what Renee kept saying. What about? It's crystal clear to me." I stepped back, out of his reach, "Renee's husband, my friend, was found by me, dead and buried. You know something about that?"

Hatton looked away and lit a fresh smoke. He was all stiff and prickly.

"And someone shut his dog up so he had to live in his piss and poop. For days! What's there to talk about, Mister Hatton?"

His jaw muscles worked. Wherever he'd spent the night, it hadn't done a thing for the circles under his eyes although his hair was damp and he'd shaved.

A whoop had us both turning to the road. A PTPD cruiser stopped beside the Beamer and Officers Ferrell and Shier got out.

"When did you call 'em?" Hatton snarled, rocking on his feet. Did he think he could make a dash for it?

"When I first saw you at my door."

"Good morning, Ms Collier." Ferrell stopped with a foot on the first step of the porch. One thing for sure, I was getting a lot of comfort lately from my servers and protectors.

"Sir, you really need to leave Ms Collier alone." Ferrell leaned over and handed me a sheet of paper. "You know there's a restraining order against you and Mrs. Birnbaum. If either of you come within five hundred feet of Ms Collier, her home or her vehicle we'll take you in and charge you." He began herding Hatton off the steps. "We're now going to escort you to the ferry."

As Renee's lover left my premises boxed in by the officers, I dashed into my office, signed the form and trotted back to my front door where Officer Shier was now waiting. He took the piece of paper and left.

"George? You there?" I yelped into my phone.

"All the time, hon. Amazing stuff, this technology. Now, can I go get a shave? Meet me at the Salal."

"I'll be there!" I disconnected and rushed back inside to give my watch dog a treat. It felt so good, not being alone anymore.

Then we walked down the hill to the bay and wandered along the pebble beach so he could sniff at what the tide had brought in, and I could keep watch for George's SUV. When I saw it park a couple of blocks away, I managed to distract my pal from all his salty stories and with him on a short leash, trotted off along Water Street.

George must have felt some of the same relief cuz once he was on his feet, he took me in for a long hug, for all the foggy world to see, something he doesn't usually do.

I wiped my eyes and blew my nose on his hanky while he loaded Porsche into his wheels. Then we walked over to the Salal where Mindy had already poured our coffee.

For our postprandial smoke we drove to the Kah-Tai Lagoon and stood under the gazebo while Porsche galloped off into the foggy landscape. After field stripping and pocketing our butts, we followed our dog's trail, arm-in-arm, along the gravel path.

It was a beautiful morning, all socked-in and eerie with underbrush and tree trunks emerging out of the grey dampness while the marina foghorns moaned away. A group of ducks with this year's hatchlings quacked and swam away into the reeds as we stopped on a little arched bridge. George pointed off to the rocks on our left where a Blue Heron was standing still on one leg, peering into the water. The far shore was covered in grey, hiding the house-crowded town beyond.

"So, Sal-the-Gal, where're you working today?" My Man rumbled, pulling me along after our dog into a copse of mossy alders.

"Up on Morgan Hill and then over to Rose." I sighed, leaning into him.

"Neither Renee nor Hatton know where, right?" He stopped and wrapped his arms around me. I nodded against his chest, and he rubbed his sweet-smelling chin in my hair.

"Think we've lost our dog?"

Chapter 20

THE LOVELIEST OF HOMES

BECAUSE MY BEST SET OF TOOLS was stuck in the Birnbaums' dumb waiter, I'd assembled another from my spares. I was going to miss my Dyson badly on the first clean of the day.

One Muir Lane is perched on the edge of the same cliffs as my home, so it was also was socked-in. The only sound I heard as I got out of my beater was the foghorn down at Point Wilson. I left Porsche sniffing out the back windows.

Beside the road, keeping out the world, is a high stone wall covered with honeysuckle which is now smothering the roses on the trellis over the cedar slat gate. With no garage, the owners park hard against that wall and their old Saab lost its passenger side mirror years ago. They're long gone to work by the time I get there.

Built before WWI, this haven is magical and exudes such a sense of peace. The wood is all silky smooth, the stone worn and the leaded windows dim. It's a single floor house that follows the contour of the ridge, with a separate guest cottage of two bedrooms and a closet of a bathroom added on in the '40s when the other homes along the road were built and the utilities laid in.

The evening I came to interview the owners they showed me the faded building plans and told me something about themselves. Doc Larry's like a bean pole favoring rust-colored shirts and green twill pants. He has a crown of ginger curls, freckles everywhere and the greenest eyes. Everything about him is long: neck, arms and hands, legs and feet.

Doc Leslie's almost as tall and as skinny, and wears her straight chestnut brown hair in a braid down to her hips. She wears no makeup or trousers, and favors Peter Pan collar blouses under blue denim jumpers, socks and Birkenstocks.

From Kentucky fifteen years ago, they finished their residencies: he in general practice and she in Ob/Gyn and drove across America to attend the annual Blue Grass Festival put on by the Centrum Foundation at Fort Worden. They'd been assigned to the guest cottage here because the owners were movers and shakers in the week-long event. When they'd mentioned they were leaving for India, the Docs decided to buy the place and set up their shingles in town. They've been part of the planning committee ever since.

The garden is a maze of stone paths around raised stone flower beds and a pond where the fattest goldfish swim under lily pads. There are no other pets, and I've never asked about there being no children around.

Beside the old pump house is a worn stone sink and scrubbing counter where once laundry must have been done. With no room for a washer and dryer anywhere in the house, they use the laundromat in the business plaza off Sims Way where they have their practices, which I also clean, on Fridays. Beside the sink is a square drying rack where sun-faded prayer scarves flutter, and the occasional hawk lands to watch the fish.

Against the protected warm walls apricot trees have been esplanaded and the tastiest tomatoes, hot peppers and green beans grow.

It was Doc Larry who taught me about composting, showing me his plastic bins brewing on the lowest terrace. On chilly days I can see the steam puffing out of their holes.

Doc Leslie always leaves me a note on handmade paper with their cash tucked inside. Today she alerts me that both sets of parents are coming in for the Historic Homes Tour. Time to air out the guest cottage, give it a once-over and set the heaters on low.

The kitchen is archaic and cramped with the original sink, draining board, counters, cupboards and light fixtures. Their ancient avocado green fridge is squeezed into an alcove I figured used to be the larder. It's full of veggies, fruit, tofu and strange brews like sarsaparilla tea, all from the food co-op. The rinky-dink freezer up top, which I have to defrost every three months, is packed with veggie burgers and frozen gluten-free bread. They love my recipe for lentil stew: minus the meat, of course.

I love their hodgepodge of bowls, platters and cups from around the world, and all the baskets and teapots hanging from the rafters. Their cooking pots consist of a copper kettle, a well-seasoned wok (which I am to NEVER wash) with all its long-handled tools, a bamboo steamer set, one saucepan, a huge Crock-

Pot and an electric rice steamer. Their cutlery is collection of bamboo chopsticks and wooden spoons they've brought home from their travels, and stuck in a wood block are very sharp paring and chef knives and a lethal looking cleaver. That's all, folks!

They eat in a booth of lumpy, faded orange vinyl at a worn Formica counter. When they have company they bring out a conference table and folding chairs in the sitting room where there's a ratty old couch and two worn armchairs with shelves behind stacked with medical and spiritual books. I've borrowed quite a few of 'em.

There isn't a telly or computer in the place though their offices have both. Here, there's a complicated sound system and a tower of CDs which I've been listening my way down as I work. And speaking of music, Doc Leslie plays the flute, Pan pipes, recorder, clarinet and oboe while Doc Larry strums on a guitar, mandolin, lute and sitar. Music stands, instrument cases and a wood chest on wheels stuffed with sheet music fill what once must have been the coat closet.

All the walls and ceilings are covered with fabric mandalas. In the second bedroom, their meditation center, there are cushions and pads and a gallery of photos of them in faraway places with people dressed in all sorts of costumes. There's a series of views of Samye Temple, the birthplace of Tibetan Buddhism, high in the Himalayas. Over their altar is a signed photo of a beaming Dalai Lama standing between them with scarves around their necks. All three have their bead-wrapt hands together in prayerful greeting.

Whenever they fly off somewhere on a natural disaster health mission, they have me watch over their little Shangri La. It smells of incense and soy sauce, and I always feel blessed when I leave it clean

THE DEAD HUSBAND 181

and tidy.

As I shut their front door at noon the sunshine is bright with the fog now hanging over Puget Sound, blocking the view of the mainland.

Porsche roused up when I set my tools in the trunk and we headed for Uptown and the food co-op. I tossed back a wheat grass juice pick-me-up and bought a pita bread sandwich stuffed with tofu, sprouts and cilantro salad. Then I drove around to the far side of the lagoon so Porsche could run free.

As I chewed my lunch, feeding my companion a nibble or two whenever he loped back from all his sniffing and drinking, I watched a flight of geese circling around on their way south. Then they started coming in to land on the still water, making me think about how my life had changed since my kids had left to go live with their Dad.

June's in Portland now and sounds busy, as centered and contented as anyone just turned 21, on the hunt for a husband, can be. Cooper moved to Seattle and earns his keep working on computers. He emails jokes yet rarely mentions his private life.

Watching those birds, who get only one summer with their young, I'd never have thought, back when my kids were little, how soon my mothering years would be over.

THEN IT'S ON TO THE GUERRERAS up on Rose Street. This one's a modern triple-decker neo-Victorian that looks out on the municipal golf course. Filled with children, I have my work cut out to be done by the time the first ones get back from school. During vacations, Mrs G rousts them all out somewhere while I set to at full speed.

I met Mrs G in Doc Leslie's office. She's the

Ob/Gyn to whom I go for all things female. Done with my yearly pelvic exam in which the good Doc alerted me that menopause was in the offing, and with nowhere to go in a hurry, I'd been chatting with a lad in the waiting room. His arm was in a cast after breaking it in a fall off his skateboard. When Doc Leslie accompanied a very preggie woman out of one of the exam rooms, she turned out to be the injured boy's Mom. Doc Leslie was admonishing her patient about doing housework, when she caught sight of me and grinned.

"And I have just the char for you!"

I followed Mrs G home where she took me on a rather slow tour, given her condition, and hired me on the spot. She needed me, badly. Mr G works for the city and I've never met him.

Mrs G could have been my sister: same height, hair color (I've never seen it down from the bun on top of her head) and body mass like mine although hidden by maternity smocks, and at the time, very swollen ankles above her flip-flops. Now she's back to her jeans and Mexican blouses and unlike me, has a loverly permanent tan, luscious lips and bosom.

She already had four boys, ranging from six to twelve and a month later made up for the lack of daughters by giving birth to identical girls. I'd come in to help as often as I could when she got home from the hospital. After I'd done the catch-up chores I'd sit in her rocking chair with an infant in each arm while the dish washer whooshed away, watching her cook wonderfully aromatic meals. I'd really enjoyed that. This autumn the girls started kindergarten.

The house is plainly painted, well lit and smells of garlic and peppers which hang on the kitchen and dining room walls. It's also a very Catholic home with lots of crucifixes, votive candles and icons of Mother Mary and Baby Jesus.

The top floor is the kids' realm: three bedrooms containing two of everything, with a huge shared bathroom. The boys' lairs are suitably masculine and untidy with lots of projects in progress. The girls' is pinkly feminine in which they've created a home within a home, complete with a tribe of dolls and a play kitchen. It's often everso neat. The bathroom is a cross between a lockeroom and a beauty salon. The genders have made peace by having one wall all female and the other all male. Everywhere else is up for grabs, or rather down on the floor. And yes, I change every single bed with colorful linens someone sets on the chair beside each, waiting for me.

The second floor has the master bedroom suite and Mr G's study, which I only vacuum once a month. The bathroom, appropriately adult, connects the two rooms. This landing serves as the family portrait gallery, perhaps to remind the parents of who all lives here, in case they forget.

Each bathroom has a drop box for the dirties that goes directly into the utility room off the kitchen, which has its own throne closet, laundry machines and walls of shelves. Here, two immense black cats, like panthers, sleep in laundry baskets and eat by the back door with its cat flap. There is no litter box, and I don't do 'em! Nor the laundry.

On the ground floor the vestibule is a clutter of shoes, hats and coats. Against two walls in the sitting room which overlooks the golf course, doors have been set on drawer cabinets for five computers, all the same make. A sectional sofa fills the rest of the space and faces the entertainment center.

There are double doors to the dining room where a

round table is surrounded by ten narrow chairs, under a wrought iron chandelier. Light streams in from a set of French doors to the back garden.

Out there, all around the fence, Mrs G grows her prize-winning dahlias. On the immaculate scrap of lawn stands a screened-in trampoline. The patio is dominated by a stainless steel propane BBQ, two picnic tables pushed together and a herd of chairs.

It's an all electric house so they have a mighty generator in its own shed next to the two car garage where freezers hum and skateboards and bikes rest.

Chapter 21

CREEPING MURDERERS

JUST AS I WAS HAULING MY GEAR back to my beater, mother and daughters arrive. After giving me hugs, the girls raced upstairs to their room. Mrs G paid me in cash and handed me a Gladware container of enchiladas out of her fridge.

I watched her boys come galloping across the bright green golf course as I started up, commiserating with Porsche who so wanted out to explore, there being a NO DOGS ALLOWED signs all around the place.

Not a wisp of fog remained as I cruised home, and then Joanne called just as I was going into the post office for my mail.

"Why so silent, Boss? But me no butts and tell me no lies, what's happening?" And so I told her. That done, I chivvied her about being unwilling to relinquish control of the meeting that weekend. We both knew I was only teasing.

"Do I want murderers creeping around looking for you?" She squawked. "Think the Gals do? Besides," her tone grew smirky. "Haven't I got everything ready, already?" And she disconnected.

When Joanne says "everything," she means it. She puts on a fantastic feast and is not shy about leaving a good mess for us to clean.

Funny thing about that: in the beginning some of my clients actually cleaned up before I came. I never object to people picking up after themselves, just leave the cleaning to me! Others took it as an invitation to hold the biggest bash of the week, using every single thing in their kitchen. Then left it all stacked on the counters, not even rinsed. While I enjoy washing dishes, even with a machine, the note I leave lets 'em know they've just paid for the most expensive dishwasher in town, and the rest of the house suffered accordingly. They get the message.

When I turned into my road, there was Mel's Cherokee in front of my gate with his daughter dozing in the sunshine.

"Yo, Claire, how's it hanging?" I asked quietly, after parking my beater in the carport and bringing Porsche around to bless my gate posts. Claire stirred, sat up and yawned hugely. I let my dog through and looked back at her.

"Just saw Mom." She got out of her car, hesitating at the gate I held open.

"If you apologize for calling me names, you may come in." I looked her straight in the eye. She pouted and scratched a bare arm. Today she was a vision in a green t-shirt and faded black jeans.

"Sorry 'bout that. Don't know why I did."

It would have to do.

"Grab your purse and come in." She leaped back to the Cherokee, reached in, came out with her backpack and slung it over her shoulder.

Porsche looked up from his tour of the garden, trotted over, sniffed at Claire's legs and sat at my heel. She bent to stroke his head.

"He's a lot happier here, isn't he." Definitely a statement.

"You thirsty?" She nodded. "Let's see what I've got." She followed me in, kicking off her shoes beside mine and dropping her backpack. It wasn't right that someone so young should have such dark rings under her pretty eyes.

We both stared into my fridge. I gave her a water bottle while I set the kettle to boil. She gulped half of it down.

"Where's your bathroom?" I pointed to the hall. She went in without closing the door.

"Your Mom's still in hospital?" I called as I set the tea tray.

"Started bleeding again last night. She's so pissed they wouldn't let her out. Do I flush?" It had been a dry summer and I'd been doing my bit for water conservation. I leaned around the jamb and pointed to the gallon bottle of rinse water in the corner.

"Where does she want to go?"

"Back home."

"Bluff View? Seattle?"

"Neither. Back east."

"Where will you stay?"

"At the Gramps."

"Ever thought of going to see your other grandparents?" I brewed the tea while Claire wandered around my home, peering here and there.

"Nice place, Sal. Like the skylights. You rent?" I picked up the tray and bore it out to the porch where I set it on the table, then sat in my chair.

"No, it's all mine."

"Cool. Didn't think housecleaning paid that well." She ignored my question and settled into George's chair, watching me fix the tea. She took an experimental sip and grimaced. "It'll never catch on. Give me ice cold Coke, anytime." She giggled. "Sal, what am I going to do?"

"What can you do?"

"Nothing. Well, that's not true. I'm good at..." Her voice faded and tears filled her eyes again. She gulped down her tea.

"What would you like to do?" I prompted.

"I know what I *don't* want to do. Does that count?" She grinned hopefully.

I nodded and lit a smoke. "It's a start. Tell me."

"I don't want to go to some stupid college or work in a dumb supermarket. I don't want to... stay here, either." She was leaving the whole world out and herself little to run with. As she spoke, she leaned over, ripped a tea rose from its stem and started pulling its petals off.

"Stop, Claire, stop!" I laid a hand over hers. "Did you smell it before you tore it to pieces?" She frowned. I picked another and put it under her nose. She sniffed. A surprised smile lit up her face.

"Wow, that's sweet!" She looked at the petals at her feet, bent and picked them all up. Then she crushed them and sank her nose into her palms, breathing deeply. "Double wow. Sorry!" She brushed her hands off into the flower tub.

"You never smelt your Mom's roses?" She grimaced. Silly question. "So what do you like to do?"

"I like working at camp, with people. I like driving. Really like driving. Would you believe I like to cook... at camp, not at home." Short as it was, her list had possibilities.

"What are your school friends doing?"

"Don't really have any, anymore." She shrugged. "Donna's going to Peninsula College in Port Angeles and Britney got married the week she graduated. I was one of her bridesmaids. Jeez, I looked like a lobster!" She shook her head, leaning her arms on her knees and staring out at my garden, lost in memories.

"Don't you ever want to get married?"

"No way! It's so dumb." She straightened up, flicking her hair back.

"Ever been in love?" I teased.

"Yuck! With boys, you mean?" She giggled. "Gotcha!" I refilled our cups. "Like your tea cozy. You make it?" She accepted her cup again as I nodded. "You asked if I'd ever wanted to meet my Mom's parents. You think I should go back east with her?"

"It's a fantastic drive. I did it once, in a Greyhound bus from Chicago."

"It's about three thousand miles, isn't it?"

"From coast to coast. Maybe three, four days of hard driving, unless you stop off to see some sights. You know the Grand Canyon's on the way." The idea was intriguing her.

"That long with just me and my Mom? No way!" She gulped some tea down. "Think the Cherokee'd make it?"

"Didn't your Dad buy it new? Take it to his mechanic, find out. You know your parents did it. When you were *in utero*, as they say."

"Yeah, I knew that. There's that dumb photo at the Gramps."

"It was an adventure... and it wasn't dumb. Speaking of which, young woman, I really don't like the way you throw that word around."

"So what?" She glared at me through slitted eyes.

"You become what you think."

"You saying I'm dumb?"

I nodded and she bolted to her feet, throbbing with indignation.

"I am not!"

"Oh yeah? Tell me, what're you going to do with the rest of your life?"

"I don't care! Whatever—"

"Sit, sit, Claire-kins, relax. We're only talking." She folded herself down and took up her cuppa.

"They're burying Dad tomorrow." She said rather casually.

"Who? Where?" I felt a pain rush up in my chest.

"The Gramps. Out at the Dungeness cemetery. You want to come? I could call and say I'm staying with you tonight. I've got my sleeping bag with."

Well now, this was a change of plans.

"What time?"

"One o'clock."

I thought about my schedule. Both homes tomorrow were up on Taft.

"Sure, I'll go. Think your Mom'll be there?" She froze and a flush rose up her throat.

"Better not be!" She snarled, then swallowed some tea. "I told her. You know what she said? 'Good riddance!'" She put her cup on the table just before the tears came. I let her weep.

"I really, really loved my Dad!" Suddenly a voice I'd never known was wailing in my head, right along with this young woman. "Why did he have to die like that?" The loss of my own Pa was something, all through my therapy, I'd never allowed myself to face.

"My Pa was killed during The War, just after I was born." Claire found a tissue in the pocket of her jeans, wiped her eyes and blew her nose. "And you better not ask which one!"

"Wasn't going to," she smirked. "You're so old it had to be WW2. So you grew up without a father? That stinks!"

I had to agree. I remembered the Mister upstairs with his brood. My best school chum Andrea's Pa. Jake's Pop. I hadn't really known what I'd missed until I saw Dwayne with our kids.

"Have the detectives said anything about how he died?" I asked. Claire shook her head. "What about your Mom?"

"Nothing!" She grimaced. "Wouldn't even let me talk about him. Told me it was none of my business. I'm his kid! It *is* my business!"

"It surely is, my dear." I took one of her hands. "Look, I've known you since you were little. Watched you grow up. Always thought we liked each other. We still do, don't we?" She gripped my hand as tears leaked from her eyes.

"Yeah." She tried to smile. "You've been like a rock. Every Monday you'd be there. Did you know I'd be late for the school bus just so I'd see you? And cuz then Dad would have to drive me. I really liked it when you used to stay over weekends." She straightened her back some and heaved a big breath. "But I'm an adult now so I don't need taking care of, right? Anyway the Gramps are real good at that."

"In a sad way, I expect they're glad for your company."

"Too much sometimes. Like they've changed their whole life around me. It gets... I need space." She heaved another huge sigh. "Their place is so... small. Feel like I'm going to step on that du—dog. You know what Gramma calls it... her? Lady Sheba!" She fake retched. "Sometimes I think I'll knock everything over if I turn around too quick."

"A heifer in a china shop." I joked.

"Exactly!" She giggled and her hair fell over her face.

"They're good people. They love you."

"I know. Just like my Dad." And there were the tears again.

"Have you ever been to a therapist?"

"What for?"

"To help you think this through. A therapist's a mind doctor. They're really useful. I learnt a lot, got a lot of healing when I did."

"You were crazy?"

"Once upon a time."

"Wow. That's... freaky." She mused, scratching her bare arm.

"Scary too. That's why I walked into that mental health clinic and got help."

"What kind?"

"Talking things out. Seeing why I did what I did when I did it. What scared me so much that I put myself and my kids in danger. Why I was so—"

"That's right, you have kids!" Claire perked up. "Junee and Coopee. I forgot... where are they?"

"Oh, they're grown and flown. Finished up with their father in Oregon."

"You let your kids go?"

"I did. They wanted it. I couldn't stand fighting 'em both, alone." Now my own tears welled up.

"But you weren't!"

"Yes I was. Sometimes grown-ups need other grown-ups to feel... well... real, better."

"And kids grow up." Claire said quietly.

"That they do. And parents grow old and die."

"Sometimes they don't. Sometimes they get killed!" How fiercely she said that.

"You think your father was killed?"

"Duh! You think he buried himself?" She was on her feet again hands clenched into fists as she stared out across my garden to Chetzemoka Park. Porsche raised his head from his favorite sunning spot at the bottom of the steps.

"What do you think happened?"

She stuck her hands into her pockets and hunched over. "Don't know, but Mom and that asshole Alan did it. I know that much!"

"You be careful who you say that to."

She scowled at me, her chin stuck out. "Just let 'em try!" She growled.

"You talked to the detectives?"

"Oh yeah. They think so too." She stepped off the porch rousting Porsche who scrambled to his feet, leapt up the steps, and headed for his bed.

Claire started kicking the tea rose tub. "You know Dad had a bruise on his back? Nothing to do with the fall." She kicked at my roses again. "Overheard them say that it looked like someone had punched him. Detective Smith was pissed cuz he said they'd only be able to prove negligent homicide. I like him."

"Smith?"

"Yeah! He... well, anyway, they talked to me some... outside Mom's room. They'd just interviewed her again. She was furious. Didn't want to talk. Told me to..." She was heaving and weaving.

"What?"

"'Fuck off, brat!'" She crumpled into her chair and started sobbing again. And then, just as suddenly, she was up on her feet clutching the porch column. "And who walks in right then? Asshole Alan. I split!"

She let go the column, crouched beside me and laid her head on my shoulder.

"Parents can be such shits!" The grieving daughter wailed.

Chapter 22

A MODERN MARVEL

CLAIRE BROUGHT IN HER GEAR as I fixed tuna salad and stuffed it into pita bread pockets. We ate out on the porch, she slurping a can of Coke she'd found in her pack. Porsche drooled and snapped up the scraps we tossed him.

Funny thing about socializing with clients. I'd always been in Claire's company in her home with her parents and their things. Now she was in my home. What would I do with her all evening long?

We went for a stroll around the cooling park, listening to the surf pound on the rocks below and smelling the first Fall scents. For a while we watched the night lights across the Sound, then a huge container ship as it slid by on its way to the Strait of San Juan de Fuca and the Pacific Ocean.

Turns out she liked jiggies, so we worked the Crater Lake puzzle and chatted about the picture and travels while she played a couple of her CDs on the my system. I let the thumping and yelling of foul language run for a bit before I ejected the disc and turned on my *Night Visions* station.

While she organized her gear in the sunroom I sorted through fabrics, thinking about baby quilts.

"I know you don't have any croissants but do you have any hot chocky?"

I looked up from the dining table to see Claire standing in the kitchen in her jammies, hair all brushed and gleaming, like a tired little girl.

"No. My... boyfriend's a diabetic so I don't keep stuff like that around anymore. You could zap some milk and put Splenda in it." I offered as I joined her.

"I so miss my Dad." she whispered.

I took her in a hug.

"I know you do, dearie. Shall I put you to bed?"

With my guest kissed and snuggled inside her sleeping bag on the lounger in the sunroom, I was locking up when George called. I stood on my porch and let Porsche have a final patrol.

"I've got company." I said feeling itchy.

"You do? Who?" George growled.

"Claire. I'm going with her to Mel's funeral tomorrow."

"In Sequim?"

"Yeah."

"Don't you have work?"

"The Wallens and Sizkorskis. Just enough time in between and it won't matter if I'm a little late getting to the Sizkorskis."

"Why's she with you?"

"No one else to talk to."

"What about her grandparents?"

"Least of all them. She was waiting by my gate in her father's Cherokee. Just been to see her Mom who basically told her to shove off. Very sad. Very lost."

"What's she doing?"

"Sleeping in the sunroom."

"What'll she do while you work?"

"Don't know." I hesitated for a moment and then plunged on in. "She told me there was a bruise on her father's back."

"Where did she hear about that?"

"Smith and Westin, at the hospital. Says they told her they'll only be able to prove negligent homicide."

"They did, did they? How unprofessional."

"I think she's got Smith wrapt around her pinkie."

"Missed you today, Sally," he said gently.

Wow! He only calls me that when he's serious.

"Me too, George."

"We'll make up for it Fri—"

"Can't." I don't remember when I'd ever rejected his company. "It's Sal's Gals weekend."

He huffed, just like my dog.

"I'll be home by teatime Sunday." I soothed.

"How's Borscht the Porsche?"

"Enjoying his nighttime sniffs. He likes it here. I certainly like his company."

"Hate to let you go but I need sleep." He sighed. "Crashed just before dinner. Got to go to the diabetes clinic so I can get these doses right."

"You take care of yourself, dearie."

"I will. See you Sunday."

I tucked my dog in for the night and then myself, all alone, thinking how George and I could change our lives so we could be together. Jeez, what a dream! Why can't women ask men to marry 'em, these days?

IT WAS STRANGE HAVING SOMEONE other than George in my home. Porsche was disturbed too. Twice I surfaced to hear his nails clicking on the floor as he sniffed at the sunroom door.

The change in the pressure of my home, the thump

of socked footsteps and cool fresh air rushing in got me up.

Another foggy morning. I showered and dressed in my uniform, gathered my phone and went into the kitchen to turn on the coffee machine. Then downed my vitamins with a glass of cranberry juice.

"'Morning!" I called to Claire as she came back through my front door. "Would you like lentil beef stew for breakie?"

Claire was munching on a squashed bagel with cream cheese oozing out the sides.

"Bought this at the hospital cafeteria." She waved it, almost smiling. "Got coffee?"

"Yup! Not your father's brew, though."

We took our mugs out to the porch.

"What're you doing this morning?" She asked as she slurped.

"Working. Be done by noon."

Porsche came up the steps, sniffed my ear and I rubbed his head. He left for a good long drink then lay down with his snout on his paws.

"What do you do with him while you work?" She chewed, watching him.

"Comes along, sleeps in the back seat."

"Shall I take him till you're done?" I did think about it for all of a second.

"Nah, he's used to it now."

Claire made a pout. "Can I come too?"

"What'll you do in your car for three hours?"

"You won't let me in with you?" She sounded surprised.

"No one else allowed in when I clean a client's home. Company policy." I decided not to look at her licking her fingers.

"Coffee's **nothing** like Dad's." I turned to her with

a sharp retort on my tongue. She was grinning. "Dunno what I'll do. Can't go home." She finished her coffee. "Detective Smith told me that."

I blew out some smoke, wondering what was hinky with this picture?

"Why're you still doing that?" She burst out in her Mom's tone. "Don't you know how bad it is?"

I stared at the girl. "Don't you start on me."

"You bitch about me using dumb and stupid!"

"You bet."

"So what's the difference?"

"My home. My rules. Take it or leave. Now!" I kept glaring until she had the grace to grimace.

"Okay, I'll drop it. But I'll tell you I told you so when you're hacking and on oxygen!"

"I'm sure you will. And I'll still tell you to zip it." I looked out at the trees in the foggy park. "I could show you the mental health clinic we clean. You could start getting some help. I'd meet you there when I'm through." What a silence as she stared at her feet.

"Okay. No guarantees. When're we going?"

I looked at my watch pinned to my uniform top.

"Fifteen minutes."

"I'll call the Gramps." She got up pulling out her phone. "Let 'em know we'll be there in time."

At the mental health clinic I left her with Laurie, the receptionist, filling out forms.

THE WALLENS LIVE IN A MODERN MARVEL four storey they built ten years ago. Their two ornamental Japanese Plum trees have shed most of their leaves already so there's no shade out front to keep Porsche cool. I opened all the windows before telling him to stay and guard the car.

Before I went up the stairs, where bulging Halloween orange plastic leaf bags with grimacing faces were set, I called GuardWell to let them know I'd be late getting to the Sizkorskis. There's no garden here, just a driveway to the garage and basement.

Mrs W's home is an all white affair laid out with open stairwells and straight lines. It also has miles of parquet floor and not one piece of ornamentation or clutter. No flowers in vases on little tables, nor any shelves of knickknacks. It's an easy clean, though I'd go bonkers living there. I carry in no tools of my trade as Mrs W's a "green" housekeeper with supplies that are dye and perfume free, and supposedly don't harm the environment.

At the front door I put my index finger on the keypad and looked up at the scan-cam. When the beeping starts, I push the door open and leap inside to punch in the code to re-activate the alarm. It's a security must. Now I'm locked in for the duration.

I was a tad uncomfortable when I first started here cuz it looked like I wasn't making much of a difference. Mrs W assured me I was, especially in the boys' rooms.

Everyone has to take off their shoes at the white wood bench and white washable rug. I leave mine, and nudge my toes into one of the sets of white cotton slippers. I say "sets" cuz they're shapeless, no left or right. I used to slip and slide all over the place before I got the hang of 'em. I leave 'em in the utility room in the same basket as the rags she provides: cotton diapers left over from the twins' baby years.

The hallway stretches from front to back with a sliding door closet on the right for outerwear. Next is the utility-cum-powder room door and behind it, another door to what I imagine are the stairs down to the basement. It's always locked. After that, recessed against the wall is the open, metal and wooden staircase. Two more flights, and there's no dumb waiter, so Mrs W has a cleaning basket on each floor. They have a central vacuum cleaner and it's one time I'm glad I'm not lugging around a heavy machine.

Leading to the back garden which is really a full size asphalt tennis court surrounded by a high fence topped with netting, is the only other outside door. On the white rug beside it, are more slipper sets.

The sliding glass door always has lots of finger and hand prints. It also has an alarm system with its own security keypad for when the back garden's in use. I peer out into the fog where, in the corner by the kitchen window, is the gazebo housing a large white covered hot tub. White lounging chairs and a table complete the little retreat. Two white urns, filled with purple and green kale cabbages give some color. When the weather's dry, I wipe down the furniture and sweep up leaves, then dump 'em into a hole with a white cover. I have no idea where it all goes.

The sitting room to the left of the hall is, of course, all white and practically empty with only two white fabric love seats on a white carpet with a white coffee table between 'em. There's no fireplace, no bookshelves, only a corner cabinet, white of course, for their CD collection and music system, whose speakers are set around the room on the floor. I get their choice of track lighting cuz the walls are covered with brilliantly colored paintings and posters, all modern, from Scandinavian artists. It opens into the dining area with its oval, glass-topped table and white chairs on rollers under a white chandelier fan.

None of the windows open, which used to bother me a lot. They have alarm strips and are covered with electronic white vertical blinds. They're the only things that take any time, and they come with their own handy-dandy duster.

And then there's the stainless steel operating room of a kitchen with every machine a cook could want, set on or under white counters and cupboards, twin sinks, and a chopping block in the center of the space over which hangs a canopy of cooking pots and pans. This is where Mrs W leaves her note, on a laptop. She banks online, so her payment will already be in the business account. As always, she greets me like an honored guest:

My dear Sally, so good of you to come. Please zero in on the boys' room. They've been busy athletes.

Today's dinner will be baked bread (so that's what I'm smelling, dough rising in the machine on the counter by the fridge), salad and salmon, with orange sherbet for dessert. I know this cuz it's on the fridge's menu screen. I've never seen blood meat in either fridge or freezer which, by the way, are recessed into the wall so their motors are muted hums. They're brushed steel with computerized inventory displays. Each is on rollers and twice a year I'll arrive to find 'em pulled out of their niches, ready for a clean. That's also the week when everything in every cupboard is packed neatly into foldable cloth baskets, in the dining room, signaling it's time to climb the step ladder and give the shelves and doors a clean and no, I'm reminded to NOT put anything back.

The house has central air conditioning and heat which has to be in the basement. I've never seen a cobweb or bug in the place. It's a strangely airless, placid home smelling mostly of clean, with faint whiffs of aftershave and perfume. I enjoy the twins' rooms, full of energy and the tang of ripe boy, when I get there.

The family room has a much more lived-in feel and occupies the entire second floor. It also has more color, even it's only orange. The U-shaped fabric couch with its pillows looks comfy. It faces a huge LCD screen above a white credenza holding their vast DVD and game library. The orange coffee table has a remote caddy, nuts and candy containers and magazines. The other wall is set up into two computer carrels with shelves in between filled with text books, mostly about child rearing, public health, the environment, and US law. Mr W's a judge and Mrs W's the hospital's administrator.

The top floor is divided into two suites. The parents' in the front, is always neat. There's a chair on either side of the mirrored walk-in closet. Their platform kingsize bed with it drawers underneath, has four pillows and a thick feather comforter. Reading lamps spout from the wall. Their books, on the bedside tables, are always neatly stacked. In the bathroom, their tile and glass shower fills one corner. The rest are the usual facilities, all white, of course.

The other door on this landing is the twelve year-old lads' kingdom with a shelving unit holding their trophies, model spaceships and airplanes, separating their beds and private spaces. Shelves of books and games fill the other walls. Each has a desk with computers under the windows overlooking the tennis court. On an old ping-pong table they make their models, and for two years now they've had a sprawling LEGO landscape going underneath it. A plastic tub the size of a riding lawn mower squats in a corner, filled with parts. I rarely find any clothes lying around though their bathroom's as messy as it should be.

I've only actually seen Mrs W in her home twice. The first, when I interviewed her and the second when she showed me the business plan she'd devised for me. She's a tall, long-haired grey-blond, athletic lady with a faint accent I can't place. If I had to guess, given the art in the sitting room, I'd say Swedish.

They were one of the families who used to clean before I arrived, still do really. It used to make me giggle cuz they made so little mess in the first place. The white plastic trash bins all over the house are always empty and all the linens already changed.

I actually enjoy every minute here. It's calm and quiet, if a tad Spartan. There are no photos anywhere, of anyone. Not even in the boys' room.

Just before noon, I pulled the self-locking front door shut and waved to the security camera.

Porsche thumped his tail as I settled into my beater. I'd have to let him out soon. Minutes later, I parked beside the Cherokee in the clinic's lot.

Inside, Claire was dozing in a waiting room chair. I touched her shoulder. She rubbed her face. Her eyes were red. "What's the time?"

"Twelve on the dot."

"We gotta talk." She grabbed her pack, "Let's go."

I caught up with her at the cars.

"I'm stopping at Gardiner so Porsche can run."

"Okay. Can't take long, though."

Chapter 23

HOW DO YOU FEEL?

THIS TIME THE WORLD ENDED in fog by the water's edge at the boat launch. Porsche loped off into the trees following his nose and lifting his leg often. I drank from my water bottle, then lit a smoke. Claire strolled over, hands stuck in her jean pockets.

"So, what do you want to talk about?" I asked as we got in step and meandered after Porsche.

"It was good." She began, staring at the ground ahead. "Got a Maureen Salter. She had a gazillion questions about stuff I'd never thought of. Jeez, Sal, like, you know, how long my parents haven't been talking. What I first remember as a kid. What music I like, don't like. Clothes. Do I do any drugs. What do I drink. What was I good at in school. What did I hate. What do I eat, how often. How do I handle stress. Do I love my Dad. My Mom. That sort of stuff."

We paused by the shore, staring out into the fog.

"I liked the way she listened. My dumb and stupid didn't bother her." She giggled. "But when I said the eff word, that did! So I said it some more, just to bug her but she didn't get pissed anymore so I quit."

"How do you feel?"

"Ah, jeez, that's what she asked... all the time. I almost lost it, you know?"

I nodded and smoked on.

"I don't know how I feel, okay? I mean, I just feel! I'm not a walking dictionary. Something happens and I... you know?" She hunched over.

"React." I murmured. "What you do is react."

She looked confused. "That's what she said."

"Did Maureen talk about the difference between reacting and responding?"

"Some. You tell me."

I patted her shoulder and urged her to keep walking. Porsche came trotting up and circled us, then loped off for the underbrush. I watched him back into the bushes. Such a modest dog.

"We react to stress," I said, remembering those long-ago seminars, "To getting hurt, by pulling back. Yell, maybe swear. That's physical stress. Basically our bodies and minds run on that. You know, self-preservation." Claire and I were striding in step, weaving through the trees. "Then we do something to ease the pain, or hit back. If the wound's bad enough we see a doctor." I stopped, looking for Porsche. Still in the bushes. "All that stuff our parents and school teach us is to override those instincts, so we won't constantly go off, like fight or kill." I slowed us down. "Mostly what your counselor was talking about was reacting to emotional stress."

"So?" Claire nudged. I was watching Porsche come out of the bushes grinning from ear to ear. And a jolly good dump was had. I stroked him, told him he was a good boy and off he went again following his nose to the water's edge. Before I realized what he was going to do, he'd launched himself in and was paddling around, lapping at the water.

"Ah, shit," I groaned.

"Reaction, right?" And we laughed. "Okay." She looked at her wristwatch. "We've got five more minutes and then we've really gotta go. Quick, tell me about this responding to... emotional accidents."

"That's a very good way of putting it, Claire-kins. Well..." My thoughts froze as Porsche made a beeline toward us. Then he shook himself dry, all over us. We leapt apart, shrieking and laughing. He was very pleased with himself. I grabbed his collar, hustled him back to my beater, dug out an old towel and wiped him down. After another good shake I told him to load.

Claire was right beside me.

"Mom would've been soooo pissed! I've always liked that about you, you just take care of business."

"Why? Cuz he made a mess of her clothes?"

"Nah, cuz she'd have to *do* something for him."

"Did she get angry when you made a mess?"

"Doesn't every mom?"

"Actually, no." I pinched the head of my cigarette, shredded the remaining tobacco and stowed the mangled butt in my pocket. "I wasn't such a good mum back then. Didn't know making a mess was part of learning how to do stuff. Didn't know we don't get born not knowing how to drink from a mug, poop in a loo, eat with a spoon. Didn't know that's what childhood's for... to learn... practice."

Claire, leaning against my beater, chewing on a lock of hair, squinted at the brightness of the fog as the sun burnt it off. Looked like she was thinking something through.

"What about marriage?"

"Never having been married, I suppose it so. Two

people having to learn how to live together, even if they've known each forever. Stuff happens. Life changes. We grow up, away. Lose jobs, make money, crash cars, get pregnant, sick, have people die on us." I watched her carefully.

"Fuck around." The pretty maiden scowled.

"That too."

"So my being angry with Dad dying is normal?"

"I can only speak from my experience. You'll need a professional to guide you through that. Do you feel like he... abandoned you?"

"Yeah! I know, I know... wasn't like his... f-fault." She gulped, her eyes dripping tears. "I mean, someone made him, didn't they? But he's gone, isn't he? And he'll never come back."

"No, dearie, he won't. Can you handle a hug?" She nodded. I reached for her and she laid her cheek on my shoulder and sobbed.

"There, there, Claire-kin. It'll hurt for a while." I rubbed her shoulders. In time her arms came around me and she returned the hug.

"Maureen said that. But I'm so angry, too! I could just kill Mom and asshole Alan!" She got all stiff.

"Ahha!" I leaned out of our hug and she backed away, wiping her eyes.

"What?" She tossed back her hair.

"Reaction." I said. Her next reaction was not what I expected. She kicked my beater.

"What should I do?"

"Right now, we should get going." I glanced at my watch. "If you can, keep seeing your therapist."

"Who's gonna pay for it?" She jiggled her keys.

"I expect your father's estate will. Oh, and ask Maureen for homework."

"You're kidding!"

"Am not. Ask for things to think about until the next session. It really helped me cuz my memories were going all over the place and I didn't feel like I was moving forward to—"

"An ending?" She said, hopefully.

"No, sorry to say." We stood side-by-side, hands in our pockets, flexing our knees and watching the fog lift. "More like an understanding, except that implies logic which getting beyond the memories that drive us, doesn't have. You know those seminars we all went to? Where I met your parents? I learnt there're four levels to it. First, you've got to realize something's wrong."

Claire snorted. "Duh!"

"No, really. How many of us step back from our lives and ask what's wrong with this picture? No, we just keep blundering on. I know I did until I re-trained myself with the tools I got from my therapist and then those seminars."

"So what's the next one?" She was chewing her hair again.

"Accept it." Another snort, which I ignored. "After that you've got to acknowledge it before you can do anything. One thing I learnt real fast though, is sometimes doing nothing works too."

"How can doing nothing be doing something? Jeez, Sal, this is so fucking complicated."

"The human mind is complicated, my dear. Layers upon layers, memories upon memories and sometimes what you remember and what actually happened are very different things." Again I checked my watch. "We really have to go." I touched her arm. "Let's keep talking? Don't disappear on me, okay?"

"I won't. Want to find out why too much."

"Then I'll warn you the why may not be what you're

expecting."

"Well, I've got something you're not expecting." She was eyeing me from behind a hank of hair.

"What?"

She put her hands on her hips. "I'm going to enlist. In the army."

I gasped.

"Gramps and me've been talking about it for months. You know he was in Korea?"

"No—"

"What?" She made an innocent face. "What?"

"That's so... brave, responsible, patriotic even. I'm so proud of you."

"Gramps said that too." She looked at me shyly. "He told me Dad missed the draft for Vietnam cuz he got such good grades. You should've seen how angry Gramps got when he talked about how Dad dropped out of college. You know, when he left with Mom."

"Why?" I asked, more to keep her talking than to query her resolve.

"Cuz she was pregnant, with me."

"I knew that! No, I meant why are you enlisting?"

She looked away. "We're at war, remember? Anyway, Gramps told me everyone in Israel, girls as well as boys, does their national service. No choice about. He thinks we should bring back the draft here too. Everyone, after school, no exceptions. Says it'd make us better citizens. Teach us about the price of freedom." She walked about a bit. "Anyway, I'm young and healthy. Don't have a job, not going to college and... well... I want to learn about cars."

"Then I have someone you should meet. Wally, out in Port Hadlock. He was a sergeant, retired from the naval motor pool at Bremerton."

"You'll introduce me?"

THE DEAD HUSBAND

"Soonest."

"We gotta go!" Claire bounded over to the Cherokee, and we were off again, speeding toward the bright sunshine of the Sequim Hole.

THIS TIME CLAIRE LEFT THE HIGHWAY at Sequim Avenue and turned north for a couple of miles, then took a left through a cemetery gate. We bounced along a dirt road between parched grass where the gravestones faced the Olympic Mountains.

We parked behind an old blue Buick and a dusty black pick-up truck.

"That's the new rabbi's wheels." Claire whispered as she took my arm. "Guess the hearse must have left already." We marched over the shorn, brittle grass to her father's coffin draped by a white flag with a blue Star of David on it.

Waiting there with her grandparents was a young bearded man in sunglasses, white shirt, black tie and shiny black trousers. He had an embroidered blue yarmulke on his bald head. He was reciting from a book in his hands. Some distance away two chaps in brown uniforms and white cowboy hats stood beside a mower with a trailer. No one else was around.

As we approached Claire whispered, "He's here from Israel." She went to her grandparents, kissed each on both cheeks and took the black lace scarves her grandmother offered, then handed me one.

In the sunny autumn afternoon while the rabbi intoned the prayers, I raised my eyes over the retirement estates and sprawling town nestled in the flood plain beside the mountains over which puffy white clouds scudded westward in a bright blue sky, casting shadows on the forested foothills.

With the rabbi's voice droning on in a language I

hadn't heard since my years in Chicago with Jake's family, I said my goodbyes to my friend.

And then it was over, just like that. The rabbi folded the flag off the coffin and presented it to Mr. Birnbaum. One of the cemetery men walked forward, pressed something under the coffin and it descended into the hole in the ground. The rabbi invited us to take a handful of earth from the pile on the carpeting and toss it in. He said another prayer and a goodbye, then set off across the dry grass.

Claire and I were silently keeping pace with her grandmother, heading back to our cars when a silver sedan emerged out of the rabbi's dust tail. Claire shrieked and took off between the graves like the proverbial bat, the black lace flying off her head. She was about twenty yards from the Beamer when it did a three point turn, accelerated back the way it came, leaving Claire prancing in the dust. I trotted over to her, picking up the fallen scarf on the way. When I got to her side her face was bright red.

"That!" The grieving daughter sneered through clenched teeth. "Was mother dearest and her—" She glanced around at her grandparents still some distance away. "Motherfucker!" She screamed after the diminishing car.

I stroked her shoulder. "Come, let's help your grandparents on their way." Claire suddenly wrapped me in a tight hug.

"Wow, easy there, you'll break my back!" I gasped, feeling a giggle about to burst out. How sad and comical of Renee. Late for her husband's funeral and dragging along her lover for moral support. How low was she going to have to go?

We turned back to where Mr. Birnbaum was getting his wife into their Buick. Claire shooed him away and he shuffled around to the driver's side. She finished helping her grandmother, folded up the walker and slid it in the back seat. Then she went around to her grandfather and bent into the window.

Claire's grandmother beckoned to me and I returned the scarves.

"Thank you, Sally dear, Claire has needed you so much this week."

"You're welcome, Mrs Birnbaum. I'm very fond of her." Her smile was so wistful, her eyes red-rimmed.

"Can you take care of Gramma?" Claire was saying, "Gotta talk to Sal some more. Be home soon."

"Take your time, *liebkin*." He patted her hand on the open window, "We're not going anywhere." She stepped away as he put the car in gear and drove off after their son's widow.

I lit a smoke and watched the dust settle.

"Give me a drag!" Claire growled sticking her hand out. I looked at the fuming young woman.

"Don't start. It's not worth it."

"I'm not going to. Just give me an effing drag!" She plucked the smoke from my fingers and sucked on it. Naturally, she doubled over coughing.

"Told you so!" I giggled taking my smoke back. Claire stayed bent over with her hands on her thighs. At first I thought she was crying, then realized she was laughing. Well, actually, she was doing both.

"I have so gotta pee!" She whined, hopping about. There was, of course, no such thing as a loo out here seeing as the occupants didn't need one.

"Me too." I let my giggle out. "Where to?"

"McD's. Follow me." And once again I did.

We raced each other from the parking lot to the restroom. She was washing her face when I came out of the stall. We stared at each other in the mirrors and giggled again.

We were the only customers ordering and without mentioning it I paid for our eats. We settled in a booth where I could watch Porsche and our cars.

"So, Sal-da-Gal, you have a boyfriend?" Claire's voice was loaded with coyness. "Anyone I know? What's he like?"

I took time to swallow and think about how silly that word was for someone my age. "He's big and... smells of orange water." I couldn't think of anything else that was PG13 rated. "It's nice. I like his company and having someone to do things with, talk things over with."

"So, what's his name? What does he do?" She was bouncing on the seat as she ate, like a kid. While that was a safer subject I didn't want to tell her about George being part of the investigation into her father's death, cuz she'd think I'd have inside information. So I told her in broad strokes, and before I was through she was licking her fingers while I still had half a fishburger to go.

George once told me after he'd finished eating and I still had food on my plate, he'd learnt to eat fast in the army. Claire would have no problem fueling up. Her cheeseburger had vanished in four gulps. The French fries slowed her down. They required chewing.

"I've got to go soon." I warned. "Want to come back and check in at the clinic again?"

"Nah." She sucked down some soda. "I'll stay with the Gramps. They need the company, besides, I have an appointment with Maureen for Monday. Right after..." When she didn't finish, I turned my eyes from the parking lot.

"After what, dearie?"

"The reading of Dad's will." She whispered. I

stopped packing up my trash. Tears were streaming from her clenched eyes.

I took hold of the young woman's forearms and stroked them.

"Can you be there? Please, please!" She bleated, her eyes big with begging.

"Actually, I got a call from Steve saying my presence was required. So, yeah, I'll be there."

"Really? Why?" She wiped away the tears with a napkin and sidled out of our booth.

"No idea."

"I'll have to drive them over in the Buick. God, I hate that whale!" She grabbed up her trash. "Grampa doesn't drive that far anymore and..." She stood stock still. "I don't want to be there alone when... Mom turns up... with loverboy."

"You think she will?"

"It's about the money isn't it?" She smashed her trash into a ball. "I better get back."

I felt a surge of love and hope for this lovely young woman.

"I didn't know," she muttered as we pushed our stuff into the bin. "That Dad didn't have any friends. I guess they were all Mom's."

"Oh, I'm sure he did, it's just who would have told them about the funeral?"

"Not her, that's for sure." She wiped her eyes again. "Well, Sal-Gal," she stretched hugely. "I hope I never see her again. Ever!" She sucked up the last of her Coke before pushing the mug through the flap. Then she belched and we started giggling again.

"Dad would've so liked this. Thanks for coming." She said as we went out the doors.

"You're welcome, Sorry he didn't get to be old."

"Me too." She whispered, blinking in the bright

sunlight.

"I'll be there Monday." I assured her, and gave her a hug.

"Thanks, Sal, you're the best!" And she actually kissed my cheek.

As I drove away I realized I hadn't asked her when or where she was going to enlist.

Chapter 24

ON TO BEDLAM

BEFORE I SET OUT on my way back to Port Townsend I called George and got his voice mail. Worry chewed at my gut as I wove the wiggly road over Eaglemont.

I took time at the entrance to a gated logging road to let Porsche out. When he returned from draining his radiator he was panting. I rummaged in the trunk, found a plastic bowl and filled it from a water bottle in the cooler. After much slurping he was ready to load up and we headed on to the Sizkorski's home.

Home is perhaps the wrong word for where they live, all thirteen of 'em: Mister and Missus, five sons and six daughters, all eleven months apart. Every one of them has a March or April birthday. With two now flown the coop for the U-Dub campus over in Pullman, they've taken in a couple of high school cousins from Gdansk.

They've been remodeling this sprawling real Victorian forever. This spring the work on all the bathrooms and toilets had finally been completed. Two years ago it had been the kitchen and utility room. Before that they'd started parking out on the street cuz Mrs S wanted to convert the basement into an office and stockroom for her Internet business. She sells colorful fleece sweatsuits, heavily adorned which her family and friends in the Old Country produce and ship to her. I see Mr S in an office at the Kah-Tai Credit Union where I bank.

Mrs S is never there when I come. She's on the Food Bank committee and it's her day for cooking and serving in the soup kitchen at Holy Trinity up on Jefferson. And that's where you'll find me on Thanksgiving and Christmas, right beside her. I'd known her as one of Clay's patients though it was Mrs W who turned her onto my work.

Just to be totally clear, I worship the woman. She's a dynamo of bleached short hair, tweezed eyebrows, startling makeup and strong perfume. She's as short as me with a magnificent bosom, just like her mother and grandmother whose studio photos hang, along with dozens of others of her Polish relatives and her children on the walls of the stairwells, all three flights of 'em.

I've never seen Mrs S wear anything other than those sweats, even before she started her company which, by the way, is thriving. In her wardrobe, painted with bright birds and garlands of flowers which she brought from the Old Country when she emigrated as a bride leaving behind five brothers and four sisters, a rainbow of sweatsuits fill the shelves. In the hanger compartment is one solitary black dress above one pair of plain black pumps. Next Spring, Mrs S will make fifty.

Her home is a cross between a thrift store and a frat house with the carpetless ground floor rooms crammed full with bags and boxes of incoming donations of clothes and bedding.

At Christmas time there'll be unwrapped gifts for needy families. Except in the dining room off the kitchen where everyone meets. They eat at a table with all its leaves in on which are two lazy-Susans of condiments. It's surrounded by a salmagundi of chairs which will seat twenty, at a squeeze. I know cuz I've eaten at it and helped clean up afterwards. Saturday night's open house. The kids always bring home friends. The Wallens and their twins join them at least once a month. I've even brought George along and he had a grand time.

Then there's the refurbished kitchen with its two fridges, vast Viking range, stainless steel sinks, dishwashers—yup, two of 'em—and a long butcher's block counter. There's enough crockery and cutlery, pots and pans stowed away in the cupboards to feed an army, and they often do.

The utility room where all the bulk food is stored on metal shelves and in five gallon plastic buckets, is as big as the kitchen and extends onto the rear porch. It has a tiny loo and two of everything: washers, dryers and freezers. Laundry is constantly being done. Mrs S told me up front that I wasn't expected to strip and remake the beds. That had been a relief! Shelves over the machines are filled with see-through labeled plastic bins for clothes. Except Mr S's who uses the Dockside Cleaners.

Husband and wife have a suite on the first floor with the visiting cousins sharing the guest suite across the landing.

The top floor has three big bedrooms jam-packed with bunks, gear, computers and two bathrooms. The smaller one, built in a closet, is the boys'.

Even though everyone has cellphones now, on all

the landings there's a working wall phone. In the hall to the kitchen is a blackboard with the clean-up schedule. Gender is no defense against doing chores.

I've only climbed the ladder to the attic once, just to see. It spans the entire width and breadth of the house and is where the kids play together. There's a jiggie table and a model train set that meanders all over the floor. Old couches are squeezed into the dormer windows and under the slanting ceiling, shelves line the walls filled with books and boxes of board games. A ping-pong table had a Monopoly marathon in progress and on an old card table packs of playing cards were at the ready. Behind the door was an ancient vacuum.

This house has no pets, at least not intentionally. About every other year, after school starts the kids bring home head lice and I'll be called in for a delousing. I've even got 'em. Tenacious little critters.

Out back is a cement basketball court. The goal posts have warped hoops and torn nets. Against the surrounding brick walls plastic storage sheds hold more freezers and donation overflows.

The Sizkorski house is bedlam, and I love it. It's not that anyone's particularly dirty, it's just that there's a lot of bodies and it takes all of my time.

Mrs S's note is computer generated and she always adds a Polish joke she's copied off the Web.

WHEN I PULLED THE SIZKORSKIS' DOOR shut I was ready for a spot of tea. Poor old Porsche looked nackered as he panted in the shade of the leg area of the back seat of my beater so instead of heading home, I drove to a part of Fort Worden where dogs can roam free.

Before we set out under the cool and aromatic

conifers I let him drink his fill from the last of the water. Then off we ambled through the forest up the old military road to the long-since abandoned bunkers on the headlands.

At the top it's open and bright and we strode fast and free against the glorious backdrop of Whidbey Island and the Cascades. All too soon we were starting down the other side of the promontory and overtook another walker and his dog.

Bob's one of the few homeless people we have. He's a skinny, dirty, mostly silent chap of indeterminable age who wears layers of grungy clothes with a black knit cap hiding his eyebrows. His watery eyes are always half closed. Up here among the warren of bunkers there's lots of places a person can hang out, and teenagers have been doing so for generations, leaving their graffiti.

Bob's particular poison's Mogen David wine. Says it gives him a little sweetness in his sorry life. I learnt early, under Mrs S's wing, that you didn't ask: So why don't you make some changes if your life's so sour?

Mrs S had heard me start with that kind of rubbish and had pushed me aside with her immense bosom, tempting Bob with a mess of macaroni and cheese. When he'd moved on along the food line she'd muttered about not antagonizing the patrons. I'd spluttered I intended no such thing and she countered that asking anything other than "Care for some peas?" would be taken as interrogation and they'd leave without eating. She'd laid her sky blue eyes on me and said out of her perfectly painted pink lips, "You're here to serve food, is all. Quit with the do-gooding!"

He'd been one of Clay's pro bono patients and

when I'd told him Clay had died and asked if he'd like the new doc to look at him, he'd bolted and I hadn't seen him since. His brown and white terrier was new. We fell into step on road.

Porsche was soon freaked by the little dog's alpha energy and the snapping sharp teeth. I called him to me and leashed him up. Bob took the hint and did the same to his with a length of kitchen rope. At heel, both dogs relaxed.

When we came to a fork in the road I dug out the rest of my smokes and a wad of singles and bid Bob and goodbye. He grunted a thanks.

OUT ON MY PORCH I WAS SIPPING on my second cuppa, with my dog dozing in the sunlight when my Man returned my call.

"I'm fine. Had to make a quick trip to Port Angeles to deliver a package." He often delivers packages. Sometimes they're in evidence bags or file folders and sometimes, if they're Clallam County residents, they're in handcuffs. "How was the funeral?"

"Nice. Simple. Just Claire and Mel's parents, and the rabbi."

"They're Jewish? Is Renee?"

"Doubt it. I've never seen a Bible around." I drank some more tea. "She actually turned up."

"The widow?"

"Yeah. The rabbi'd just left. Did a U-ee and beat a retreat. Claire says Hatton was with her."

"How's she coping?"

"Okay. Took her to the mental health clinic. She rather liked it. Oh, yeah, she's going to enlist. Did you know her grandfather fought in Korea?"

"Doesn't surprise me. But Claire's news does. Good for her! It's a whole 'nother Army since I was in. Lots of career opportunities for women now. She won't get stuck clerking or nursing if she doesn't want to. Where's her BTS?"

"Her what?"

"Basic Training Station."

"No idea. She kind of threw it at me before I drove home. Oh, Steve called. Says I've got to be at the reading of the will Monday morning."

"Is Renee going to be there? Any news on that?"

"He says she is. Haven't spoken with Smith or Westin since..."

"Yesterday, hon, just yesterday."

"Really? Seems like ages ago." I gulped some more tea, feeling awfully alone. "George? Any chance I could see you tonight?"

"Sure, Sally, is that all you want or do you want food, too?"

"That would be loverly."

"Golden Gate?"

"Yum-yum."

"In thirty?"

"I've missed you, sweet man."

"Me too, honey girl."

AND THEN, NATURALLY, the Cosmos dealt another card. As I was getting up I saw a silver sedan cruise by on Jackson. Then it came by again, slowed and when I stepped to the edge of my porch, moved on.

I keyed in George's number.

"The Beamer's circling again."

"I'll get on it. Go inside and take the dog. Lock your door. Stay away from your windows."

"Damn!"

Porsche was about as happy as I was to go inside. We hung about in the sunroom, he asking silent questions and me dead-heading the last blossoms on a geranium, there being nothing to tidy out there.

The whoop made me jump. I crept out of my front door to peer up the road. A PTPD squad car had stopped behind the Beamer while another had squeezed beside it.

That's when I heard a flat bang. There was shouting. Officer Ferrell stepped forward with his weapon drawn.

Hatton got up out of the driver's seat with his hands over his head. Renee tumbled from the passenger side, her purse in hand. The coppers surrounded them, bellowing orders. Hatton and Renee leaned over their car.

My cellphone chirped. "What's happening?" George rumbled and I described the mean little scene.

"Someone's coming." I told him as an officer started trotting along my road.

"Keep me connected."

Ferrell strode up my path. "You got the Captain there?"

I gave him the phone and he walked away into my garden. Soon he returned and handed it back.

"You have a nice evening now, ma'am." He touched the brim of his cover and left.

"Jeez-louise, isn't anyone going to tell me what's going on?"

"Sure!" My Man said in my ear, "Load up and bring our dog."

Chapter 25

A COPPER IN MY CORNER

I SHUT MY HOUSE, loaded up Porsche and drove off wanting some serious hugging time with my very live lover. What I got was a peck on the cheek and an invitation to slide into the booth at Golden Gate where bowls of soup waited.

I was torn between feeding my face and drinking in my Man's presence. Once in a while, when he'd catch me watching him, he'd throw me a kiss and shovel in another load of the hot stuff. I finally dug in too.

After George took a toothpick from beside the register he ushered me out into a foggy orange evening.

"What if we smoke at your place?" He suggested as we walked arm-in-arm to our wheels. "Let me have Porsche for the ride, okay?"

I watched dog and man hie off to the gleaming Escalade on the other side of the parking lot. I giggled at Porsche's reaction to the overhead moan of the foghorn. He eagerly leapt into the SUV and as they pulled out behind me I felt comforted with that hulk following me home.

I opened the utility room door and George came in first making a beeline for Porsche's bowl where he upended his doggie bag of meaty morsels into the kibble and stirred it up. Our dog ate with much grunting glee.

In no time me and my Man were on the porch enjoying a smoke, watching the world end at my fence in dew-laden fog.

"You rattled Smith and Westin some." George said after a while. "Embarrassed them all to hell. They know they dropped the ball about having the whole house worked over the first time. Lucky for us no one's been there and the security company recorded the front gate traffic. Weird place, Bluff Haven. No deliveries. No wives. No kids. No visitors. Just the same six autos leaving at the same time each morning and returning in the evening. We're checking on who all lives out there. Ever meet anyone?"

I shook my head. We smoked a while in silence.

"I'm taking some leave next month." He said, stubbing out his butt. "Three weeks. Want to go for a drive with me?"

"Where to?" I was amazed at how my wishes were being granted.

"Was all set to run the ALCAN up to Alaska. Never done that. When I asked Triple A for an itinerary they said there's an early snow warning. So then I thought of going south to the Four Corners area. Never been there either. It'd be a good time to check in with my step-sister and brother on the way."

"Where're they?"

"Ellen's in Palm Springs and Kev's in Berkeley."

"Where're your children?" I asked before I thought it through.

"My kids?" He shrugged. "Dunno. Sue left the state after the divorce. All I did was give our lawyer the alimony and child support check. The year I moved up here she told me Sue'd remarried, and I didn't have to pay anymore."

"You never got any Christmas cards, school photos?"

"Nope." He shrugged.

"Ever thought to do a search on the Internet for them?"

He bent over and gave Porsche a belly rub. "Never occurred to me."

"Did you like them?"

"Sure! George Junior was a good kid. Eight the last time I saw him. Er... Danny still sucked his thumb and...Jenny was a little doll." He shook his head. "Hon, it's been too long. They're all growed up by now."

"Think you're a granddaddy yet?"

He gave me a startled look and then made a grimace. "Now you're making me feel old!" He shook his head again, focusing on Porsche. "Think I should check 'em out, after all this time?"

"Maybe they've been looking for you?"

"Let me think about it, okay?"

"What about your father?" I hoped I wasn't being too nosy.

"Which one?" He sat back up, rested his hands on his head and blew out a breath. "Never knew if Mom was a widow or divorced. Saw a wedding photo in her bedroom once. Wouldn't talk about him or anyone else in her family. First I knew his name was when I enlisted and had to get a copy of my birth certificate."

An orange ball of fur leapt right over our dozing dog and landed in George's lap. Porsche's nose twitched, his ears perked up, eyes opened. Then he got to his feet and regarded Ronnie. George chuckled and stroked the cat. Porsche walked behind our chairs to my side and sat down with his jowls on my thigh. I stroked him too. What domesticity!

"I was twelve and we were living in an apartment in Palm Springs. My Mom was a bookkeeper in a realty office." George continued. "Figured that's where she met Ray Mason Tullock because he ran an upscale mobile home park nearby. He was a good man. The strong and silent type. Retired Marine and a Korean Vet. His wife had just died of cancer leaving him to raise Ellen and Kev." He lit a smoke. "After my Mom and I moved in to his ritzy double-wide he adopted me. Then she got all churchy. You know, baking and praying and rushing off all the time to do something for... the less fortunate. She'd drag Ellen with her. Things got bad when Kev and I hit our teens. Seemed like she nagged on us all the time. And then she quit, just like that! Always figured Pop had had words with her." He cocked his head and winked. "Tell you more if you come with. Want to head out at first light October sixth."

"Love to, George. What'll you do about shaving?"

His chair groaned as he stretched out his legs dislodging the purring Ronnie who leapt to the ground, turned to eye our throbbing dog and streaked off through the bushes. With his nose to the ground and tail stiff behind him Porsche silently took after.

"Maybe grow a beard."

"Really?" I looked at his beloved face imagining what that would be like. "Is Porsche going too?"

"Of course!"

"Can I ask you one more question?"

"Sure."

"Could we stop by Crater Lake?"

He grinned. "Beat me to it."

Then he stood up and bent a leer at me. "I've got one for you, sweet thing. Want a spin in bed?"

"Thought you'd never ask."

WHEN WE FIRST STARTED MAKING LOVE I'd wanted George's baby something fierce, which was odd cuz I hadn't had that kind of feeling with Clay. So while my hormones had howled my tubes stayed severed. George hadn't been thrilled with the idea of babies, him being so old and all.

All good things come to an end and too soon our dog and me were standing in the foggy dusk as the Escalade purred off with a little toot on the horn.

I locked up and tumbled back into the bed where George's scent still lingered.

My dreams were filled with parched blue cemeteries and purple people on silver stairs, while bleached tombstones scudded in a blazing green sky and bodyless white shirts danced around orange Dayglo lamp posts.

Next morning my dog and I woke bright-eyed and bushy-tailed and pounded our way around Point Hudson with an amber dawn coming over the Cascades and the Sound smothered in mauve fog.

Back in my office I stared at my calendar. Now where was I supposed to be?

THE GOOD DOCS keep their clinics open late week nights so they can take off Friday for a long weekend.

Their offices are at the end of the plaza where a monster QFC bought out the family supermarket a while back. The plaza also contains a UPS depot, a bicycle and kayak rental business, and a drugstore hanging on by the skin of its teeth. The gift shop next door to the clinic packed it in last year, and the Docs tell me a graduate from John Bastyr College will be opening his naturopathic practice there in January. So my choice in music wasn't disturbing anyone.

When I'm up to speed, the clinics are a fast clean. I wasn't, and my music wasn't doing a thing for me so I found one of the Docs' Bluegrass CDs and danced around the foyer a while so the perky plucking could kick me into gear.

By noon I was famished. So while the floors dried and before I buffed 'em, I took a break for a real sit-down lunch at Kathy's Korner at the other end of the plaza, where you turn off from Sims Way. I scarfed down a cup of yummy veggie soup along with a cheese, tomato and sprout sandwich on freshly baked dark rye bread and, cuz I needed a treat, a slice of Kathy's infamous pecan pie. I washed it all down with a glass of water, ending with a high octane latte which, naturally, had me so wired I could have ignited my beater without the key.

I burnt some of it off taking Porsche for a fast walk around the headlands overlooking the Olympic Trail which, one day, I'll take him on. Twenty years ago when the pulp mill closed (the one featured in the movie *An Officer and a Gentleman*) local folks ganged together and converted the abandoned timber railroad track into a walk-and-bicycle trail.

Porsche trotted beside me, ears flat, tail between his legs. As I puffed along I'd catch him warily eyeing me. So I found a bench under a tree and had a smoke. My dog sat beside me sighing, his head on my lap. I stroked him so much and so hard there should have been a worn patch in his fur. Stout hound!

Now I was ready for the clinics again. I put out

some water for Porsche and leashed him to the bicycle rack outside so he could hang out near me in the shade. After all that food I worked even slower. As I was closing up, it dawned on me I hadn't heard from anyone all day long. I checked all my pockets. Oops! I'd left my phone in its charger.

Back in my office I had calls from George and Joanne, two wails from Claire and a panic attack from Renee.

"So, are you a free woman, Boss? Do we get the pleasure of your company? Will you be here for dinner at seven?" Rock steady Joanne. I left a message that I was still on the loose.

I was in no mood for either Claire or Renee.

"Where've you been?" George rumbled.

"Forgot my phone. Had the clinics today." I settled into my porch chair while Porsche was busy under the bushes. Chetzemoka Park was gold and green. "Did I say yes to your invite?"

"Sort of."

"Well, I'm saying it now, with bells on!"

"Ooookay, hon. Had a thought. What're you going to do about Porsche?"

That brought me up short real fast.

"Thought we were taking him with."

"No, while you're at your pajama party." My Man said, heavy on the patience.

Joanne didn't like dogs. Oops!

"Maybe he could hang out in my car?" I dithered.

"No he can't!" Said my Man, all prickly. "I happen to know this guy who's at loose ends cuz his gal's off with a bunch of broads. What say I stay over?"

"Oooh, would ya?" I giggled with relief.

"Be my pleasure." He smirked right back.

"You're such a gent." I cooed.

"When are you leaving?"
"Um… six-forty-five-ish?"
"I'll be there six-thirty, with no "ish" about it."

Chapter 26

HOSTESS WITH THE MOSTESS

I'D FINISHED PACKING MY STUFF into my beater, had backed it out in front of my gate and was having a smoke when the Escalade rolled up and backed in to my carport. Porsche leapt up the stairs, galloped into the utility room and moments later I heard man and dog greet each other.

George was all casual in his shirt and jeans, looking pleased with himself. I was almost reluctant to leave, almost. My Gals would've never let me live it down. The only thing they'd so far allowed to get in the way of attending our monthly sleepovers was contagion, like the 'Flu and Zoe's bout with adult-onset Mumps, caught from the commune kids. Now Joy was about to test that, what with her buns in the oven. It would be interesting to see how much guff they gave her.

George made no bones about wanting me gone. He put his books on the table by his end of the recliner. Stuffed his insulin and sodas in the fridge. Set his pills out on the counter, and stood there waiting.

"Time to kick you out, Sal-the-Gal." He was grinning and rubbing Porsche's head. And that's what he did with lots of loverly kisses rolled up into a great big bear hug.

I drove off ready for some serious time with the nicest, funniest and rudest women I know.

I GOT TO JOANNE'S IN THE NICK OF TIME with her up on her stoop clanging away at her "Come'n'Git It" triangle. I found a spot within the herd of Wally's Wrecks all around the corner yard. The cloudless apricot-hued sunset over the purple Olympics was magnificent.

One of the things we agreed upon after our first disaster of a potluck weekend with its duplicate casseroles and salads, was that the hostess catered. And we brought none of the tools of our trade either, so all I'd needed were my business machines, pillow and sleeping bag, my personal stuff and towel and a change of clothes.

We also bring no booze, and in deference to our co-workers, we smokers: Joanne, Judith, Lois and me retire outside for our nicotine fixes.

The first thing Joanne likes to do when she greets you is slap you on the back with a sticky name tag. Then you have to find out who you are. No cheating in mirrors. As we sidled along filling our plates from the splendid smorgasbord, we gave each other clues. The first to guess gets to choose where she sleeps. It's a fun way to get us all going. I couldn't think of a name, so Judith finally had to tell me I'd been tagged Lizzie Borden. I was not amused.

One of the things about charwomen is their homes are very different from ordinary folks. Most tend not to live in clutter and Joanne's is about as Spartan as it gets.

Ethel and Joy are the exceptions. Ethel's Uptown Victorian is crammed with antiques in various stages of restoration and Joy's, being a 28 foot Benford Scrimshaw classic moored at the Point Hudson marina is all shipshape and utilitarian neat. I'd had a case of claustrophobia when I'd interviewed her. I had a feeling once the twins arrived, she'd be looking at some terra firma real estate.

After we put away the leftovers and washed the dishes we milled about, using the facilities and kowtowing to Joanne's three fat, long-haired white cats as they wound themselves around our legs. When we reconvened around the dining table. Joanne shooed her felines outside and latched their door flap.

Joy's news can't wait. She'll be the first to have children since the Gals joined up. She also lets us know she's got the contract for the club house at the marina, which she says she'll continue to do herself now that she won't be sailing so much. We all have a chuckle at her expense. She brought in two of the four downtown penthouses in the original brick buildings built at the turn of the last century. The owners are sailors too, except you could fit Joy's little boat in the staterooms of their yachts.

I hadn't cleaned a penthouse since the three over in San Francisco when I'd taken them on during one of my kids' alternative school teacher's maternity leave. I'd enjoyed working on the umpteenth floors of those ivory towers overlooking the Bay and Alcatraz Island, so I offered to take Joy's from her fifth month on. Ethel signed on for post-delivery. Joy said that was enough cuz by then she'd be wanting to get back to work.

I enjoy watching all my Gals together. They're

funny, foul-mouthed and bright, and I've never heard one of 'em be unkind or bitch about another.

Annie, Judith and Lois, living together, have an easy rapport and make sure they sit separately among the rest of us.

Joanne keeps us on track, leading us through last month's Minutes, then proceeds to income and expenditures.

In any given week, Sal's Gals cleans:
17 homes
11 condominium
9 timeshare units
7 cafés and restaurants
7 taverns
6 realty offices
5 motels and hotels
4 Historic Home Tour business buildings
4 doctors' practices
3 banks & a credit union
2 penthouses
1 mental health clinic

Oh, and we'll groom your partridge in your pear tree if you've got one, on our lunch hour.

Joanne informs us she's taken in ten applications for new Gals, and come up with four possibles.

One is a philosophy graduate in need of some cash, willing to work afternoons and evenings. She wants taverns and cafés. Lois takes her on.

The second is an English major wanting to make enough to go to England next summer. She can do weekends and three evenings, and prefers offices. If she works out, she'd like to join us again when she gets back stateside. Sandra takes her

The next is a mother, relocating from Georgia to be close to her grown Navy son and his family out by

THE DEAD HUSBAND

Indian Island. She can work weekday mornings and likes homes with children. Zoe takes her.

Number four is a guy. That gets us all giggling. Zoe's quite keen on him. He already works Chez Cherie and The Landfall cafés.

"He's super clean and neat." Zoe says grinning. "Got a great sense of humor. Oh yeah, he's gay."

So why does he want to join an all-female company? Figures we'd treat him right and not give him a hard time about his lifestyle. He prefers restaurants and motels. Zoe and Lois want to train him. After much talk in which the silly subject of gender bias comes up, our wise Business Manager, seeing some of us have stuff on this applicant suggests we sleep on it.

When Joanne asks for any new business, giving me a stare full of innuendo, I know it's time to talk about the Birnbaums. That takes the rest of the session cuz between her questions and Annie's prompting I have to repeat all the gory details. Sure enough, Ethel swears up a storm, except no one knows enough French to get offended. Lois adds some juicy tidbits she's gotten out of her deputy sheriff and Zoe starts belting out some damn song that has us in stitches. Joy grouses about lousy landlubbers. Sandra shakes like a rabbit and yup! Judith worries about the plants at the bottom of the garden.

It sure felt good to be laughing instead of crying.

After we discuss the likelihood of losing that job, Ethel reminds us of her pilgrimage to Paris in six weeks. She's got a couple of realty offices she'd like to start when she gets back.

Annie's places are all humming along, nothing new to report. Her domestic life is uneventful except the yard has been magnificent this year. We all give

Judith a round of applause.

Judith's got another home to bring in and as she gushes over the garden, I know that one of these days we're going to lose her as a char. She's also met a Carol Flauberg who wants training. Married to a fish boat captain and with depleting catches they really need the extra income. Now that her last child's in first grade she can take on the work, mornings only.

Lois has a tavern she wants to drop cuz the new bartender's an a-hole and too slow in closing up and won't take no about dating. She's got two more she'd like to work. Taverns are my least favorite cleans.

Zoe pipes up that she's been asked to inspect two new homes in the Happy Hippy Hollow near her commune. She also tells us one of the men's divorce has been finalized and they've started dating. The ex has left town and his two kids are staying on. And no, they're not getting married. Yet, everyone teases.

Sandra gives her financial report and lets us know she's got the health food store on Water Street. Ever since the theft episode she's cleans only empty places of business. She takes a while to join in and let her hair down, literally. She keeps it in a horrendously tight knot on top of her head. We know when she's gotten comfortable cuz she'll unwind that amazing black veil.

It's going on eleven by the time we close and we're all tired. There's a traffic jam in the hallway to the guest bathroom until Joanne opens up her bedroom and we overflow into it. Soon we're all settled in our sleeping bags, the cats are on Joanne's bed and all's well with the world.

THE DEAD HUSBAND

SATURDAY'S DAWN is brilliantly sunny with a stiff breeze off the Bay. The view from Joanne's porch is spectacular: the water, islands and the purple Cascades to the east. In the west the timber-covered Olympics. After such a long, hot summer, there's no snow left on 'em.

Joy, Judith and I go for a walk around the neighborhood and return in time for the second breakfast sitting. We clean up and settle in for the next part of our meeting.

How better can we run our company. This is when new tools are introduced and when I hand over any new uniforms I've finished. There's a problem-solving session about such things as homeowner habits. Joanne and Sandra talk money and prospects. We decide to give the gay guy a go.

Then it's time for a break before starting Yoga and brushing up on our self-defense.

Another walk about and it's time to fill our bellies and clean up. Then we're ready for our pjs and a good movie. This time Zoe wants us to watch *Gosford Park*. Joanne makes popcorn and the cats are passed around until they get too hot and heavy.

When Sandra asks me to interpret, I'm almost as lost as she, no matter which class is doing the talking. Twenty minutes into it though, my ear for English English kicks in and I'm hooked. Soon we're doing the grooming thing, watching the story unfold.

After talking about the kitchen in the movie and what all it must have taken to keep that huge mansion sparkling, we sleepily head for bed.

During the night the fog rolls in and when we awake the world ends beyond Joanne's front yard. She's already lit her woodstove.

With breakfast done we go out into the fog and

stuff our gear back in our cars. Then it's time to give Joanne's home a good clean, banishing her to the patio, bundled up with her cats in her lap. Working all together, this clean is fast and fun with a lot of bawdy jokes and teasing.

As we meet for our closing circle, I remember George's invitation. I'm surprised at how silent my Gals get.

"When's the last time you took a vacation, Boss?" Joanne drawls, herding us back to the dining table where everyone scans their schedules, volunteering here and there until my work is covered. Come Monday I'm going to have to start making calls.

As I drive home, still feeling all the hugs from my friends and co-workers, I'm very, very glad to know these women. They make our company sing, earn good money and work well at what we like doing. What more could a body want?

And I hadn't thought about my two males once, tut, tut!

Chapter 27

AND THE EARTH SHOOK

SO HOW MANY TIMES WOULD YOU SAY George thinks about me while he's at work? Or Porsche, when I'm not around?

The greeting I got when I opened my gate told me they'd thought of me a lot. Both man and beast. Porsche kept sniffing and sneezing as he got whiffs of the cats. He even goosed my crotch which sent me into giggles.

George was on his feet on the porch and took me into a hug garnished with lots of kisses. Ray Lynch's music wafted through the open front door. All was right with my world.

"Not the same without you, sweet thing," he growled. He looked tired.

"Had a crash?" He nodded. How I hate that.

"Doc Tell's ordered another kind of insulin. Should be in the mail midweek."

"You reached her on the weekend?"

"Nah, left a message on her emergency number right after you vamoosed Friday. Hey, you want to come to bed?"

Of course I did!

THERE'S NOTHING QUITE LIKE a loving man with hands that like to touch and caress, in your bed. On his part, George tells me there's nothing quite like a woman in bed who enjoys his bod and attention as I, nor who loves to do what we do between the sheets. We dozed off, like comfy spoons, with our dog out on the porch, guarding our front door.

Eventually Porsche brought his cold nose in from the garden and stuck it under the covers, sniffed around, sneezed himself into a tizzy and bolted, dragging the comforter with him. George and I rolled out and dressed, rewarding our dog with a turn around the park under a magenta and pink sky. Then I grilled the last of the steaks. George gave Porsche the juicy morsels we left.

As our dog and me saw our alpha male off, I comforted myself that soon we'd all be together on that road trip.

There's nothing like coming home to your own things, your own space. Didn't have any calls to return and couldn't concentrate on sewing or reading nor wanted to watch telly, so I locked up, got into my robe and worked my jiggy, thinking about my Gals and the upcoming adventure. It took me a while to realize how many more pieces had been put into place. My, my, hadn't known George liked 'em, too. Then I thought about seeing Crater Lake for real.

When I hadn't found a piece in ages, I patted my snoring dog, turned off the lights and rolled into bed.

SOMETIME LATER, Porsche's whining roused me.

After I peed and flung on a set of sweats I raced to the bay window to see if the silver Beamer was circling again.

All was quiet and still, with no car exhausts pluming in the street lights. The sky was bright with stars to the east. Somewhere a dog howled, and it seemed to go on forever.

I nuked a cup of tea, put on a wool cap, wrapped myself in a blanket and went out to my porch.

Then I felt it. It wasn't any animal howling, it was a trembler and from the sound of it, a biggie. Porsche tried to get between my legs as the roaring came toward us from the east over the water. Then suddenly car alarms started going off.

The porch boards creaked and my whole home squeaked and groaned. Porsche pressed close, the whites of his eyes glowing. I stroked and stroked him. Had he been smaller, I'd have taken him on my lap.

The Spruces in Chetzemoka Park jiggled. There was no wind. Then the lights of my little town blinked off, and came back on.

It was over in seconds, and the waves of Admiralty Inlet went on thudding into the rocks at the bottom of the cliff.

A PTPD cruiser with lights flashing prowled past on Jackson. People started coming outside. Someone must have had a radio on cuz a metallic voice was ricocheting around. I couldn't make out a word.

Next door, Mr J was wrestling with his picket gate, got it open and shuffled along the sidewalk toward me with Ronnie tucked under his arm. He tried to push my gate open and gave up. He just stood there in his jammies and slippers, his hair sticking out like Einstein's.

"Not such a bad one this time, eh?" He yelled at me, the dazed look on his face belying his nonchalance. I wondered if he'd remembered to put his hearing aids in. "Thought our street lamp was a goner there. You got any damage?"

"Haven't looked yet, Mr J, Want a cuppa?" He stood stroking Ronnie, staring back down the road. Then he shook his head and shuffled home.

Mr J worked at the paper mill all his life, except during WWII, when he spent the duration on a barren Aleutian Island way off the Alaskan coast. Now he's waiting for his wife Clara to come home. Their two sons are retired in Florida, and they've a grandson in the Navy; another working oil in Alaska and a granddaughter making babies in Bellingham. Mr J doesn't own a car anymore: says he can't remember which pedal does what, so I take him shopping whenever he asks, otherwise he rides the bus which stops every hour at the end of our road.

He's very lonely since Clara's been away. I've had him over for a pot of tea now and again. We have nothing in common, mostly cuz all he does is watch telly. Before Clara broke her hip, he'd ask me a couple of times a year to keep an eye on his house and Ronnie while they took off for Reno with their seniors club. I'll have to ask him to watch mine when I go on George's trip.

THERE'S NOT MUCH ANYONE CAN DO when a trembler comes through. Being on the Ring of Fire and right where one tectonic plate is sliding over another, we actually get quite a few, though most are hardly noticeable. The mountain peaks on the mainland are dormant volcanos except Mount St. Helen, which blew back in the '80s. Some say it's only a matter of time before Mount Rainier and/or Baker does. All you can do is sit tight and pray.

It's the storms coming out of British Columbia that scare me. Last winter a ferocious dry wind had come down on the heels of a freezing fortnight.

"Boss?" Joanne had said when she called. "Do you have extra water? Food? When the power goes, it's gonna be for days."

I'd joined the crowd in the hardware store buying water tanks, Mexican candles in their tall glass jars and matches. I got bags of ice from the gas station, two of the last ones left and stuffed 'em into the freezer compartment of my fridge. Then I filled the water tanks in the kitchen and set 'em on the counter. From the hose, I filled up all old milk jugs for my thrones.

The second night I couldn't sleep, what with my little cottage out on its promontory, groaning and creaking in the roaring wind. I lit my woodstove, put a bucket of water on and my big old Brown Bessy teapot filled with steeping tea.

Then I worked my jiggy until the power went out, when I lit the candles and dragged my then single recliner over to the woodstove and camped out in it.

None of us Gals could work with no power and no city pump, so everyone just hunkered down to wait it out, and the sound of a hundred generators could be heard throughout the land. Then visitors started dropping by bearing all sorts of food they needed cooked on my propane stove. It had been kind of fun as we collectively went back to the days of yore, before we'd learnt how to light the night.

George had been busier than usual. Seems folks had crime on their minds. He'd come over whenever he could for food and warmth. His place being all electricity and restaurants weren't serving. He'd even slept over. There's always a silver lining, isn't there?

He'd been at work when the giant Spruces in the park bit the dust. I'd nearly jumped out of my skin when the three separate cracks sounded above the wind. Seconds later they thudded to earth and ancient body memories of the noises I'd heard as a child during The War kept me shivering.

All over town trees were down, and two elder citizens were felled by heart attacks. Burst pipes flooded homes and businesses alike and then froze, making it a prosperous, if exhausting season for plumbers and utility crews. The power came back on to everyone by the fifth day.

SUNSHINE SHAFTING through the park trees woke me. I was chilled to the bone. Inside my wide open front door, Porsche lay curled up tight in his bed ring.

Before I flushed and took a shower, I tested to see if all was working. After I'd warmed up under the loverly hot water, I took care of my morning rituals, then sat at my office desk with Porsche underneath. I brought up my phone lists to start making calls to clear the way for my first holiday, no vacation since... that cherry picking trip with Clay.

Before I could speed dial the first number, my phone chirped.

"Mom? You okay? Just heard about it on the news." June was breathless.

"I'm fine, dearie. Was going to call you. George and I are going on a trip. Down to California. Can we stop by and see you on the way back?"

"Sure! So, I'm finally going to meet him! You've got both my numbers?"

"I do, dearie."

"Okay, gotta go. Love you, Mom!"

"Love you, too." I was already talking to thin air. I sipped my coffee and was thinking about my grown daughter when my phone chirped again.

"Momma? You okay?" Cooper in Seattle.

"I'm good. You must be at work."

"On the way. Can't talk long." A motor roared in my ear. "That's the bus. Just wanted to know if you're all in one piece."

"I am. Did you feel anything?" When he said nothing, I told him about our trip.

"Freezin'! I'll work so—" I took the phone off my ear at screeching of brakes.

"What?" I said rather too loudly.

"...a dog?" Coop's voice suddenly came in clear. "...shelter. Zena's ten months old. Golden... computer belly... walk... what?" More squeals and roaring. "Gotta go ... me when... get... you!"

Again I was listening to airwaves. The idea of seeing my kids had landed on the surface of my mind like those geese coming in on Kah-Tai Lagoon. I took a leak, got more coffee and set about checking in with my Gals.

Joanne, naturally, was roaring with laughter cuz her cats had freaked, climbed the curtains and torn 'em to shreds.

Sandra was on her way to the mental health clinic, saying she needed a booster session after watching everything in her little cottage dance about.

Ethel was swearing up a storm, knee-deep in broken crockery at her first job of the week.

Annie was already at work at one of her many-windowed homes. Her route had been empty of traffic, lots of fallen stuff. She'd left Lois sleeping.

Judith was rescuing something in someone's

garden. She'd bicycled over, lots of toppled fences.

Joy was on her boat and wasn't about to set foot on our not-so-terra firma.

Zoe was home with her boyfriend and his kids, school having been cancelled. They were in the middle of rounding up escaped pets. A tad hysterical cuz Lola, the boa constrictor, was on the loose.

When I began calling my clients, the Birnbaums' number came up and I just stared at it. Then I scrolled on down to the next.

After Mrs W had hung up, the clock on the wall told me I had only minutes to get to Steve Milnik's office. I dialed his number, just in case, and Susannah assured me it was business as usual. I was heading for the door when George called.

"Slept through the whole thing. Something just came up about the Birnbaum case. Thought you should know. You okay?"

"Safe and sound. On my way to Steve's. Hey, I've been calling all my clients about going with you."

"Good. Given any thought to seeing your kids?"

"Actually, they just called They're eager to meet you. Said we'd catch 'em on the way home."

"We'll plan it on the drive. How's your neighborhood?"

"Nothing serious. What about yours?"

"A couple of those sports field lights're leaning. What?" And I heard nothing more.

Something told me to leave Porsche home. I shut my door on him looking all abandoned and set out feeling excited about being with George all the time, watching the world cruise by.

Chapter 28

LAST WILL AND TESTAMENT

BY THE TIME I CAME AROUND THE CORNER of Taylor Street, downtown was a-buzz with a clutter of utility vehicles parked in the delivery lane on Water Street. People were everywhere, surveying and stringing up hazard tape around piles of bricks that had tumbled off the facades of the old buildings at the crossroads where the traffic lights blinked yellow.

I parked beside Mel's parents' Buick in the diagonal slots in front of the Rose Theater. Claire was helping her grandmother out while her grandfather was looking at the posters under the marquee, showing a retro festival of '40s movies. I couldn't be sure if the silver sedan parked way over in a lot by the print shop was Renee's Beamer.

Claire and I walked beside her grandmother as she slowly pushed her walker. I wondered why they didn't get her a wheelchair. Mr. Birnbaum followed us, eyeing the store windows. At the entrance to the Proxall Building we helped Mrs. Birnbaum up the four steps and into the bright and shiny vestibule where the refitted freight elevator trundled us upwards. Four flights I knew rather well.

Once upon a century ago, when this brick building and the three others at this intersection were going up (you could see their progress in the faded framed photographs all through the public rooms) the upper floors had been taken over by the "Ladies of the Night" (as the tour guides coyly call 'em) and their customers: the carousing sailors, explorers, gamblers, grifters, loggers, fishermen and eventually civil servants who'd settled this land. And a jolly wild time was had, if the spare, ungrammatical and imaginatively spelt police logs in the museum down the street by the Town Hall were anything to go by. All four buildings have secret passages that allow escape to the next which, on the twice-yearly Historic Home Tours, are left open for inquisitive tourists.

Nowadays, it's all sanitized and very smart with the red bricks reclaimed from decades of paint, and huge green ferns and dainty trees thriving in brass spitoons and oak barrels. Artifacts from the town's ribald past hang, spotlit, everywhere.

Sal's Gals has a contract to clean the public rooms and hallways, daily during tourist season and the Holidays. Sandra and Lois usually do it, with any one of us dropping by to assist. To keep their inner sanctums shipshape, most of the receptionists have taken my training.

"Nice place you've got here." I teased Susannah as she watched Claire bring in her drooping grandparents.

"Had a good teacher." She winked at me and then came around her desk, reaching for Mr. Birnbaum. "You must be Mel's parents." She took his elbow. "Come on in, it's all ready for you." And the three

Birnbaums shuffled into Steve's office.

Through the hinge of the ajar door to the VIP holding room I caught sight of a pacing Alan Hatton with his cellphone stuck to his ear.

I was scuttling after Mel's family when I heard a sharp cough ahead, much like a deer does when danger's afoot.

The first time I'd seen Steve's corner office suite was after Clay died and George brought me here. I'd been surprised at how large and bright it was. Where the two outer walls come together, tall windows let the light in. Volume after volume of law books lined the interior walls. At the other end of the room was a vast captain's table with library lights, file folders and thick tomes laid open on reading racks.

Susannah was settling the Birnbaums in red leather armchairs to the left of Steve's desk. He was already coming around it, drawing Claire to a folding chair on the other side of her grandparents.

Susannah indicated I should sit beside Claire, and when I turned around, there was Renee, sitting across from us in a copper silk suit, head down so her hair hung over her face like a hoody. Her hands were clasped on her lap, no handbag in sight. Cast in bronze, her feet were everso slightly pigeon-toed. I couldn't see a piece of jewelry on her, not even her wedding ring.

Beyond her, against the inner wall, crouching at antique school desks, a brace of sleekly groomed young gents had money, the making of it, written all over 'em. They didn't look up from their laptops.

Sitting with their backs to the windows in a row of folding chairs were some of Port Townsend's movers and shakers. I know this cuz I'm religious about reading *The Leader* each week. Even been in it a time or two.

Though I'd seen Jesse Wiegant coming and going at festivals and benefits, I had yet to speak with him. He was in a plaid shirt and a down-filled vest. He had a great summer tan still and his tawny short hair had golden glints. He wore rimless glasses that enlarged his grey eyes. He's a favorite son of this neck of the woods having graduated from PT High, left for parts unknown and come home a Microsoft Millionaire at the ripe old age of forty-one. Then he built an amazingly complicated timeshare estate with a twelve-sided conference center for retreats and symposiums in the middle of a hay field (which had been paved over for parking) out by the Jeffco Fair Grounds. The whole place operates only on alternative energy experiments. He also started the town's first cyber café in the old five-and-dime on Water Street. Downtown, where all The Money is. I read he now spends part of each year taking computers to the Third World. Wow!

He was listening to Paula Hensel-Hall in the next seat. To me, she's the winner of the last three years' Best In Design at the Sandcastling Festival. She favors 3D spreads of fruit and veggies, and they are spectacular. To everyone else, she's a favorite daughter about the same age as Jesse. She owns and runs two motels (which we clean), owns the one and only cheese and wine store in the county and operates a catering company out of the back of her restaurant, which we clean. She's been on the Board of the Humane Society for years. Double-wow!

Beside her were two Senior Citizens who I couldn't place. The chap had the air of The Uniform about him, maybe police. The suntanned lady with a halo of white hair whose ear he was bending was fitted out in a familiar set of purple fleece sweats. Had I seen her at the Soup Kitchen with Mrs S?

Steven Milnik, Esquire, a long-ago New Mexican, stood behind his desk scanning the room. He's always had a lean and hungry look about him, and is therefore a take-charge kinda guy. He's got a burnished brown complexion and a marvelously hooked nose between glinting brown eyes under black brows. His turquoise shirt showed off his neatly trimmed black beard and the long braid that hangs down his back. He always wears pressed black pants, Birkenstocks and thick, woolly white socks.

Then I saw the full color studio portrait of Mel set on an easel in front of Steve's desk. Once upon a time, he must have posed for a press release cuz he was fitted out in one of his white shirts and thin black tie, with none of the gray in his moustache I'd seen in the last few years. He looked so clean, so charming, so vital. My heart hurt at how very much I'd liked him.

As Susannah left, closing the door behind her, Steve sat down and studied a thick wad of papers in front of him.

"Let's get started." He didn't looked up at us, "There's a lot to cover and I've just received notice to be in court at one o'clock, so we're going to have to move along and save any questions for another time."

He paused to read something. "As you know, we're here to read the last will and testament of Melvin Aaron Birnbaum. As he didn't die a natural death there'll be some complications I can't go into at present. Suffice to say the contents of his will are going to affect every one of you. Do you understand so far?" Steve lifted his eyes to look around at us all gathered there.

"With the exception of Messrs. Cargill and Steinman," he nodded at the laptop gents. "None of you know the full extent of his... fortune. The last time we talked, back in July when he made me his Executor, he wanted it kept that way until his daughter reached twenty-five years of age when he said he'd tell her about it. Now he's not going to get to do that, is he?" He glared at Renee's bent head.

"As per his last instructions, I must inform you that Melvin Aaron Birnbaum's financial worth as of the opening of the New York Stock Exchange this morning, stands at..." He nodded to the watching the Messrs C and S.

"One hundred ten point seven." One said, eyes now on his laptop.

Steve cleared his throat. "That's... one hundred and ten million, seven hundred thousand dollars," He said slowly, keeping his eyes on the pages in front of him. "Even with the current economic down-turn."

I joined in the collective gasp. Claire squirmed beside me. Her grandparents looked bewildered. Opposite us, Renee clutched her hands to her chest and grimaced, as if she had a toothache. I forced myself to look at Mel's portrait again.

"Now, this is what Mel updated on July tenth." Steve lifted the top sheet of paper. "Article One. I am as of this date of sound mind and body, and am married to Renee Rose Rainey Birnbaum, Citizen, with one adult child, namely Claire Ruth Rainey Birnbaum, Citizen, residing at Number Four Bluff View, Bluff Haven on Discovery Bay Road in Jefferson County in the State of Washington. As I must be dead by this time, I am sure my parents will have taken care of my earthly remains. For that I thank them."

Mrs. Birnbaum rattled her walker, her husband

coughed and Claire blew into a hanky.

"Article Two. I made my money by the following. A) founding the Ahimsa Organic Food Co-op and Distributor based in Oakland, California in which I still own forty-five percent. B) trading on the stock markets and currency exchanges of the world. C) authoring several computer programs. D) the Bluff Haven estates. E) my sunset photography." Steve laid down that sheet and took up another.

"Article Three. I have decided my estate be distributed as follows: to my parents, Leo Victor and Rachel Miriam, I give all and every financial need until their deaths, funerals and upkeep of their grave sites." Mrs. Birnbaum moaned while her husband rocked in his chair, eyes pressed shut, lips moving. One hand, curled into a fist, was gently tapping against his chest.

Steve kept reading. "To my wife, Renee Rose, I bequeath the aforementioned Ahimsa Organic Food Co-op and Distributor shares because she founded it with me and worked hard to make it successful. I also bequeath her a stipend of three thousand dollars a month free and clear. Should she re-marry, said stipend is to cease."

Mel's widow, still looking down, crossed her legs and stuffed her hands in her jacket pockets.

"To my dog and faithful companion, a nine-year old black Labrador we call Borscht, I bequeath a stipend of ten thousand dollars a month free and clear for his complete and lifelong care. Mr. Williams who owns Wally's's Doggie Heaven and has seen to Borscht's welfare assures me that with good care he could live another six or eight years."

There was utter silence in the room while we all calculated what that meant. When I got the full count, I had to choke back a giggle. Claire couldn't suppress hers. Her mother grunted, as if that tooth had been pulled.

"It is my hope," Steve read on as if he hadn't heard, "that my good friend, Sally, no middle name, Collier will accept this charge as I know she likes him and, more importantly he likes her."

Steve lowered the page and peered at me, "Is this so, Ms Collier?"

"It is," I blurted out. "I took him home with me... after I... last week."

"Good. Let's set up a meet to talk about that, yes?"

I nodded.

"I want to take a moment," Steve went on, staring at the clock over the door, "To explain what Mel meant by 'free and clear." He read from a separate page. "All associated withholdings and taxes for said stipends so encumbered are to be paid by the estate." Then he went back to the original pile. "There's an addendum which Mel insisted be included: Upon her acceptance and the eventual death of said beloved dog, Sally Collier is to continue receiving said stipend free and clear for the rest of her life. When she dies said stipend will be paid out free and clear equally between her daughter and son, June Collier and Cooper Collier whose current addresses I am sure she knows. This is to be for the rest of their lives." I sucked in some air when Claire poked an elbow into my ribs, her face hidden by her hair.

"There are other one time free and clear bequests of various amounts," Steve continued, "of interest to the rest gathered here, to whit: the American Red Cross; the Public Broadcasting Service; the Jefferson County Domestic Violence Prevention Program; the Olympic Peninsula Law Enforcement Officers

Memorial Fund; the Jefferson County Animal Shelter; the Nexus Computer Café; the Annual Port Townsend Rhody Parade Fund; the Annual Kinetic Sculpture Race Fund; the Annual Sandcastling Festival Fund; WOW, the Wild Olympic Women's Quilting Bee Fund; Free Kibble to Animal Shelters.com Fund, and Wally's Doggie Heaven Rescue Fund. Each of these entities will receive a notarized contract of settlement. At this time, the other un-designated funds are to be made available at my parents' discretion."

Steve took a gulp from his water bottle, then picked up another page. "To my daughter, Claire." Now her hand gripped my elbow. "I gladly and sadly give and bequeath the rest of my estate, both real and personal, with the stipulation that she receive, free and clear, a stipend of two thousand dollars a month while she completes community work of her choice until her twenty-fifth birthday.

"The upkeep of and taxes on our family home and its environs will be maintained by my estate. When Claire reaches twenty-five, Cargill and Steinman will advise her as to the disposition of said estate. I request that Claire not sell the family home until then. Should Claire not wish to live there, I request that she rent it, for no more than twelve dollars a year, to the Jefferson County Domestic Violence Prevention Program to be designated as a Safe House for battered women and their children.

"Should Claire die before reaching that age, my estate is to be split between my cousins Aaron Samuel Baruch and Amy Ruth Baruch Burnett whose last known domiciles were in Asbury Park, New Jersey, with the same disposition conditions of the house and environs."

Steve sat back in his chair, not looking at any of

us. "There is a coda I insisted he add which states: Any contest of anything in this document by anyone heretofore named, nulls and voids said bequest. Mel then signed the coda and added this: 'Choose now, and now, and now.' I have no idea to what he was referring."

I did, and so did Renee, if she hadn't forgotten what her husband, she and I had learnt at those training seminars where we'd met. It was Mel's way of reminding us that we have the opportunity to transform the quality of our lives by choosing how we react or respond to whatever is affecting us.

A deep ache washed through me as I watched Mel's elegant widow sprint for the door.

Chapter 29

CONSPIRACY TO MURDER

I WASN'T FAR BEHIND RENEE, feeling a bit ashamed at abandoning Claire to take care of her distraught grandparents.

Only to come to a full stop in the reception area where Renee and Hatton were trapped between Smith and Westin. Hatton was as stiff as a board, glaring at me. Renee, face red and eyes on the carpet, clutched his arm.

And there was George at the door to the landing, his jacket open, arms akimbo, badge and weapon in full view.

"We're requesting you accompany us to the Court House." He rumbled. "There's something we need you to see. Mr. Hatton, you'll go with Detective Westin. Mrs. Birnbaum, with Detective Smith, if you please. Ms Collier, would you be so kind as to follow us?"

Hatton took a step toward George, dragging Renee with him. "We don't have to go anywhere! Not until our lawyers get here."

"I'm afraid you do. Now, under your own power? Or

in these?" He jiggled his handcuffs.

"My lawyer's going to rip you a new one!"

"I'm sure he'll try," my Man said calmly, turning away and tucking his manacles back in his belt. Smith and Westin herded Renee and Hatton after him, and I took up the rear.

George had the elevator open, waiting. I stepped in and tucked myself behind him. Then the detectives and their charges crowded in.

What a seething, silent ride down. Smith and Westin stood in front of Renee and Hatton while George silently worked the old-fashioned controls. When he pulled the horizontal loading doors apart, I snuck around him and loped ahead through the vestibule out into the fresh air.

I stood by my beater watching as the coppers loaded their the widow and her lover into separate squad cars idling at the curb. Then I followed George's Escalade to the landmark Court House up on the bluff overlooking the new ferry terminal.

Smith and Westin were already guiding Renee and Hatton down the ramp into the basement offices when George, with a frown between his eyebrows, held me back.

"This is going to be tough, Sally." He turned me so we were facing away from where the foursome were walking. "We went through Jerry's security discs. They pretty much line up with Claire's memories. Then Steve gave us Mel's passwords to get into his computer. Our geeks found some really interesting things there. One's off his camera. You know, above his monitor? The other's from someone in Perth, Australia. A streaming video, they tell me. Don't think we'll have to run that one, though. We'll see how Renee and Hatton react."

He kept a firm grip on my elbow as he maneuvered at a fast clip through the crowded law offices to a dimly lit conference room where four long tables were pushed together, surrounded by metal and cushion folding chairs. At the far end was an LCD screen beside a DVD player. George guided me to a seat on the opposite side to where Renee was settling herself beside Hatton, who had his phone to his ear. Sheriff Morrow and Doc Nelson slipped in and stood against the wall in the back. Smith closed the door, then positioned himself beside Westin in front of it.

"My lawyer says not to answer any of your questions till he gets here." Hatton snarled across the wide tables.

George's face creased in a mirthless smile, "Why, Mr. Hatton, we're not going to ask you anything. We're only going to have a little show and tell. You remember show and tell, don't you? We're going to start at the end and then go back to when this sorry mess began. When you're ready, Detective Smith."

Smith pointed a remote and Westin clicked off the overhead lights. A silent, full color movie bloomed on the screen.

It's a scene I've seen many times: bright daylight outside Mel's home. Seconds are ticking by in the upper right corner of the image. At the bottom of the screen, the top of Porsche's head (who was then Borscht) passes from right to left. Seconds later, he comes back and stands beside the wall of windows, looking back out of frame.

I gasp when a person's torso in mauve and green comes into view from the right. It's me! I see myself go to the left and then to where Mel's dog waits. I pull the sliding glass door open and stand watching as he bolts across the patio into the sunshine, sniffs around the terrace flagstones, then takes off down the slope.

I exit stage left, re-entering moments later, walking into the camera, looking down. It's eerie watching myself inspecting the camcorder on its tripod then stepping outside, looking all around and following Porsche to the edge of the terrace.

I descend out of sight.

Time ticks away.

Now, the still scene fast-forwards a full nine minutes. There's my head coming up the hill. I've got the dog by his collar. I put him inside, closing the sliding door. He goes left, comes back and flops down inside the glass.

I sit in Mel's hanging chair. Soon there's a puff of smoke. I must have pushed the ground cuz the chair swings around while I'm talking on my phone. Watching it, I can taste Mel's Sobranies.

The cigarette done, I get to my feet, stub the butt in the bucket and peer at that for a while, moving things with my purple-gloved finger. I take my baggie from my uniform pocket and put something in it. I leave stage left. Inside the house, Porsche rears up and follows me out of the frame. Then he returns to his spot at the right of the screen and settles down.

The minutes flick by as the movie fast-forwards.

Eighteen minutes and thirty seconds later, I'm arriving from the left, leading Deputy Sheriff Haffey and Detective Westin across the patio out to the terrace. Porsche gets to his feet. The deputy gestures for me to stay put. The two men descend out of view. I return to Mel's chair. Porsche lies down again.

Again the scene speeds up through ten minutes and six seconds, and slows to normal speed as Deputy Haffey comes up over the edge. I get to my feet, repeating the cigarette stub out.

Deputy Haffey opens his notebook and we stand talking. I gesture toward the camera. Porsche paces. Then I'm digging out my wallet and handing him something. He inspects it, writes as I talk. He listens to his radio, then points to the steps. I point to the camera, walk to the sliding door and open it, grabbing Porsche's collar. Me and the dog exit left, and Deputy Haffey stays on the terrace writing in his pad, bending his head to speak into his radio, then he descends to the bottom of the garden.

The scene fast-forwards fifteen minutes to slow down when the paramedic crew with their gurney and cases, roll in from stage left. They cross the terrace and head down the hill.

"Lights please." George rumbles. Everyone blinks and shifts about. Renee's curled into a ball hugging herself, eyes closed. Hatton has shrunk too. "Now we're going back forty-eight hours to Friday night." George nods at his detectives and the lights dim as the screen blooms again.

My heart leaps at the sight of a very alive Mel, brightly lit, sitting in front of the camera. Behind him it's dark outside and the windows are filled with reflections of his home.

He looks up, a frown on his dear face. He takes off his headset and looks down for a full fifty seconds. When he stands up his white shirt fills the screen before he steps away. Porsche arrives. Mel bends over and rubs his dog's head for a while, points right and Porsche leaves. Mel turns and exits left. This time Smith fast-forwards the still scene through twelve minutes... eighteen... twenty-nine.

Suddenly something comes hurtling down in the right of the frame and the exterior security motion detectors light up.

"Rewind that, please," George says quietly, "And play it in slow-motion."

Again the dimness outside, the sparkles of raindrops and then everso jerkily, a body cartwheels from above. Floodlights blaze on as the body in a white shirt smashes onto the terrace flagstones, head bouncing, arms splayed out, legs in black trousers sprawling, one slipper popping of a bare foot.

Leaning forward, with my eyes glued to the scene, I'm sure the fingers clench on the hand I can see before my friend's body goes still.

"Pause, please," George's voice is hard. The scene freezes. "Dr. Nelson?"

"Mr. Birnbaum was certainly injured. Both clavicles broken, left shoulder dislocated, left cervix and patella fractured. Internal organ bruising. Skull and brain damage. He was alive and likely could have survived."

"Continue," George growled.

The time in the corner of the screen flicks to 11:27:10 PM. Mel lies on the stones, head turned away. Porsche enters stage right, pawing at the glass, silently barking.

Suddenly someone rushes in from left frame. It's Hatton, in blue pajamas and brown loafers. For all of ten seconds he stands looking down at the body of his lover's husband.

Here comes Renee, in her pink robe and slippers. She swipes at Hatton's arm, then beats her clenched fists on his back, and when he turns around, his chest. He slaps her hands away. They both turn toward Mel's windows, where the dog is prancing in a frenzy.

Faces set in black and white masks, Renee and

THE DEAD HUSBAND

Hatton freeze for a full eighteen seconds in the pouring rain. Then she's screaming at Hatton, stamping her foot.

He steps under the deck, into the dry and pulls Renee to him. He digs in her robe pocket, coming out with a pack of smokes and a lighter. He lights up. Renee plucks the smoke from his lips and starts puffing like crazy, saying something as Hatton lights another. They stand there hunched over, heads together, talking and smoking.

"Pause, please," George rumbles again. "Had you dialed nine-one-one right here, you might have been free right now. Because of what you chose to do next, Mrs. Birnbaum and Mr. Hatton, you turned a probably explainable accident into an indefensible conspiracy to murder."

Time ticks on. Renee tosses her butt in the sand bucket and bolts to the left. Hatton stays put, lights up another cigarette from his butt and drops that in the bucket. He just stands there with his back to Mel.

Three minutes and seventeen seconds later, Renee re-enters lugging a spade in her hand. She thrusts it at her lover and points out into the dark. He takes the shovel. They talk. She shakes her head. He wants to know something. She turns her back to him, head bowed, hands over her mouth. She faces him again and answers. Hatton nods once, repeats the chain smoking ritual, shaking some cigarettes from her pack and taking the lighter, drops them into his pj pocket. With his butt between his teeth, ignoring Mel's body he walks across the flagstone and disappears into the dark.

Renee uses her butt to light another smoke, and stands there hugging herself.

Porsche is still prancing and barking. Three

minutes later, she turns around, and drops her smoke in the bucket, wraps her robe tight and comes to the sliding door. As she pulls it open and steps inside, closing it behind her, Porsche backs out of sight. She follows him. Soon he's back, running across the bottom of the frame with Renee in pursuit. At the left of the screen with arms wide, she corners him and grabs his collar. Even with her back to us, we can clearly see her hitting him with her clenched fist, again and again. He cowers. With his collar at the choke point, she drags him, fighting all the way, off to the right.

The scene fast-forwards another seven minutes and thirty seconds. Now the exterior lights have gone out. When Renee returns reopening the sliding door, she steps out into the patio and they blaze on again. She has one of Mel's towels wrapped around her head, another around her shoulders. She's smoothing her hands on her robe, and stands looking into the dark. Then she takes up her butt from the bucket and lights a fresh one from it. Smith fast-forwards through two more smokes. She never once goes over to her husband's body.

Suddenly Hatton rises out of the dark, like a muddy specter. He doesn't have the shovel. Renee hands him a lit smoke. They talk. She rubs his upper arms and throws the towel around her shoulders, over his. She seems to be pleading, maybe urging. It goes on through another cigarette, after which it looks like Hatton's made a decision. He tosses the towel back at her and with a fresh smoke between his teeth, he grabs Mel's ankles, turns around and starts towing the body behind him. Mel's head bounces, his arms flail, and then they're gone into the dark.

Renee waits, smoking again. She goes over to her

husband's chair and pushes it, setting it swinging and spinning. She takes up pacing.

Fast-forward twelve minutes of Renee frenetically going back and forth, lighting up and puffing smoke.

"Doc Nelson says there was dirt under Mr. Birnbaum's nails and in his mouth, nose, throat and lungs." Westin says in a high, hard voice, "You buried him alive."

The screen jerks to normal speed as Hatton again clambers into view. The frame freezes on him standing in the floodlights, his pjs covered with mud.

"I'm curious," Smith drawls. "Why didn't you just throw him off the bluff? The fall would've explained most of the damage. Except why he was walking around out there in the middle of the night. Oh yeah, we found the shovel, twenty feet down, blade first in a ledge."

Mel's silent testament starts again. Renee dashes to the deck pillar and pulls the garden hose out of its reel. She points her lover to a spot on the patio and opens the nozzle. As she hoses him down, he kicks out of his shoes and strips off his sodden pjs, rotating in the spray, shivering.

Someone in the room makes a wolf whistle.

Renee shuts off the water, drops the nozzle and hands him a towel. As he dries off, she waves him toward the camera. With his loafers in hand, Hatton lopes nakedly through the door and exits right. She picks up his pjs and wrings them out. With them held forth like some offering, she follows her lover into her husband's kingdom and without closing the sliding door, disappears.

Thirty-three fast-forwarded minutes later Renee comes hustling from stage right. Now her hair's fluffy and she's dressed in a fresh purple glory suit. She tiptoes in puce pumps onto the patio, her arms in the air for balance, triggering the flood lights. She picks up the hose and starts spraying where Mel had lain on the stones. When she backs in under the deck, she bumps her husband's hanging chair. She doesn't notice, intent as she is on washing away her lover's muddy trail clear up to the door. Soon she cuts of the water and throws the hose down.

    She steps daintily inside, pulls closed the door and passes out of view.

    A couple of minutes later she's back, hauling the vacuum system hose. She scours the carpet in front of the sliding glass door. At the camcorder tripod she presses a button on it, extracts something and stuffs it into a pocket, then resumes vacuuming, backing out of frame.

    Now the lights in Mel's home go out and all that's left is the floodlit exterior with my friend's favorite chair gyrating in the night.

Chapter 30

AFTERMATH

SO HERE I AM HOME AGAIN on a crisp and clear November morning with pale sunshine slanting through the trees in Chetzemoka Park. Porsche is sitting on our porch sniffing the stories on the air and listening to the surf pound at the bottom of the cliff.

That trip with George was three weeks of "getting to know you" tourist fun: cuddling in motels, driving the highways through spectacular landscapes and mazes of cities, and doing a lot of deep talking about life, liberty and the pursuit of happiness. George and me and Porsche together all day and all night. Wonderful!

Meeting George's step-sibs down in sunny California was a chance to see him in action with people he'd known as a kid. Far as I could see, they were complete strangers.

Kev was a shock, even though George had warned me he was disabled, having lost an arm and leg in Vietnam. By the smell of their rundown home in Emeryville (NOT Berkeley) filled with medical gear, he's also into the medicinal properties of weed. After he ignored me, I stepped outside for a smoke so I wouldn't say something rude when he ordered his wife, Gail, around. I'd never heard anyone talk to another like that. No wonder she's all caved-in and shut down. Then a hairy chap in a black t-shirt and jeans with tattoos all up his arms got off a motorcycle and clomped up the ramp to where I was smoking. He told me he was the visiting nurse. George took his arrival as a signal to leave. That visit lasted all of forty-five minutes.

Down in Palm Springs, Ellen and I found a few things to talk about as we worked a dim and dreary Kincade jiggy on her dining table in a her double-wide overlooking a golf course. George and she shared some memories of their parents while we ate microwave dinners and watched the Golf Channel. She wasn't keen on Porsche although she invited us all to stay the night, then took us for breakfast in the club house before she set off on a round with her friends. She said it hadn't rained in three years, and I was already missing the misty moistness of home.

So much for my fantasy of any tender Hallmark family moments!

We didn't get down to Four Corners because of a snow storm, so we lazily toured through the parched mountains and fertile interior valleys on the way north to Crater Lake.

It was all I'd hoped for, even if it had already snowed a lot up there at six thousand feet. We stayed at the lodge during a sunny break while the staff closed up for the winter. We wandered about the ploughed road, filling our eyes with views of the Cascade Mountains strewn before us and the intensely blue lake. Then we'd simply sat, all bundled up against the chill, and taken in the smells and feel of that special place. All that my jiggy promised, only so much bigger!

I almost cried when I saw June for the first time in six years. All grown up and so like my Mum in that one photo I have. She was at work in her bright and crowded skyscraper Portland office and when we took her for dinner, she flirted with George who loved it and got all avuncular and old-fashioned. I got the giggles. We talked about how we looked (she's into cosmetics and fluffy hairdos and high heels) and memories of our years together. As she hugged me goodbye she whispered that I had a keeper.

Cooper, in a grubby downtown Seattle building, was all bristly and on guard, looking so like his Dad when I'd first met him. Porsche liked how he smelt when we got into the Escalade to drive down to the waterfront for a seafood special. While George and I ate silently, Coop regaled us with tales of his work, new dog and roommates (all chaps) in a house they're buying out by Green Lake. His parting hug was long with a lot of rocking, during which he whispered how he'd missed me and was sorry he'd been such a pain.

We were a weary couple as we edged onto the Bainbridge Island ferry and headed home in a darkening, damp afternoon. It had been the longest vacation either of us had ever taken and when we did talk it was about missing our work, our nests and how strange family was.

After helping me and our dog settle back in, George stood around confused to be leaving. Me too! I'd known the first night on the road, I wanted us to live together for the rest of our lives. I'll just have to wait for him to catch up.

Neighbor Mr J did watch my place even though his wife got back from the convalescent home while I was gone. Clara asked me to do a clean after all those months away recuperating from that fall in her kitchen. Joanne has found a carpenter to build a ramp to their stoop and install grab bars everywhere.

Ethel got my tools back from the Birnbaums' dumb waiter when she took over the job. I'll find out how much I've missed the place when I fill in for her when she's on her annual pilgrimage to France.

Steve tells me Mel's widow and her lover are lawyered-up to the gills. They're out on bail and prohibited from going near Bluff Haven, or me.

So now I'm about to load up Porsche for a run to Sequim to check on Claire's grandparents, as I promised I would when we saw her off to Basic Training, just before we left on our trip. Their char, Marti Graber, wants to meet me. Says she's interested in starting a branch of Sal's Gals there. Hey, hey!

THE END

About the Author

R. J. Brown, a WWII adopted orphan, was born in London, England and as a secretary emigrated to Chicago, Illinois where she worked in the Union of American Hebrew Congregations until joining the Counter Culture in 1969.

A decade later, she moved her family to Berkeley, California where she took trainings in the Human Potential Movement, put her kids in alternative schooling and started her cleaning company.

Upon relocating to Port Townsend, Washington, she continued cleaning and trained as a Children's Advocate for the Jefferson County Domestic Violence Program where she created the Stepson Walk & Talk Safety Course. For nine years she was the Managing Editor of the *Townsend Letter for Doctors*, a magazine written by doctors in alternative health practices.

She is now a grandmother, living on the Olympic Peninsula's West End with her husband. Together they created the book review site RebeccasReads.com and took care of her ailing father-in-law. Her first book, STANDING THE WATCH: The Greatest Gift is a memoir of those years. She is a contributing writer for the SENIORS SUNSET TIMES, monthly newspaper.

She'd love to hear from you at these websites: rjbrownbooks.com or bigriverpress.com

Printed in the United States
216336BV00002B/4/P